THE DARKEST TIME OF NIGHT

THE
DARKEST
TIME
OF
NIGHT

JEREMY FINLEY

ST. MARTIN'S PRESS

NEW YORK

THE DARKEST TIME OF NIGHT. Copyright © 2018 by Jeremy Finley. All rights reserved. Printed in the United States of America. For information, address St. Martin's Press, 175 Fifth Avenue, New York, N.Y. 10010.

www.stmartins.com

Designed by Omar Chapa

Library of Congress Cataloging-in-Publication Data

Names: Finley, Jeremy, author.
Title: The darkest time of night / Jeremy Finley.
Description: First edition. | New York : St Martin's Press, 2018.
Identifiers: LCCN 2017060168| ISBN 9781250147301 (hardcover) |
    ISBN 9781250147318 (ebook)
Subjects: LCSH: Missing children—Fiction. | Grandparent and
    child—Fiction. | Family secrets—Fiction. | Conspiracies—
    Fiction. | Human-alien encounters—Fiction. | GSAFD:
    Science fiction. | Suspense fiction.
Classification: LCC PS3606.I55345 D37 2018 | DDC 813/.6—dc23
LC record available at https://lccn.loc.gov/2017060168

Our books may be purchased in bulk for promotional, educational, or business use. Please contact your local bookseller or the Macmillan Corporate and Premium Sales Department at 1-800-221-7945, extension 5442, or by email at MacmillanSpecialMarkets@macmillan.com.

First Edition: June 2018

10 9 8 7 6 5 4 3 2 1

For Linda Howerton and Pam Finley,
who inspired this story.

And for Rebecca, Eve, and Charlotte,
who inspire everything else.

THE
DARKEST
TIME
OF
NIGHT

ONE

Even before I learned about the boldness of blue, the vanity of purple, and the purity of white, the bell taught me the meaning of red. *You go any farther than that bell, Lynn Marie Stanson,* Daddy had said, pointing to the Faraday original shining like an apple at the pitch of the greenhouse roof, *and you're as good as dead.*

He'd made the threat on a Sunday. I remember this because I was wearing half-size-too-small saddle oxfords, shined to the best of Daddy's ability, which hurt my toes. I'd meant to take them off as soon as we got home, but Mrs. Ross, who watched me sometimes after Mass while he worked, had insisted that I immediately help her with the double wedding ring quilt for Ruth Mosely's daughter. After a few agonizing moments of trying to thread a single needle, I mentioned that Daddy would be drowning in sweat if he were in the greenhouse. Mrs. Ross raised one eyebrow and said she'd put the lemonade in the icebox.

Ice clinked in the glass as I ran across the lawn and threw open the door. Momentarily overwhelmed in the heat generated by the glass panels, I took a sip of the drink, knowing

Daddy wouldn't mind. I assumed he would be inside, puffing on his pipe, as he had walked in the direction of the greenhouse when we got home, quickening his step when he looked at his watch. Instead, I smelled only fertilizer, with no trace of tobacco. I was tracing my name in the soil spilled from a repotted spider fern when I heard his voice.

Hoping the mower was acting up again and he would soon mutter one of the words that made me giggle and Mrs. Ross frown, I crept out the back door, glaring at its weary, squeaking hinges.

I expected to see him alone among the burr oaks, perhaps having moved the Atco mower into the shade. Instead, he stood with his hands on his hips, one eye narrowed, encircled by three men holding lanterns.

I froze in place and then inched back inside, careful to leave enough of a crack in the door to peer through. One of the men, wearing a wool suit too hot for a Tennessee summer, made a sweeping gesture of an arch. My father frowned, scrunched his forehead, and pointed to the skies. The man in the wool suit nodded once.

"We brought these to show you," the man said, holding up the lantern. "You'll see. We really need you to show us where it is. You agreed."

"I know I did," Daddy muttered.

I had been out of school for a month, so I'd had plenty of time to get to know all of Daddy's customers, and he always let me hand out cigars to his friends at Tuesday night's poker games. I knew with certainty the three men in the woods were strangers.

Don't do it Daddy, I wanted to whisper in his ear.

He made a beckoning motion to the men, and I felt the

sting of hypocrisy. After all, he was the one who filled my head with terrors: wild animals, thorns, sinkholes, bear traps, snakes, and monsters.

Monsters? I'd asked.

Especially monsters, he nodded. *Lynn, we never, ever go in the woods.*

Not even you?

Not even me, peanut.

I almost called out for him, but something about the way he walked with the men caused me to hesitate. Daddy was never in a hurry, his hands usually deep in his pockets, his boots lifting and falling in a routine rhythm. He now seemed to scurry along with the three men, deep into the foliage, all carrying lanterns despite the midafternoon sunlight.

When he had almost disappeared into the green, I threw open the door and followed. Mrs. Ross would have her head thrown back and would be deep into a snore by now anyway.

The rule about the woods was for both of us, Daddy.

Last fall, I brought home a balloon from the Davidson County fair, and the string had slipped from my grasp despite my taffy-coated fingers. I watched it float into the woods and become ensnared in a low-hanging cluster of branches. I could see the bobbing of the purple balloon not far from where I'd stood. I'd called for Daddy to fetch it for me. It couldn't have been more than a yard away. He'd just shook his head and took me by the hand into the house.

I told myself I'd watch him and the men from a distance, enough to know that he was all right. If something happened, I'd go for help. Pretending to be some sort of lookout helped temper the gnawing feeling in my stomach.

After a ten-minute walk, they stopped in a small clearing.

Daddy looked around and motioned to the man in the suit. He pointed to a corner of the grove, and the man hurried over and nodded in grim acknowledgment.

I hid behind the trunk of a maple tree that had squeezed itself into life among the oaks. Squinting, I could not only see what the man was looking at on the ground, but could read what was written upon it. My narrowed eyes widened.

On a count of three, the men lifted the glass canisters above their heads. The two wearing glasses clearly struggled, their doughy triceps trembling in short-sleeved shirts. The man in the suit held his own, as did Daddy. All began to walk, holding the lanterns, peering into the glass intently.

Inside, black spots began to sputter upwards, just as a batch of twigs beneath my uncomfortable shoes betrayed me.

At the sound of the snapping wood and the sight of my blue pleated skirt peeking out from behind the tree, the lantern fell from Daddy's hand, shattering to the forest floor.

I gasped, covering my mouth in a futile attempt to hide myself. I watched as small beetles began to crawl on the large pieces of broken glass now scattered between the men. Ladybugs drunkenly flew in unexpected escape, unsure of what to do with their newfound freedom.

I braced myself, as all children do when their parents' eyes simultaneously become too white and too pinched. Daddy reached me in seconds, his hands gripping my arms with unfamiliar fierceness. "What are you doing?"

He scooped me up and carried me back through the trees. Although my vision bobbed as Daddy's shoulder threatened to crash against my chin, I still saw the men gaping, straining their necks to watch as I was hustled away. Only when the man in the suit kneeled on the ground where Daddy had pointed did the other two tear their gaze from me. The last thing I saw was the man in the suit looking at the forest floor, covering his mouth in shock.

When we were once again on the lawn and free of the trees, Daddy set me down so abruptly I almost bit my tongue. I wanted to run away, frightened by this stranger suddenly embodied by my father.

He slapped me across the face. The same man who, as a single father, learned to paint my toenails, gave funny names to my earlobes, carried a curl of my hair in his wallet, and fluffed my pillow at night. I broke into tears, and I saw his hand tremble, threatening to strike again. Instead, his fingers curved, with only his index finger remaining, pointing up towards the greenhouse roof where, last summer, he had installed the bell that had once hung in the fire hall on Holly Street.

"Never, ever, ever again, do you step foot an inch beyond that bell. You go any further than that bell, Lynn Marie Stanson, and you're as good as dead."

"But you—"

"It doesn't matter what I do! You are never to enter those woods again!"

Tears pooled in my eyes. He leaned in closer, taking my chin roughly between his thumb and fingers. "Don't you know—you go in those woods again and you won't come back. Do you understand me? Do you?"

I nodded repeatedly in his grip, and he hissed at me to get inside the house. I ran and didn't look back.

Even now, decades later, if I stray too close to the woods, I seek out the bell. Even after Daddy died, and Tom and I added three thousand square feet to his house, painted it white and added a wraparound porch where I'd rocked each of my three daughters to sleep. Even after the girls grew up and started their own lives, and the glass from the greenhouse came down, the sign changing from "Bud's Greenhouse" to "The Rose Ped-dler," the bell remained. The contractor we hired to turn the greenhouse into a gardening shop had practically insisted it be removed. He declared the concept Daddy had implemented, of wiring the store phone to the bell so it would ring if a customer needed him while he was tending to his vegetable garden, was unnecessarily outdated. He suggested I have my business calls forwarded to my cell phone if someone was trying to reach me while I was watering the coneflowers and peonies that grew where Daddy's green beans and tomatoes once flourished. I had given my husband a look. "The bell stays," Tom had said to the contractor, with a wink. "My wife hates change."

The two had exchanged knowing glances. I let them be-lieve it.

It is not by chance that boxwoods stand as sentinels around the house, that roses and lilies fight for dominance in my for-mal garden, that hostas rest under four different willow trees, and that the front of the Peddler is flooded with coneflowers and daisies, yet I plant nothing remotely close to the tree line. The blot of red beneath the black shingles, on the verge of the trees, still holds sway.

I am a mother and grandmother, with my seventies on the near horizon. I should have let go of those fears long ago. But in all my life, I never entered the woods again. I may have been jarred that day Daddy hauled me out of the trees, but I know what that man in the wool suit had examined, then lifted from the ground of the clearing. I should have asked—and almost did, several times—but I never could find the courage to ask my father why the gravestone of a child was so deep into the woods.

TWO

The sound of Tom's sleeping kept me awake. It wasn't that he snores, or incoherently mumbles, or twitches under the covers. It was his even breathing, his bottom lip slightly jutted out, that made me want to shake him. Even if I had knocked over our dresser, he would just turn over. *How can you sleep after what you told us—?*

The first ring of the phone was like a jolt of black coffee. I quickly looked over at the clock. Almost midnight. My husband's soft breathing continued, even when it rang a second time. Despite having to make the biggest decision of his life, a decision that will impact generations of our family, and getting an ice-cold silent treatment from me, he proved yet again that he is a champion sleeper. Nothing rattled him, not the cry of a newborn daughter, not our veteran tomcat Voodoo scratching at the door, and obviously not the phone ringing in the middle of the night.

I, however, practically leapt for the phone. Any call this late is most certainly Washington with some sort of crisis. Either that or something was wrong with the girls. I snatched the phone and hit the answer button.

"Mama." Anne's voice was so thin I could hear her straining for oxygen. "We can't find William."

Ten minutes later, Tom and I were hurrying across the damp grass and past the pergola, our flashlights dancing off the pine and oak that lined the perimeter of the yard. Tom reached his hand back for me to take. Instead, I paused at the edge of the woods.

"OK, let's get this over with," he folded his arms across this chest. "Let me have it before we go a step farther."

"Let's not talk about that now."

"You don't want me to accept it, do you?"

"Please, Tom." I squinted, even though it was pitch black.

"William is probably curled up asleep on the dog's bed; the one obvious place neither Anne nor Chris have looked yet. We need to talk about this, Lynn. This would change our entire lives—"

Not our lives. My life. Your life is in Washington. My life is here, with our family, my shop, my house, my garden, and my friends. I don't want to leave any of that. I love my life. I don't love your life.

I sighed. "I'm still in shock about it. But right now, I'm worried about William."

I looked from the trees to the Rose Peddler on the other end of the property. Somewhere in the dark, at the pitch of the roof, the bell watched.

"I'm sure he's fine," Tom said. "But I know William is your favorite—"

"Stop that."

"And he's the one thing that could get you in these woods. We'll find him, and then you and I can have a long debate over waffles and coffee in the morning."

I was grateful when he took my arm. Together, we waded through the treacherous boundary of acorns the size of golf balls. I shined my flashlight on the soggy ground, forcing myself to keep walking despite my pounding heartbeat. *I'm sorry, Daddy.*

Tom held his arms up high to push back any branches. "Now, may I ask, why on earth would William be out here this late at night anyway during a thunderstorm?" he asked. "It poured hard after dinner for a minute"

"I told you, Chris let the older boys camp in the backyard when it looked like the weather might clear. William was upset he couldn't be with them. Anne thinks he opened the back door."

"How many times have I told them to install an alarm system?" he growled.

"Now, don't start on that, you'll only upset them more."

He snapped some twigs away. "I should have had a path put in between the houses a long time ago."

I would have never let you. It couldn't be more than a ten-minute walk through the trees to Anne's house, but no one, especially their boys, was allowed to use the forest as a short cut. Too much poison ivy and wild animals, I repeated to anyone who would listen. Even in the well-populated neighborhoods of west Nashville, swatches of dense forest were not uncommon. Tom occasionally kidded me about my fear of the forest, but stopped when he saw the shade in my glances.

"There, I see their flashlights."

As soon as Anne saw us she rushed over, her face ruddy with tears, speaking in a pitch usually reserved for theater majors. "We can't find him, Mom. We can't find him."

"Anne, are you sure you've checked the house thoroughly?" Tom asked wearily.

"Dad, I'm not overexaggerating!"

"He's here somewhere."

"He's not, he's not." Anne covered her mouth, looking around frantically.

"Where's Chris?" Tom asked.

"He headed off that way, there's his flashlight," Anne pointed. Tom nodded and walked in that direction.

"Explain to me again what happened," I asked.

Anne stifled a sob. "I don't know how William got out of the house, but he was so mad that he couldn't camp with his brothers. Chris has been promising Brian and Greg that they could camp all summer, and after we got back from your house tonight and the phone showed the rain had stopped for a minute, Chris set up their tent. You know he grew up camping, and he said a little rain wasn't going to hurt them. We explained to William that he wasn't old enough yet, and he threw such a fit that I thought he'd cried himself to sleep on the couch. I left him there; you know how he likes to sleep on the downstairs couch. Then Greg came to get me and said William had somehow gotten outside and wanted to get in their tent."

Anne cleared her throat. "Then there was something about them daring William to touch a tree in the forest, and if he did, they'd let him in, so he ran off. It started raining heavier, and when he didn't come right back, Brian followed him in."

"Who is watching the boys?"

"You remember our neighbor Ralph Swift? He's with Greg at the house. And Ralph's new wife, Peggy, is with Brian just over there."

"Brian is out here?" I asked, turning to where Anne motioned.

"He knows he's in big-time trouble, so he's not talking."

"Keep calling for William. Don't stop."

I hurried through the trees towards Brian, the top of his head illuminated by the screen of a phone.

"Thanks for coming, Peggy. I know it's late," I said, kneeling in front of Brian.

"It's no problem at all, Lynn. But I can't get Mr. Brian here to say a word."

Brian's freckled face was drained of color; it was obvious even in just the dim light from Peggy's phone. "Hey, buddy. You aren't in trouble with Nanna, Brian. You were just trying to find your brother. It's OK. Tell Nanna where you last saw William."

Brian said nothing, continuing to vacantly stare as if I, nor anyone else, existed in the world.

"Brian, look at Nanna."

He didn't move, didn't blink.

I looked to Peggy's concerned face and stood up. "Can you stay with him for another minute?"

"Of course," she said, placing her hand on Brian's shoulder.

"William!" I called out, hoping that the sound of my voice would cause William to stop, wherever he was, and call out to me. "William!"

The forest seemed ridiculously large, even though it couldn't be more than a mile in any direction. For heaven's sake, I thought, there was an Exxon not a half-mile away from where the trees ended.

That thought frightened me even more. What if William made it through the forest and to the road . . . ?

"Tom!"

I followed the sound of my husband's booming voice to find him shining a light under a fallen tree. "I'm worried William may have made it to the Harding Road. He's only seven, he could easily get turned around. I'm going to get in the car and drive, see if he's walking. Have you called the police?"

"Chief Stacks is coming with a few of his guys. They know to keep it off the scanners."

I felt a bit of anger flare, but I swallowed it as I hurried back towards the house. What Tom was saying was right. Once it hit the scanners that a boy was missing in Belle Meade in the middle of the night, the overnight photographers from the local stations would be jarred from where they napped in their news cars. Live-broadcast trucks would soon follow.

We'll find him long before that, I promised myself. Feeling my pants pocket, I pulled out the key fob to the Volvo, pushed the button, and saw the headlights flare to life.

I tried not to think about how relieved I felt stepping free of the trees.

When I drove back up the driveway a half hour later, two unmarked squad cars and an old Dodge pickup sat with their headlights on. I pulled up behind and hurried out. The beams from the vehicles shined on Anne frantically talking to one of the officers, who was taking notes and trying to calm her down. When she saw me, she once again burst into tears.

"We're gonna find him, we're gonna find him," I whispered as she collapsed into my arms.

"Ma'am, we're quietly calling in metro police to help comb these woods. If he's here, we'll find him," the officer said.

"If he's here? Of course he's here!" Anne cried out.

I petted her hair. "Shhh, Anne."

"Are you suggesting someone has him? Mom, what if someone was in the woods? What if he got to the road before you, and someone picked him up?" she asked.

"Excuse us, officer." I took Anne aside. "Honey, call your sisters. We need everyone's help. I'm going to get Brian and bring him into the house. He doesn't need to be standing out there."

"He won't talk to the officers, Mom. He won't talk at all. It's like he's in shock."

"Just call your sisters."

At the clearing, I was not surprised to see my daughter Kate had already arrived. She was pacing back and forth, talking on her cell phone in the same suit coat she had worn home from Washington. Tom and Belle Meade's police chief were kneeling in front of Brian, who looked exactly as he did when I left him forty minutes ago.

Kate reached out and gave my arm a squeeze, continuing to talk quietly on her cell. Tom spoke in a low voice at my approach.

"Brian's not speaking. Kate is on the phone with the feds."

He explained volumes in those two brief sentences. He believed Brian was in shock after experiencing something traumatic. And the fact that Kate, who along with being our daughter was the chief of staff in Tom's senatorial office, spoke intently on the phone with Washington meant she was talking to the FBI.

I headed straight for Brian. "I'm taking him to the house. He doesn't need to be out here anymore. Come on, baby."

I scooped him up, knowing he looked comically large in my arms.

"I'll carry him—" Tom began.

"Keep searching. William's here, we just haven't found him yet."

I could feel the heat from Brian's body as I whispered soothing words to him on our way out of the trees. Thankfully, as we reached the yard, I saw that the officer and Anne had returned to the woods. I didn't want her to see me carrying her son like a limp doll.

We entered the house, heading straight for the back rooms

where I kept spare pajamas for all my grandchildren. I quickly
found his favorite: a pair of Avengers shorts and a T-shirt. I un-
dressed him and slipped on the pajamas.

We went into the kitchen next, where I poured him a glass
of cold milk and handed it to him with an Oreo cookie. He held
the cup in one hand and the cookie in the other, continuing to
stare, bringing neither to his mouth.

"Let's take them upstairs," I said, relieving him of both,
knowing I was moving too fast, that I needed to calm down
myself. But instead, I hurried us up the stairs to my bedroom,
turning on one small lamp. I peeled back the quilt on my side
of the bed and guided Brian inside, kissing his forehead, then
rounded the bed, took off my shoes, and climbed onto Tom's
rumpled side.

I took a deep breath and gently turned Brian's rigid body
towards me, looking directly into his eyes, brushing his hair
with my fingers.

"I love you, Brian bear. I want you to go to sleep. But we
have to find William. Can you tell me where was the last place
you saw him?"

He closed his eyes, and I rested my head on his pillow. His
eyelids then slowly drifted open, only for a moment.

"The lights took him," he said softly.

THREE

My hands tested the strength of the ceramic mug as I watched the flashlights move in the trees. I'd come downstairs after Brian had rolled over and refused my repeated questions to explain what he meant about the lights. I'd covered his shoulders with the quilt, even though I was the one who was suddenly cold.

I almost wished to experience Anne's bold and unhinged panic, weeping and crying out William's name. Instead, my fear manifested differently, in horrible thoughts of my grandson, hurt, lying on the floor of the forest, unconscious from tripping, his bright red hair tangled with leaves, unable to alert even the police officer who stood unknowingly a few feet away. Or perhaps he was wandering in some nearby street having long since left the trees, his face flushed in tears, unaware of where home was and why no one had come to find him. In the darkest parts of my mind, I thought of William in the backseat of some stranger's car, a stranger who coaxed him through trees, loaded him into the car with promises of going to see his parents, and was driving him farther away with each passing minute.

I glanced at a sudden series of snaps from one of the out-door lights on the porch. I expected to see a singed cicada, or perhaps a wounded moth, drifting to earth. Instead, the lantern was nearly covered in a mass of movement.

Ladybugs swarmed the light, popping like kernels in oil. I realized why all the lights were so dim on the porch: All the other lantern sconces were also covered in the beetles.

When I was a little girl, Daddy brought them to the prop-erty. Since the beetles were known to kill other plant-eating insects, he purchased hundreds of them through one of his mail-order catalogs. They'd been in the lanterns my father and those men had carried that day in the woods—

The coil on the screen door squeaked. Tom, Chief Jeff Stacks, and another officer walked out. I inhaled sharply at the sudden recognition. Paul Strombino was the metro detective I always saw on the news, with his fierce, full mustache and sunken eyes, the one who was always assigned to investigate the most disturbing crimes in the city.

"I can't get Brian to wake up," Tom said. "I'd forgotten what's it's like to try and rouse an eight-year-old when they're dead asleep. But he has to wake up, Lynnie; he's the last one to see William."

"What, again, did he say to you?" the police chief asked.

I cleared my throat, the words like thorns in my throat. "That the lights took William."

"Could be someone with a flashlight. Or the headlights of a car," the mustached detective said quietly.

"Lynn, this is detective Paul Strombino, with Metro PD," Chief Stacks motioned. "He's the best detective in town, maybe in the entire state."

"Not true, but thanks." The detective nodded in my direc-tion. "I hope I can help, ma'am."

"Thank you for coming," Tom said. "I certainly hope you're not needed."

"I am not an alarmist, Senator. But I do not like the sound of this."

"He's got to be out there."

"I'm sure he is. We just haven't found him yet," the police chief said, his hands on his hips. "We have thirty men in the woods right now. Those trees aren't more than a square mile. We'll find him. And our patrol units are combing the neighborhood. We haven't issued an Amber Alert yet, but your grandson's photo is quietly being distributed throughout all police channels."

"Why would it be quietly sent out?" I asked. "Shouldn't we let as many people know as possible know that he's missing?"

Chief Stacks lowered his gaze and Tom squared his shoulders to me. "Because we have to be smart about this, Lynn. William is in those woods. Or he's wandered somewhere in the neighborhood. If we go sounding the alarm, and he's quickly found, never in harm's way, it will reflect badly upon Chris and Anne."

What you mean is it will reflect badly upon your political career—

A car came tearing up the driveway, squealing its tires as it came to an abrupt halt behind the police cruisers. Our youngest daughter leapt out of her Honda Accord, dropping her cell phone from her ear as she ran towards the house. Stella's hair, usually styled professionally for morning television, was pulled back in a hastily assembled ponytail. "Why didn't anyone call me sooner? Oh my God, Strombino? Why is he here?"

"It's OK, Stella. Detective Strombino is here as a precaution," Tom said.

"No sign of William?" she asked. "I couldn't reach Kate or Anne on their phones."

"They're in the woods with everyone else."

"Where is Greg?" Stella asked.

"Anne just checked on him. He's asleep at her house with the neighbor watching him."

"Oh my God, William," Stella bit her lip.

"Go, Stella, we're right behind you," I waved her on.

"Do I need to call the TV station? Get William's picture out?" she asked.

"No, not yet," Tom responded. "Go to your sisters, Stella."

Stella dashed across the lawn with the speed of the former track star she was in college.

"Let's all go," Tom took my hand. "We all need to keep searching."

"Brian shouldn't be up there alone."

"There's an officer stationed here," Chief Stacks motioned upstairs.

"Come on, Lynn." Tom tugged at my hand.

I swallowed, looking up at the bedroom window. I still wasn't convinced Brian was sleeping.

Once, when we were teenagers, my best friend, Roxy, stole some cigarettes. We snuck off towards the tree line with them when Daddy saw us from the nursery. "Lynn Stanson! Roxanne Garth! You take one more step and you'll wish the only trouble you were in was because of those smokes!"

I remember tilting my head, a rare flash, especially for me, of teenage defiance. But I saw Daddy approach with all the intensity of a bull, and I snatched Roxy's hand and dragged her back to the house. I'd glanced over my shoulder at Daddy, but he wasn't looking at us anymore. He was staring into the woods.

I should have asked you then. I should have made you tell me what happened that afternoon. Why those men wanted to go to that clearing with the gravestone. It was a gravestone—a child's grave-stone. I know what I saw. Why did they carry lanterns with ladybugs inside? There was so much I wanted to ask you, but I didn't learn to only fear the woods that day.

After Daddy died, and Tom and I moved into and remod-eled his house for our growing family, I made sure to read fairy tales to my girls of haunted forests where witches lived and children got lost. I routinely emphasized Lyme disease, and I sighed with relief when Anne declared she wasn't the nature type—and her younger siblings were thankfully in the throes of older sister worship.

But decades later, it was the grandkids who salivated for the woods. When Tom finally succumbed to years of whining, he tried to sneak them out back. I saw them through the dining-room window and came out blazing from the kitchen.

Poison ivy! Chiggers! Ticks! Underground caves! Old bear traps! I tried to remember every line my father used on me. I held back on telling them about the monsters. They would have laughed, and I would have lost ground. Instead, I got a lot of groans, but ultimately the sad parade marched back in the house, with my husband shaking his head.

But there was nothing I could do to keep Anne's boys from entering the woods from their own property. I knew Chris and Anne were wishing they had heeded my warnings, considered, up until this point, unwarranted. I had seen my son-in-law briefly in the last hour, and I wanted to grab his arm, tell him everything was going to be all right, that we would find his son. But Chris's face was so full of despair I let him go. His voice was already growing hoarse.

I tried to banish the thought of William unconscious, dirt smeared over his sweet face, lying on the ground. He's wan-dered off, I told myself. He's asleep on someone's screened-in porch. There are so many sprawling properties out here, mansions and estates filled with gardens and guesthouses and pergolas. Country-music executives, lawyers, doctors, and a few celebrities were our neighbors. There were so many places for William to go.

My phone began to vibrate again. Stella's name came up on the screen.

"Mom, my overnight assignment editor called. I let it go to voice mail. They know something is going on; the cops are everywhere. It's only a matter of time. I'm not returning the call. Dad needs to know it's started."

"I'll tell your dad. Keep looking."

"Mom." Stella's voice quieted. "Has Dad had the cops run the addresses of the registered sex offenders in the neighborhood?"

"Stella, there are no registered sex offenders around here."

"Mom, there are registered sex offenders in every zip code in the city. We have to think about these things. I'll find out myself if I have to."

"Keep looking, Stella."

I hung up and saw Chris's face among the flashing lights in the clearing, his fingers laced behind his head.

I hurried over. "Chris, where's Tom?"

"It's my fault, Lynn. I shouldn't have let them camp out tonight. Especially with rain still in the forecast. Will was so upset, he cried himself to sleep. I should have brought them all inside, if only to calm William down."

"Chris, I don't want to hear you say that again. No one is to blame. We will find him. Where is Tom?"

"I'm here," Tom said, walking up with Detective Strombino.

"Stella called. Her station knows something is happening.

She says she won't return their call. But they'll figure it out. They may already have cameras outside."

Tom whipped out his phone, turning his back to us.

I looked to the detective. "Has he told you yet?"

Strombino paused, and Tom looked back at me. He whispered a few more words and jammed the phone into his pocket. "Lynn, this isn't the time."

"Tom, these detectives need to know everything."

"Lynn, I will handle this."

Before I lowered my chin, I saw Strombino look at us, obviously uncomfortable in the simmering air.

"I'm not sure what the two of you are talking about, but I advise you to go public. The first twenty-four hours a child goes missing are crucial, and yours has already been gone for roughly two. I don't want to rattle off the statistics of how many children are actually found after that twenty-four-hour window closes—it ain't pretty. The longer this goes on, the more concerned I'm becoming about what your other grandson said. Lights don't take children—people holding flashlights or driving cars with headlights take children."

No, Detective. My throat was suddenly so tight I couldn't have spoken if I wanted to. *Not always.*

"I just ordered my staff to reach out to the TV stations, the papers and the radio stations, and to get it on social media. We need the most recent photo of William possible. But no news conference yet. Only that our grandson is lost in the woods," Tom said.

I almost didn't hear my husband; I was so alarmed by what Strombino had said about the lights.

It can't be. After all this time . . . it cannot be.

"Find a recent picture and send it out with the alert," Strombino suggested.

"We have the family picture on my dresser, but William was only a baby," Tom said. He then snapped his fingers. "Get the magazine cover. It has a huge picture of William."

"The boy was on the cover of a magazine?" Strombino asked, and then cleared his throat. "Get that photo out now."

AP NEWS ALERT—NASHVILLE, TENN.

The seven-year-old grandson of U.S. Senator Thomas Roseworth is missing and a massive search is under-way in the woods directly behind the Tennessee law-maker's home.

The metro police department confirmed the identity of the boy as William Thomas Chance, the youngest grandson of Roseworth.

Police said Chance was last seen Friday night en-tering the woods.

William Chance is the son of Roseworth's oldest daughter, Anne, who lives on the other side of the wooded area behind the Senator's home in Nashville.

The neighborhood is known for the estates of other prominent politicians, including Al Gore.

Chance was recently appeared on the cover of *Southern Living*, for an article profiling the home and garden shop of Roseworth's wife, Lynn.

Senator Roseworth is in Nashville to help in the search.

—*Copyright Associated Press*

"The lights took him."

I awoke to Brian's words, the last memory of a disturbing dream. I lay in a pool of morning sunlight, already hot from the August sun.

I slid out of bed, almost stumbling in my haste. I'd come up to check on Brian and found him tossing, so I sat down to pat his back as I had when he was a toddler with the croup. I'd lain down for only a moment.

How could I have done that, knowing William was out there somewhere? And if it was because of the magazine, it was all my fault.

I'd known, even then, the cover had been a terrible idea. A freelance writer for *Southern Living* had showed up early one morning in early spring, gushing about the store, my garden, and the house. I declined an interview and repeated over and over again that there was nothing special about any of it. Roxy, who managed the shop with me and had not had her coffee yet, wordlessly led the writer outside, took me by the hand out the front door, promptly went back inside herself, locked the doors to the building, told me through the glass to enjoy the early May heat wave, and to come back in the air conditioning when the interview was done.

After conferring with Tom, I consented. I had to admit, the end result had been a beautiful spread on the Peddler and the garden.

The writer thought the garden might make the cover, but none of us expected the photograph that was ultimately chosen. William had been corralled along with his brothers to the front lawn while the photographs were taken, but he had begged his mother for sweet tea after a while, and Anne had snuck him into the house. As they exited, the photographer cried out for silence (mainly directed towards Roxy), and snuck up on the little red-haired boy wearing only overalls carrying a glass of sugar-drenched tea, wandering through the garden. The end photograph was William looking back towards the camera, surrounded by calla lilies.

I should have been thrilled by all of it. But I could barely look at the magazine; horrified by the customers who asked me to sign it, inquiring if Tom knew how famous his wife was now.

With a quick glance at Brian to confirm he was still sleeping, I bolted across the bedroom and hurried down the stairs while hugging the rail like a car driving too fast on a curve.

The stairs led to a hallway off the kitchen, and the first person I saw was Tom, leaning on the counter and intently checking his phone.

"Was it all orchestrated?" I said, startled at the volume of my own voice.

I then saw the police officers crowded around maps on the kitchen table, with Kate in the center. By the refrigerator, two men in suits stopped their conversation with Detective Strombino.

Kate moved around the table quickly. Tom put away his phone. "Lynn—"

I waited till he was near enough for him to hear my whisper. "Your operatives, did they send that writer to the shop? Was that all part of some campaign?"

"What?"

"It's true, isn't it? The magazine cover. The profile of our family. It wasn't by chance that writer came. And now William is gone. How could you let me sleep?"

"It's only been an hour, Lynnie. Honestly, I didn't even know you were up there until about thirty minutes ago, when I couldn't find you—"

"I don't need to sleep. I need to know if that's how William ended up on that cover."

"What you need to do is calm down and not make a scene." He stepped in close.

"I have never made a scene in all my life."

Kate rubbed my arm. "Mom—"

"Where is Anne? I need to see her." I felt delirious from the swell of anger and exhaustion.

"Stella made her lie down in the back room. She's asleep, finally, and so is Stella, beside her. I think Stella strongly suggested she take a Xanax," Kate said.

"Then who's out searching?"

"Seems like half the police department," Kate looked out the window. "We came in to look at some of the geological maps in better light. We're all about to go out again. Roxy is here."

I walked past them and the police officers, heading out the screen door. I knew neither Tom nor Kate would follow.

I instantly heard Roxy's voice as I moved across the dewy grass that would soon become bone dry in the oppressive heat.

She was railing into her phone, which was barely visible amidst her mess of black hair streaked heavily with gray. She wore a white T-shirt with a Beethoven face, his eyes peering out from beneath her denim vest. There was some kind of embroidered flower on both the vest and her matching shorts. She slipped her feet in and out of her Birkenstock flip-flops.

"Get your ass over here, Rick. I'm calling the entire garden club. We're all going to help in the search. See you in a minute," Roxy said. She turned to see me walking across the grass.

"They can't find him."

"Don't start saying that." She pulled me close and patted the curls on the back of my head, just as she had done when Marty Throw broke up with me before the eighth-grade Sweetheart Banquet. Those same hands would later punch him in the gut in the alley behind the gym. "He's gonna turn up any second now."

"I wanted to call you, but I kept telling myself we would find him by now."

"You should have. I've already told the cops they need as many trusted volunteers as possible to comb the woods and the neighborhood. So I've already called the sewing group, the garden club, and the Roseworth Democrats, and they're all headed this way. I'm going to the shop to make coffee for everyone, then I told the cops I'd screen all the people showing up, to make sure no media types get in. No offense to Stella."

"I keep thinking about William, hurt out there or in some stranger's car—"

"Don't go there yet, Lynn."

"I have to get it together," I rubbed my face. "I tore into Tom about that damn magazine article."

"I doubt very much you tore into him. In fact, you haven't raised your voice to him in decades."

"If I wasn't so afraid, all I would be is angry. Let's just say we learned last night that the magazine was coinciding with a big announcement Tom would like to make."

Ever active in the Democratic Party, Roxy raised her eyebrows. But she quickly shook her head. "Go wash your face and change your clothes. Then get back out here. We'll find him, Lynn. Look at me. We'll find him."

I nodded once and turned back to the house. As soon as I began to hurry away, I heard Roxy once more on the phone. I could still hear her as I crossed the porch and entered the kitchen.

Kate and Tom were standing and talking to Detective Strombino, their arms identically crossed in front of their chests. The two men in suits were looking at a laptop computer and conferring with the police officers.

Kate approached me. "They're FBI."

"Strombino thinks he's been kidnapped, doesn't he?"

"He's not said that yet."

"That's what he thinks. That's why you've called in the FBI. Kate, you have to tell them about—"

A scream came from upstairs.

I scrambled up the stairs, everyone else in my wake. One of the officers said something about letting him go first, but I ignored him and pushed open the bedroom door.

Brian was sitting upright on the bed. Barely audible under his screaming was the sound of static coming from the television in the open armoire. I'd forgotten to turn off the alarm. The television was programmed to turn on automatically at 5:30 A.M. Instead of HGTV, all that buzzed was a grainy white-and-black screen.

"Baby, it's OK, it's OK," I swept him into my arms. "Tom, turn off the TV."

Tom scrambled for the remote. Brian continued screaming as I rocked him. Finally, Tom found the device and the TV went dark.

My grandson immediately stopped crying, but continued to stare at the screen.

"It's OK, it just scared him," I said. The cops and the FBI agents looked around the room to make sure. Tom came over to the bed and sat down, patting Brian's back.

"Hey buddy. You're OK. You got spooked."

"Must have been a power surge last night," Kate rubbed her eyes. "All the clocks in the house are blinking."

"He's asleep again," Tom noted.

I looked down to see Brian solidly passed out. I laid him down, brushing his hair from his forehead.

"We really need to talk to him," Detective Strombino said quietly from the hallway.

"Lynn, we have to wake him up."

"Not until one of his parents is here. Kate, go get Chris. Let Anne sleep."

I continued to stroke Brian's hair as the minutes dragged on. The clock in the room ticked irritatingly loud. Tom stood by the window and looked out at the large gathering of volunteers and police.

"You told them, didn't you?" I asked. "That's why the FBI is here. That's why you didn't tell me I was wrong about the article. They know, don't they?"

He kept staring. I buried my nose in Brian's hair.

"They know what?" Chris asked, wearily walking in, with Kate and Strombino behind him.

"About what I told everybody last night." Tom looked out the window. "The agents know what that means—"

Chris sat on the bed and put his arm under Brian, a little rougher than I would have liked. "Wake up, son. You've got to wake up."

I couldn't watch, hearing the frustration and desperation in his voice. I also feared that if he successfully woke Brian, the boy's only response would be a dense stare.

"You think this is all connected?" Chris asked.

My husband waited a moment before answering. "When you agree to run for vice president, you make a lot of enemies overnight."

FOUR

"Mom, are you with me?"

As my youngest daughter leaned in closer to apply a heavy coating of concealer under my eyes, I realized how haggard even she looked in the bright lights of the makeup mirror, although her face was void of wrinkles and age spots.

"If I can make myself look awake at four in the morning to read about car wrecks and shootings on TV, then I can surely make it seem like you haven't been awake for twenty-four hours," Stella said.

"I did sleep for a while. They shouldn't have let me sleep."

"Mom, you were probably asleep for fifteen minutes. You need to rest. You're going to bed right after the news conference—"

"I will not do it, Stella. I told your father that, and I told Kate that. I cannot do it. I am in no shape for it. The only reason I am sitting here now is because you practically strong-armed me. I should be out looking for him."

Stella put the makeup brush on the bathroom counter. "One thousand people, including members of the National Guard, combed over every foot of the woods. It's not that big of an area. Every house in the near vicinity has been searched. William is not in the woods. He is not in the neighborhood. You have to realize that. We have to reach a wider audience."

"I can't do it."

"Yes, you can. You've done a million election nights."

And I had hated every one. Sitting nervously in the room at the Hermitage Hotel watching the results come in, Tom pacing even though he knew he was a shoo-in every time. The Washington staff flown in for the election, complaining about the slow pace of the servers in the restaurants and checking their cell phones frantically.

"You have to do it, Mom. For Anne, Chris, for William. For Dad. It will be hard enough as it is for him to make the statement. All you have to do is stand beside him and hold that picture of William."

"I will start crying."

"You're not a big crier. You know that. I'm the same way. So is Kate. Anne got all the waterworks genes. You stand up there and know that what you're doing is getting William's picture out all over the country. It's urgent that we do this now. This news conference will be carried by every cable channel and will be in every paper in the morning. It will be the top story on every news website and will be all over social media—Twitter, Facebook. There is no place in the world that won't know he's missing. It will bring him home."

I looked down. "How much time do we have?"

"About ten minutes. But we should go down. All the stations in town will be taking the news conference live at the top of the six o'clock news. That's good, Mom. Most people will be home from work, if they work on Saturdays. And it's so hot tonight most people will be indoors. It's the best exposure you can get. And we need the exposure. Pretty soon, William will be missing for twenty-four hours. And you heard what Strombino said about that."

I looked back in the mirror, horrified at the yellow tint of my skin in comparison to my white shirt. My cheeks looked sunken, my eyes dark.

"Come on." Stella pulled on my hand softly.

I took my hand back gently to indicate I was fine to walk on my own. As soon as we walked down to the kitchen, I heard the screen door snap, and Kate was there, wearing a dark business suit. "Are you ready, Mom?"

I left the mug, thinking the caffeine might make me even more jittery. *If that were possible.*

The screen door exited to the north end of the wraparound porch. Tom, smoking a cigarette, paced beneath large Kimberly ferns. Another man and a woman, also smoking, stood nearby.

"Lynn, this is Tony and Deanna from the Washington office, they both just flew in." He quickly snuffed out the cigarette. "Tony, Deanna, this is my wife, Lynn, and my youngest daughter, Stella. You remember, Lynn, that Tony works with Kate in our press office. Deanna is kind of a surprise; I didn't know she was joining us. This is her first day. Some hell of a first day," Tom said, straightening his tie.

"I'm so sorry for all this," Deanna said, trying to hide the cigarette in her own hand.

Stella walked over and stopped her father's efforts, taking the tie into her own hands. He thanked her quietly.

Kate rounded the corner of the porch, motioning for us all to follow. Tom walked over and took my hand.

"My wife isn't a fan of the cameras. Or any attention, for that matter."

"I'll be fine," I replied, so softly only he could hear me.

"Oh Mom, wait." Stella rushed back into the house. She

appeared seconds later, holding a large framed photo of William's magazine cover.

"Oh my God, I almost forgot."

As we crossed across the porch, the woods beyond seemed to vibrate in the summer haze.

The lights took him, Brian had said.

You know you've heard it before.

My family called my mind a steel trap. I remember the ever-changing shoe sizes of my grandsons, how much aluminum to add or subtract in soil to change the color of a hydrangea, the names of quilt patterns. I am everybody's first choice on teams for Trivial Pursuit. Roxy commented she would give me psychedelic drugs if it meant I would stop recalling the time she admitted she found George W. Bush attractive.

How long can I pretend I haven't heard it?

Live-feed vans and satellite trucks, with tall masts and enormous dishes, lined the street in front of the house. I scanned the call letters on all the trucks, failing to recognize several of the stations, which had come from all over the state. Some of the larger trucks had no writing at all, which, I remembered from Tom's election nights, meant they were local production companies hired by the networks.

From the trucks rolled long black cables, stretching across the yard like snakes, leading to the sea of cameras standing in a row. It felt as if we were approaching a firing squad.

Tom gripped my hand and led us towards the microphone stand, a silver rod where more than a dozen mic flags were fastened, decorated with garish colors and numbers. Standing among the cameras were reporters, armed with notebooks. I could hear several of them talking, broadcasting live off the top of the six o'clock news.

". . . Marcus, Senator Roseworth is now approaching the microphone . . ."

". . . I can see his wife and two of his daughters with him . . ."

". . . One of them is Channel Four's own Stella Roseworth, who is obviously taking some time off to be with her family . . ."

". . . It doesn't appear the parents of the missing boy are here, and none of the other grandchildren are here, including the one we're told who last saw William Chance . . ."

". . . Let's listen in and see what the senator says."

Tom stopped before the microphones, squinting in the brilliant last light of day.

"On behalf of my wife, Lynn, our children, and our grandchildren, I want to thank you all for coming here tonight. And thank you to all the volunteers and police officers who have helped us try to find our William."

The lights took him.

Of course I remember. But I didn't even dare mention what I suspected; I just hoped we'd find him by now. We all just need to focus on alerting everyone to his disappearance—that's what matters now.

"As you all know, my youngest grandson disappeared in these woods late last evening. We have combed every inch of the area, spoken with all our neighbors, and there is simply no sign of him. We have no other choice but to assume he has somehow been taken."

The lights took him.

I can't tell them now. They'll think I'm hallucinating. Tom will rush me to the hospital, fearing I've had a stroke.

"We are asking everyone watching to take a good look at our boy. Our William. He is everything to us. His momma misses him, his daddy misses him, his brothers miss him, and his grandpa and nanna really miss him. He's our baby boy, our

Will, and we need all your help to find him and bring him home."

Like fireflies in evening shadows, the lights on top of the cameras started to glow. The sun had faded behind some powerful clouds, and the photographers scrambled to keep enough light on our family. The satellite truck operators turned on the large lights on stands that stood behind the row of cameras, to light both the press conference and the reporters who would soon turn back to the cameras to repeat what had just been stated. The lights bathed my family in white, causing my eyes to flare.

The lights took him.

With that, I admitted to myself what I'd worked so hard to bury. There was no use denying it.

William had been taken, just like all the others.

FIVE

I walked into the kitchen, pulled my sunglasses from the tangles in my hair, and glanced out the windows above our banquette. The purse that I intended to set on the counter slid off my shoulder and landed with a thud on the floor, and the keys I always carefully put in the drawer under the microwave crashed to the floor with it.

The window provided a wide view of the satellite trucks that had doubled, maybe tripled in number since I left that morning. The monstrous vehicles now appeared to line both sides of Evelyn Avenue. More photographers had arrived to stand on our side lawn, their lenses following investigators walking in and out of the woods. Heavy traffic prevented the trucks from parking on Harding Road, which is why I'd taken it when I'd returned a few minutes ago, fearing but not fully comprehending the chaos surrounding our home.

I should have known when I'd driven to Anne's before eight and found another crop of cameras waiting to document me hurrying into their house. I had never been so thankful that she drove a Subaru with tinted windows, so we could pull out of the garage and none of the cameras could get footage of Brian in the backseat.

I heard Tom's footsteps approach from the other room. He always scuffed his feet when he was anxious.

"Has Brian spoken yet?"

I wrinkled my nose. "Please don't smoke in the house."

"I was in the study with the door closed. And who the hell cares at this point, Lynn? How is Brian?"

"I care, Tom, because Ginger Roth from church died from lung cancer last year."

"Tell me about the doctor. Did he get Brian to talk?"

"No, Tom, he didn't. He wants Brian to come every day and do some experimental therapy to hopefully open him up to discuss what happened. But he thinks the same thing the police think: that whatever Brian saw stunned him into silence."

"Experimental therapy? My God, we don't have time for experiments. It's been almost twenty-four hours, Lynn. You heard what the detectives said. Every minute that passes means our chance of finding William diminishes. Brian needs to talk. He's the only one with answers. I should have gone."

His used that tone primarily when he was in Washington, with everyone from his staffers to Republican adversaries. It indicated that he knew everything about which he spoke. There was no room for debate.

"If you had gone, you would have ended up in a shouting match with the doctor. So no, Tom, you shouldn't have gone. I know you want this to end—"

"So I can get back to Washington and the VP offer? That's not true, Lynn."

"I didn't say that."

"But you were thinking it."

"This is my fault. I'm the one who allowed that photo-

grapher to take his picture and put it on the cover of that magazine. My God, what was I thinking? I just wished I'd known
the truth."

"If this magazine had anything to do with William's disappearance, I will live with that for the rest of my life. It's not
your fault. It's nobody's fault but my own. It was my idea. Even
Kate didn't know. I didn't think it would do any harm. I keep
saying it, over and over again. I know the agents are tired of
hearing me say it."

"But if you'd just told us about the formal offer to run for
vice president the night William disappeared, how could anyone else have known?"

"It's the worst-kept secret in Washington. And the FBI does
not hesitate to point out that you could fill a phone book with
the names of the people who hate me."

I actually sat in during the first meeting with the investigators from the government and local police, but became so upset
I had to leave in the middle of it. When the vice agents began to
talk about the desire of pedophiles, I couldn't hear anymore.

The likely culprit was someone who had staked out the
family, the investigators believed. It was no random act. Someone either had become fascinated with William from the article,
or wanted the deepest revenge possible on my husband.

"Could someone hate you that much?"

Tom's face took on a weary look. "Shall I begin stateside or
overseas?"

"I can't believe someone in the United States would do this
for political reasons."

"I never thought it was possible either, Lynn. I still can't
fathom it. But people are so angry now, they are so fired up by
the pundits on both sides . . . All it would take is one crazy
zealot who listened to one of the conservative commentators

call me an enemy of the state. The FBI played it back to me, a recording of what's-his-name, the bigheaded guy, looking at the screen, pointing. 'Take back your country. Do whatever you have to do stop Roseworth and his liberal agenda. Don't let him into the White House. Do whatever you have to do.' All it would take is one nut job to come up with the idea to hurt my family. Because that's about the only thing that would cause me to turn my back on politics forever. They know that."

"This certainly can't be an act of terrorism."

Tom twitched his lips. It meant he was craving a cigarette.

"Terrorism . . . do they really think . . . ?"

"It's been tense in DC. It's by design that I don't bring you or the kids there anymore. I have almost constant security now."

"Since when?"

"Since I started coming down hardcore on needing more ground troops in the Middle East. I knew it would be controversial when a Democrat called for it, but I didn't expect to become public enemy number one. ISIS obviously hasn't taken responsibility for William—that would have been plastered all over the internet. But domestic terrorism is a different story. We've seen what these extremists have done. It's all about seeking revenge. And there've been no calls, no letters, nothing demanding a ransom for William. I've had every theory thrown out to me by either the CIA or the FBI, and I get a real feeling they don't know a damn thing."

The lights. Tell him about the lights. What you heard, what you did all those years ago.

Instead, I nearly threw up, something I'd never done in my life, despite living through countless stomach flus with the girls. I hadn't even vomited with Anne, my only girl who had prompted late-term morning sickness. Anne's pregnancy had been so different than the others. . . .

"Lynn, listen to me." Tom placed his hands on my shoulders, leaning in close. "I need you. I need you to be the person you've always been for us. We need you to be solid, to be unwavering, to be calm. No more outbursts like the other morning, asking if the magazine spread was a setup. I can't have you acting like that. Anne and Chris need you to be supportive and encouraging. Brian and Greg need their grandmother to be loving, not frazzled. Greg especially is having a hard time. Being nine-years-old and having one brother missing and the other refusing to talk is weighing heavily on him. Kate and Stella are tough, but they need their mother too. And I . . . I need my rock. The person I can depend on for everything."

He pulled me into a tight embrace.

And with that, I decided to keep lying.

It was Roxy who broke me free. Leaving the house wasn't an option, with investigators and police still combing the woods, and Tom receiving hourly updates on no potential leads. All this meant there was no way to avoid the cameras, the calls from earnest-sounding producers from the *Today Show* and *Good Morning America*, the neighbors bringing food and insisting they were refusing all sorts of financial offers from the tabloids to gain access to a better view of our house.

Roxy showed up late in the evening. She scowled at the photographers who'd flicked on their lights to capture her arrival in her pickup truck, took one look at me pacing in the kitchen, and ushered me out the back door towards the Rose Peddler.

Our garden shop was already closed on Sunday anyway,

but she'd made a sign that read "Closed Indefinitely. This means you, *National Enquirer*."

As Roxy unlocked the door, the familiar smell of the lavender candles and fertilizer brought the first moment of peace I'd had since Anne's frantic phone call two days ago. I inhaled deeply as she led me out to the back to the small screened-in porch we added on a few years ago as a place for me to read magazines and for Roxy to drink margaritas after a long day.

"No one can see you here. No reporters, no investigators, no husband or children. Turn on Nina while I pour the tequila."

"My God, Roxy, I can't do this. What if the police find something, what if Anne needs me, and I certainly can't have alcohol—"

"Sister, that tequila is for me. I wouldn't waste it on you, you're drunk off half a glass of wine. And you know as well as I do that your phone is in your pocket set on the loudest ringtone possible. Tom saw me haul you out, he knows where you are. We need to talk, and we need to do it in private. And your house happens to be crawling with the FBI at this moment. Simone. Now."

I reached over and pushed play on the ancient, yellow CD player. The piano rift that began "I Want a Little Sugar In My Bowl" was barely audible above the cicadas outside. As Nina Simone began to sing about her heartbreaking longing, Roxy returned from the mini refrigerator with a margarita in a pouch, something she routinely stocked up on at the liquor store.

"Now." Roxy took a long swig. "Tell me everything."

"There's nothing to tell. No leads. No ransom notes. No threats. No homegrown terrorist taking credit. All the sex offenders in a twenty-mile radius have been questioned and their homes searched. Now—as Chief Stacks warned us—the attention is turning to us."

"To you?"

"To the family. You can't imagine how awful it is. Here are Chris and Anne, in the midst of the worst moment of their lives, having to answer the most awful questions. They asked Anne if Chris is abusing the boys. Not only physically, but sexually. She almost hyperventilated, especially when they said they'd tracked down her old fiancé from college, who claimed that Tom was mentally abusive to all of us."

"He said that because Tom told him at Thanksgiving dinner that he doubted the punk would ever make more than $12,000 a year." Roxy raised her index finger before taking a drink. "But regardless, how terrible."

"And they just circle the boys. They try to talk to Brian, who only sits in his chair and stares. I sat in when they interviewed Greg, and they asked him if he was ever afraid of his mom and dad. He looked at me and Tom in confusion and answered yes. You should have seen the FBI agent stiffen, and when they asked Greg why, he promptly told the story of when the dog pooped in the house, and he used the robot vacuum to try and pick it up, and it spread feces all over the upstairs carpets."

"He should have been afraid after that. That poor boy."

"And they know everything. All the times Chris has been sued by unhappy clients, when Brian was suspended from school for a day for bringing a pocketknife, what Anne posted on Facebook about her anger at people who complain about public breast-feeding. About that weirdo from Antioch who kept sending Stella those love letters at the TV station, demanding she friend him on Facebook. Anything—anything at all to indicate problems with our family, or who would hate us."

"Oh Sis, I'm so sorry. And it probably took them thirty

seconds to interview you. You have no enemies and you've never made anyone mad, except for me—those pastel garden hats we wore at my wedding were your idea. You may have put off a few of your fellow English students in college when you critiqued their awful short stories, but that's it. You're as noncontroversial as anyone could possibly be."

At that moment, I wanted to take the pouch from her and drain it dry. *You've been my best friend all my life, and even you don't know what happened.*

Roxy took another long drink. A wasp darted above us. Somewhere nearby, a lawnmower from one of the yard services roared to life.

"No family can survive this."

"Don't say that."

"We won't. We can't. Who could? We can't have Christmas. We can't have birthdays. How can you celebrate anything when you know he's out there? How will we ever recover? How can we go on without him?"

"You'll recover when William comes back. They will find him, Lynn."

"How? How can they find him? What if they don't know what they're doing? What they're even looking for?"

"Lynn, this is the FBI. That's what they do."

"What if they don't know? I'm so afraid they don't know."

"I know you are. We're all afraid. What do you think they don't know?"

I rocked instead of answering, and I knew Roxy understood what that meant, just like she knew what it signaled when I ate chocolate at midnight or crunched ice after watching Matthew Crawley on my DVD box set of *Downton Abbey*. When I rocked, it meant I was trying to work something out.

"Do you remember my father not allowing me to go into the woods?"

"Hmmm?" Roxy leaned back, folding her arms, a nap rapidly approaching. Ever since we were teenagers, it only took a little bit of alcohol to put her right to sleep.

"He absolutely forbid it when I was growing up. Once he told me that when you go into the woods, you don't come out."

"Your father was the sweetest and most overprotective man I ever knew. You were his only child. He raised you as a single father after your mom died so young. And let us not forget that he almost lost you too."

I reached up and let my fingers trace the back of my head, just behind my right ear. I was five when Daddy said the doctors discovered the brain tumor and insisted it be removed, even if the risks were great. My very first memory was waking up and seeing a man smiling at me. I asked who he was, and he barely could manage to say, "Your Daddy."

Some parents would have crumbled, but Daddy soldiered on and taught me everything about my life before the procedure, repeatedly showing me pictures of my mother to try and prompt me to remember her, which I never did. When I returned to school the next year, my friends (none of whom I remembered either) thought I'd moved away. Nashville was a lot smaller then. Daddy bragged to my teacher that I relearned to read in a week, and I was probably too advanced for kindergarten, but the school made me repeat the grade. Twelve years later, I graduated at the top of my class. In every picture from graduation, Daddy had tears in his eyes.

"He adored you. He didn't even want you riding in the car with me when I got my license, which, in retrospect, was a real concern. But honestly, do you think your dad could have foreseen this? Because that's impossible. I know you're running over every possibility in your mind. Don't torture yourself."

"Was that it, then? Him being overprotective?"

"Mmm hmmm." Roxy spoke in almost a hum.

"Maybe he was just being a helicopter dad. Remember when I came home from Illinois even though it was Tom's last semester in law school, because I was determined to have my first baby in Tennessee? Daddy never even told me how sick he was. When I was up north, he refused to let me come home and visit, saying that I needed to stay and support Tom in his last year. Even when I told him over the phone I was pregnant, he said I needed to start a new life there. I didn't even tell him I was coming home, and when I did, he had practically wasted away. He couldn't speak, write, or even eat on his own. All that time, he was protecting me from the truth about how sick he was."

I looked over to say more and saw Roxy's mouth was open enough for a soft snore to escape; her glasses had slipped down her nose. The tequila had kicked in.

"And do you know what else?" A hot wind blew through the trees, and I watched the leaves stir. "Do you know just before he died, he did speak to me? Only once. He said, 'Don't you raise that baby here, Lynnie. You go, and you never come back.' What did he mean by that?"

Roxy's chest rose and fell.

"I want to tell you." *I want to tell you everything. But once that door is opened, it can never be closed. And you would immediately begin to worry that I'd lost my mind.*

"What's that?" Roxy mumbled. "What . . . did you say?"

"Nothing." I took the pouch from her hand, placed it on the floor, and continued to rock. "I didn't say anything at all."

SIX

I could feel the encroachment of night, even though daylight saving time hadn't officially ended. The only solace to the early dark was that I could go to bed a little earlier each evening, pull up the quilts, and close my eyes. On this night, though, sleep had other plans.

I thought of Kate talking in hushed tones on her cell phone in the corner of the kitchen, on the rare weekends she was home from Washington. She had twice now booked earlier flights to return to the capital.

Of Stella's resignation from the anchor desk and her agreement with her news director to take a pay cut to join the investigative unit. How she held the mic like a weapon on the six o'clock news tonight, thrusting it in the face of a minister who took money from his congregation then promptly closed the church and purchased two sports cars and a boat. "I need to nail some bad guys," Stella said quietly last week, over lunch.

Of Anne, who slept away much of the day. Of Chris's leave of absence from the law firm, spending his days poring over information on sex offenders in Nashville and pacing through the woods.

Of the alarm going off at 6:00 A.M., so I could be at Anne's house by 6:30 to get Greg ready for school. Of 3:15, when I picked him up, took him home, and peppered him with questions about school. *Don't you think you should rejoin scouts? Don't you think you should get back into flag football?* He preferred to sit in front of the Cartoon Network instead. I didn't mind. That programming was never interrupted with news updates, which occasionally pertained to our family.

Of Brian, vacant and wooden, staring out the window of the psychiatrist's office, refusing to engage with the doctor or anyone else. He was unresponsive at school, so Chris and Anne had to pull him out and hired a tutor to come to the house to try and work with him. Yet every day I brought Greg home, the tutor only shook her head. Chris had flown into a rage on Monday, screaming at Brian to tell them what he saw. Brian had gone into his room and laid on top of his bed. I hurried in, hoping to find him crying. His eyes were dry.

Of Tom's absence from the neighborhood Labor Day parade, which just last year he, Brian, Greg, and William had led, the boys tossing candy from Tom's 1990 soft-top Jeep Wrangler. How he disappeared into his library to stare at a photograph of the four of them, each holding a Jolly Rancher in their teeth and grinning like hyenas. He emerged smelling like smoke and whiskey.

Of our family's offer of $500,000 for any information that led to the safe return of our grandson. Of the hundreds of false leads that followed.

Of the flowers in the garden that I had abandoned at the end of the brutal summer. I felt like I had done the same to

William, in denying that I remembered where I had first heard the words.

The lights took him.

I have a difficult relationship with memories. I still remember how it felt to be five and know nothing. How I stiffened when Daddy went to hug me, until I was convinced he was, indeed, my father. My hesitantance to eat broccoli until I believed what Daddy had told me, that I did in fact love it cooked, but not raw. Forgetting memories is a task I have yet to master. Max Riddle lifting my skirt in front of the junior-high football team. What it was like to have three daughters, each with the stomach flu. The early morning call from Roxy about the cancer diagnosis for her husband.

Pushing aside memories, I have found, is easier. They're sneaky, though. When someone says to me they're so sorry about William, that they wish there was something they could do, memories start to sneak in. When Chris shares his latest research on his detailed spreadsheet of all the known sex offenders in the five surrounding zip codes, they try to dodge around the protective barrier I've put in place.

I've tried, I thought as I rolled over in the bed, seeking a cool spot on the pillow. I can't pretend anymore like I don't know.

The lights took him.

It seemed like it was always cold in the days I first heard those words.

The landscape had slowly altered outside the window of the Oldsmobile Cutlass, from the still-green trees in Nashville, to the relative lushness of Kentucky and Southern Illinois. *I will like it here*, I remember thinking. *It looks like home.* Three hours later we entered the cornfields of Central Illinois standing beneath the gray skies.

Tom, my husband of two weeks, had smiled sheepishly and kissed my cheek. "If I told you how terrible it is, you'd never have agreed to come."

We arrived in the town of Champaign-Urbana, the home of the University of Illinois. As picturesque as the university appeared, it still paled in comparison to my alma mater, Vanderbilt, which I'd only been able to attend thanks to a full academic scholarship. When we found our new apartment, I followed the landlord into the building and was nearly struck by the swinging door. It was the first time in my life a man had not held the door for me.

By Christmas, the snow piled high, along with our bills. My father never had much money, but I had never been this truly poor. It soon became apparent that Tom's life would have to become the law if he were to pass the bar. He was gone most of the day in class and was often away at night, studying at the law library. He wasn't on scholarship, and there wasn't time for a job. Tom's mother was dead, and he wasn't close to his father.

That meant I had to find a way to make money if we were going to eat. Stopping all attempts at writing my first novel, I took a job as a waitress at a late-night diner. I had a degree in English and graduated with honors, and I was serving up coffee.

When we returned to Nashville for Christmas, I went straight to Daddy, who took my face in his hands and told me that this was just part of marriage; that my home was in Illinois now and coming home wasn't an option; and that through the plant circuit, he knew a professor in the university's agriculture department who might be able to find me a job.

A few weeks later, I got a call from the university, thanking me for my interest in an office-manager position and saying that I had been given a job. It was decent money that would pay the bills, with a little left over for used books and cheap wine. I wasn't thrilled, but it meant using my brain, and I was proud that I was the sole breadwinner for my little family. I was given directions to the building and instructed to start work the following Monday.

At first, I thought I had the wrong building. But sure enough, there was an office manager job not in agriculture studies, but in the astronomy department, of all places. When I reacted with surprise, the dean of the department said he could certainly offer the job to someone else, but I quickly lied that I had always been interested in the stars. Once I had even located the Big Dipper, even though I had no idea how to find it again.

Yet the professors in the department didn't care. They were thrilled that they now had a full-time office manager. At first, I thought it was strange that a department with only five professors would even need such a position, but soon I came to understand why. There were, of course, the demands of students and scheduling, but there was also need to proof articles for industry publications, and near constant requests to book time in the university's planetarium. I took all of the tasks in stride, quietly enjoying being among the academics who seemed to constantly push up their horn-rimmed glasses above the bridge of their noses and thank me for completing even the smallest task. They had long dealt with bored undergrads assigned to man the front desk as part of their student work programs.

The only exception was Dr. Steven Richards. The young professor never picked up his messages from his students, never made eye contact with me as he walked briskly from his classes, and always kept his office door closed, even when he was inside. No one beside him ever entered. Sometimes, as he shut his door, I swore he lingered, staring at me while I typed.

And then there were the phone calls from nervous people anxious to speak with him. When he wasn't in, they insisted I write down bizarre messages to pass along to him. "Five stars on the horizon tonight," was a particular repeated message, and then their names and phone numbers. They called from all over the country—sometimes the world, based on the various accents. I started to think it was one big joke, and began to grow weary of the ridiculousness of it all.

While Dr. Richards always treated those messages with urgency, snatching them out of his mailbox and stuffing them quickly into the pocket of his tweed jacket, he would let messages from students pile up without responding.

Finally, when a student called for the fifth time, practically sobbing, saying she couldn't graduate unless she could talk to Dr. Richards about her final research paper, I'd had enough.

Granted, it had been a bad day. I'd broken the coffeepot at home, spilled ink on my white blouse, and the laundry Tom had promised to fold remained mounded up around the apartment. I took Dr. Richards's messages and marched to his office door. I knocked.

A soft response. "Who is it?"

"It's Lynn at the front desk. You have several students who need to speak with you, Dr. Richards."

"I'll get to them."

I turned the handle, expecting to open the door just enough to stick the messages in and then quickly close it. Instead, the knob turned easier than I thought and the door flew open.

"What are you doing?" Dr. Richards said.

"I am so sorry," I replied, my face flushed. I held out the messages. "I really feel like you should call them—"

I stopped in midsentence. The maps covering the walls all had red pins with connecting strings, making the room feel like a bizarre spider's web. Each of the pins seemed to have a note with some kind of furious writings. The maps continued all the way across the ceiling.

"Miss, you're going to have to leave. You're not allowed in here. And I will call those people back when I can."

"Those people?" I found myself firing back. *Stop talking! You need this job!* "They are your students! You don't even know my name, do you? I've worked here for four months."

It was clear he didn't. He ran his fingers through his hair, which was in desperate need of a cut. "I'm sorry, I'm very busy."

Be quiet! "Students are asking for their grades. Some are waiting to graduate."

"I will respond to them all today."

I nodded once and began to close the door when he spoke again. "You are Lynn Stanson, married name Lynn Roseworth. Vanderbilt graduate, English lit major, 4.0 grade point average, from Nashville, Tennessee."

I looked back at him in surprise, only to see that he was back to reading the papers in front of him. "I wouldn't let you take my messages if I didn't know who you were."

I turned to walk away and then stopped. "Why are those messages so strange? Is it some kind of joke? Are they friends of yours trying to be funny? Because they don't sound funny. They sound angry."

"They are colleagues of mine. Take down the messages and make sure you write them down exactly."

Get out of this office. "I'm the office manager, not just a secretary. The other professors even use me to proof their research papers. Dr. Long is sending me to the library now to do research for him. So I don't need to be told how to do simple tasks." *You are going to get fired, and Tom will have to drop out of school.* "I'll tell you what: From now on, if someone calls for you, I'll see if you are in. And if you are, you can take the call. If not, I'll ask them to call back later. That way, you'll never doubt that your messages were taken down correctly." *Thank you for the four months of employment.*

I had hoped the dean wouldn't call me immediately with the termination notice. I might have a day or two to find a new job—

"Mrs. Roseworth, do you think . . . you could do some work for me? Obviously, I'm a little disorganized. I don't mean to be aloof. It comes naturally."

When he smiled, it was almost childlike. He was clearly unaccustomed to it, like an awkward boy sitting for a school picture. Dr. Richards couldn't have been more than seven, maybe eight years older than me. *Shut up and thank him and agree to help.*

I stared over the rims of my own glasses. "Get those students straightened out, and I'll be happy to help you. What kind of work do you need me to do?"

"Just . . . keep taking the messages accurately for now. And I'll let you know when I need you for something more."

I closed the door, hoping he would never make the request. If my old babysitter, Mrs. Ross, had seen that mess of an office, she'd have said, "Bless his heart."

I'd gone back to the library and come back with so much research on solar flares for Dr. Long that he looked at me in astonishment. I wanted to explain that what I did two hours ago in Dr. Richards's office could have gotten me fired, so I needed to earn some goodwill among the other professors. Instead, I returned to my desk and prayed.

When I arrived the next day, two large boxes were stacked

on my chair. A note on top read: "Start with these. Organize by date. Only date.—Dr. Richards."

I put the boxes aside, thinking it would take me no time flat to organize the files by date, even though the boxes were quite heavy. I would do as Dr. Richards asked and politely thank him for the task. *Be sure to let me know if you need anything else,* I would say quietly.

The day had been busy with arranging meetings for students and the professors, fetching coffee, and copy editing an article about the gases around Saturn. The boxes stared at me like a hungry dog.

Before I prepared to leave, I peeked at a few of the files, knowing that my calendar tomorrow appeared freer, and I could tackle the project, maybe even finish it by late afternoon.

The first few pages in the file had most of the words blacked out. So many of the words were marked through I couldn't comprehend even what was typed or written on the pages. A quick glance through the files found them all to be the same.

Dr. Richards had to be in on this joke. My face grew hot. I strode down the hallway. Tom hadn't even thanked me for staying up late the previous night to prepare his lunch. He'd also washed my favorite blouse with a pair of his red basketball shorts.

I went to Dr. Richards's office and knocked on the door. When he didn't answer, I turned the handle.

He sat at his desk, several books stacked in front of him. He didn't look up. "Apparently, that lock is broken. I'll have to have maintenance come fix it. I didn't say enter."

"I saw you come in a few hours ago. You should respond when someone knocks on your door. So, is this a joke? There isn't a date on these, and they're all blacked out."

"There are dates. You won't find them in their usual locations. You have to look within the paragraphs."

"Why? What is this? Why is it all blacked out?"

He looked up, irritated. "When I feel like you can do this job, I'll explain more. If you can't do this job, then there's no need to explain."

I wanted to take his stupid boxes and stack them outside his door so when he opened it, he might trip on them. I flushed at the thought. "Yes Dr. Richards," I managed to say.

I returned to my chair, trying to ignore the boxes jeering at me. Tom would be working late. I had no interest in or desire to spend another night eating alone.

It was nearly seven o'clock when Dr. Richards left. As usual, he didn't acknowledge anyone or even note that I was still at my desk, hours after I was typically gone.

I immediately began pulling out the pages from the first box and began reading.

Two hours later, I was completely lost. At times, I could almost make out a few sentences, but even those made no sense. And what made it even more ridiculous was that none of it seemed to pertain at all to astronomy or his students' work.

Was he just crazy? Did he suffer from some kind of medical condition? I'd come across several dates that were not blocked out, but hundreds of other pages and letters had nothing to decipher.

I looked over at the picture of Daddy and me from graduation on my desk. Give a Stanson a job and we'll get it done, he always said.

This sudden attitude of mine could cost me this job. And I hated confrontation. Tom rarely became angry with me, and when he did, I quietly tried to even his temper to end the argument. I certainly never fought with Daddy. Perhaps it was that no one had ever totally dismissed me before or spoken to me like hired help.

I am wasting my time, I thought. I could be working on my writing. I leaned back in the chair, holding up two pages. *These are the last two. I'm dumping this all back outside his office and apologizing for my inability to finish the project.* I imagined sending all the students inquiring about him back to his office, and telling them to knock loudly because, despite being in his late twenties, Dr. Richards is a little deaf.

The fluorescent light above flickered. I sat forward and began to toss the papers into the box, when I stopped. I read the page again and found nothing. Then I leaned back and held up the pages.

The paper was so thin, I could easily see through to the blocked out words on the first page. I had encountered that problem myself before, when I tried to black out one of the professors' home addresses on a handbook that all the students would see, only to find the address could been seen when angled correctly in the light. But this time, it wasn't an angle that revealed what was marked through. When I held the two pages together, I could not only see the blacked out words, but also saw the words on the page behind it. The words from the second page fit the sentences from the first page perfectly.

I held the pages up to the desk lamp. I read them over and over again. The second page wasn't a second page at all.

I reread the sentence on the first page:

"I had noticed (blacked out) were blowing, so (blacked out) outside, and that's when I saw the (blacked out) and I (blacked out). The (blacked out) had (blacked out) him."

Dr. Richards—or someone, I guessed—took the time to type out a key for every single page. When I held the pages up to the light and matched up the paragraphs exactly, the words on the second page were, in fact, the words that had been blacked out on the first.

I had noticed (blacked out) were blowing.

The word behind the blacked out word was "trees."

I had noticed trees were blowing, it read. I smiled.

The words "trees," "ran," "streetlight," "panicked," "knew," "lights" and "taken" had all been blacked out on the first page and placed strategically on the second.

I snatched a pencil and wrote the words above the blacked-out smudges, and read the sentence in full:

I had noticed trees were blowing, so I ran outside, that's when I saw the streetlight and I panicked. The lights had taken him.

SEVEN

I had stayed until midnight the night I first unraveled the code of the files. It had not been dedication that had kept me glued to the pages.

The letters were not always written to Dr. Richards. Many were firsthand accounts, all had most words blacked out. I knew all I was supposed to be doing was finding the dates to figure out some kind of order, but I quickly realized it would be more complicated than that. While some were dated in the upper left-hand corner in standard letter format, the rest required full readings to find some mention of a day, a time, or even a month.

Soon, even if letters were clearly dated, I found myself reading them in their entirety. Several I read more than once. I had to put on my sweater due to the goose bumps on my arms.

When the clock hit 12:30, I grabbed my coat and hurried home, fearing Tom would be pacing in alarm. But he wasn't home either, which meant he was out with his law-school buddies, blowing off steam.

I made angry laps around the apartment. I'd never been a drinker, and while I didn't disapprove of alcohol, I certainly didn't like how it was contributing to my solitude. He hadn't even stopped by to leave me a note to say he was going out.

The next morning, I left without leaving him a note, making his lunch, or waking him, since had slept through his alarm.

I got to work early and waited. When Dr. Richards arrived, I practically blocked his entrance into his office, holding up one of the files.

"What is this?"

The professor's head was down as usually, but upon seeing the letters in my hand, he glanced at my face and told me to come in and close the door.

He sat down, folding his fingers behind his thick, dark-red hair, which was already streaked with silver, even though he wasn't yet thirty.

"You can read them?" he asked.

"Of course I can read them." I hoped the bags under my eyes didn't give away how long it had taken me. "I don't know how else to say this: It's disturbing. These are letters about people disappearing, being abducted, losing their loved ones. This has nothing to do with astronomy."

"It has everything to do with astronomy," he responded quietly.

I stood with my arms folded across my chest, waiting for him to continue. "I'll be honest with you, Miss Stanson—"

"It's *Mrs.* Roseworth."

"I suspected you were bright, but I actually didn't think you'd figure out the system this quickly."

"Well, you thought wrong. And I'm wondering if you should be giving this to police instead of to me to organize for you."

The professor reached deep into his pants pockets, and then fumbled in the interior of his coat, finally locating his keys.

He pivoted his chair around and unlocked an old file cabinet behind him, pulled out a drawer, took out a thick envelope, and slid it across the desk.

"Open it."

I picked it up and lifted the clasp. I expected to find more blacked-out papers, but instead saw what looked to be hundreds of photographs of varying sizes.

"What is this?"

"Those are the people we're trying to help. They've had someone disappear, or are missing themselves. I keep that envelope close by, and about once a day I open it, to remind myself why it's so important to keep all this so . . . shall we say . . . cryptic."

I once again looked around at the posters of space and maps of various states and countries, connected with pushpins, notes, and coordinates.

"What's going on here?"

Dr. Richards chewed on his lip.

"I will tell you one thing: The second I think you're up to something illegal, I'll go to the police."

"It's nothing like that. But you have permission to do so if I ever break a law. I suppose you could say that some people come to me when someone they love goes missing."

"Why would they come to you? You're an astronomy professor."

"Because they can't get answers from police. And they know something is wrong. I believe we have the ability to tell— to sense even—that something has happened beyond our understanding."

I raised my eyebrow.

"Has anything ever occurred in your life that you can't explain?"

"Honestly, no."

"Then you're lucky, and I hope, for your sake, that the rest of your life goes that way."

"I don't understand. Why would they come to you if someone is missing?"

"They don't just come to me. They come to all of us who are trying to find the truth."

"What truth?"

"That the government is aware of people disappearing and refuses to acknowledge it. I really shouldn't discuss this anymore until you agree to keep what we do silent. I had to see first if you could even decipher how we communicate—it can get complicated. Maybe I should have you sign something."

"Does the university know about this?"

"Oh, no. I'd be fired if they knew the amount of time I devote to this. They pay me to teach students about stars; students who actually don't care about stars and only want to fulfill their undergraduate demands."

Dr. Richards then added quickly, "I'll pay you to do this on the side."

I tried to not let on that at that very moment, I was ensnared. The student loans Tom would rack up by graduation seemed insurmountable.

"I won't do anything that's illegal, and I won't keep quiet if I even think you're doing something that harms someone."

"There's nothing harmful about anything we're doing. Honestly, most people would laugh if you told them what we do."

"And what is it, exactly, that you do?"

"Start organizing all those papers by date. You'll find the reference to a date on every other page. I'll pay you a $1.50 an hour."

I started doing the math in my head. It didn't even meet minimum wage standards for 1969, but it wouldn't be bad extra money. "I still don't know what this is about. Why are these people disappearing? Who is taking them?"

Dr. Richards stared hard at me, and then pointed up with one finger. I looked up at the ceiling covered in maps of the stars.

Like all children of the fifties, I'd seen the movies featuring the campy music, the flighty women, and cardboard-cutout heroes who fought against invaders from other worlds. When I had read over the documents from Dr. Richards's office, I tried not to think about those films. Because the people who documented the missing were real, and they were afraid. The letters, the bizarre phone calls, all came from very serious people.

I only told Tom that I was doing additional freelance copy editing work for a professor. It meant I would be staying later at the office. He certainly didn't object to the extra cash flow.

So I combed through the papers, leaving the neatly organized stacks in boxes outside the professor's office each evening. When I arrived the next day, the boxes would be gone.

One night, with the campus silent with snow, I had set a box outside Dr. Richards's door, surprised to see the light still on. I knocked. He looked up and motioned me in.

"You've been getting the checks in your mailbox?"

"Yes, thank you."

"No, thank you. It's unacceptable, the conditions of those files."

"Do they really think . . . ?"

He put down his pen and rubbed his eyes. "Think what?"

"That . . . aliens . . . took their loved ones?"

"You've read it all. What do you think?"

"I know they're afraid. They're really afraid. And I know

they're desperate to believe in something that explains what happened. But if you read the newspapers, you know that terrible things sometimes happen: drugs, alcohol, mental illness. I wonder if you're feeding them false hope."

Dr. Richards jutted out his jaw. "It's a fair criticism. Something I've wondered myself. But it's the commonality that keeps me up at night."

"Commonality?"

He leaned his chin on his right hand. "How can someone in Malvern, Arkansas, describe the same kind of being that someone in a remote village outside Kenya, Africa, says they saw as well? It's all the same, with some small variation. Look here."

He handed me two pieces of paper. "You know this family. The Gobels."

"How can you forget? It's terrible."

"Farm family. Outskirts of Cape Girardeau, Missouri. Wake up one morning to find their two-year-old daughter gone. Massive search, police, FBI, everything. No one finds anything. The mother, Sarah, is so distraught, she hires a hypnotist to force her to remember everything about that night. And when she's put under—what does Sarah see?"

"It's not what she sees. It's what she feels. Something probing her body. Large eyes. Wide forehead, gray skin. Then bright lights . . ." I paused, finding the words on the page, ". . . and her daughter going into them."

"The Semitacalous, from the Zakynthos Island in Greece." Dr. Richards slid me another folder. "You know their story too: Elderly couple. Go to bed one night. Anna wakes up the next morning, her husband, Georgios, is gone. But she doesn't need a hypnotist—she remembers everything. The probing, the wide head, the irregular eyes. The bright lights and her husband rising into them."

He placed the folders on top of each other. "The Gobels' daughter went missing on August 20, on the same night Georgios Semitacalou disappeared. Neither has ever been seen since."

He looked down, his pen scratching across the paper before him as if I had never interrupted him. "Now you tell me what to tell these families."

I looked out his small window. "I . . . hate it for them. How long can they keep looking? How long do you tell them to keep hoping?"

"Forever."

"Why? How can you even encourage them?"

"Because sometimes they come back," he said, continuing to write.

EIGHT

At first, I found the laminated cards that Dr. Richards gave to me to pass along to the families of the missing quaint and sweet. I had praised him for being compassionate enough to come up with the poem written on the front. His response had been an academic frown.

"It wasn't my idea. I honestly don't know why we hand them out. We started doing it about five years ago. I suppose it's supposed to be comforting, but I think it's a bit much. We're all instructed to do it, so it's become our calling card. Every family gets one."

I often sent them by mail, always with a handwritten note. I reread the poem each time I placed one in an envelope.

PRAYER FOR THE MISSING
You are not gone, as long as I remember.
You are not away, as long as I weep.
You have not vanished, as long as I can picture your face.
You are with me.
You are in the rain.

You are in my tears.
You are where the water falls.

Being an English major, I wasn't overly impressed with the poem, but it was a nice sentiment. And knowing Dr. Richards was atheist, handing out anything that resembled a prayer was a real stretch for him.

He told me to send one to Barbara Rush when she insisted on meeting with him.

"Her family is against our involvement," he said.

"She wants your help," I replied, flipping through her brother's case file.

Barbara was only eighteen, four years younger than me. Her twin brother, Don, had gone missing in a snowstorm in St. Joseph, Michigan, a small tourist town on a dramatic arch of Lake Michigan. Her parents had fallen apart after his disappearance, leaving the girl to search for her brother on her own. That led her to a missing-persons support groups, and ultimately to one of Dr. Richards's colleagues who attended such meetings to seek out questionable disappearances. When he heard her story, he encouraged her to call to the University of Illinois's astronomy department.

She had asked for Dr. Richards, and I took the call.

Don had casually smoked marijuana, Barbara explained, so the St. Joseph police thought he got stoned and wandered into the storm. Probably got too close to the lake, they surmised. His body will wash up soon with the ice balls, she heard one whisper to the other.

But she insisted that her brother—despite being a lifelong Michigander—hated the cold. Even high, he would have never gone out. And when she had awoken that night and found light streaming through her bedroom, she'd assumed a car was shining its headlights into her room—maybe one of Don's friends from the bowling alley had come to pick him up for a quick nip at the bar. She had parted the curtains and saw Don standing on the street, in the snow, looking up. Then the lights were gone, and so was Don.

"I told my parents," Barbara had said. "They thought I was sleepwalking. But I don't sleepwalk. Never have."

I had talked to her off and on for several weeks. But then her parents listened in on one of the calls and forbid her from calling "those whackos in Illinois" again. So she called from pay phones when she got off work at the restaurant around the corner from her house. I stayed late at work to accept her calls.

A month after her first call, Barbara showed up at the office.

"I took the bus all night. I had to see your face," she had said to my astonished expression. "You're as nice as I pictured."

Barbara sat and talked with Dr. Richards and me for hours, pleading with us to come to Michigan to help her search. The more she talked, the more she twisted a strand of hair on the back of her neck. "Nervous habit," she said, smiling sheepishly.

Dr. Richards had explained they didn't have a budget for traveling. She vowed to give them all her money. Steven shook his head. "I can get you in touch again with my colleague at the University of Michigan, who told you about us—"

"I don't want him. I want you. And Lynn. He talked about theories of missing people, including something called . . . Argentum? Am I saying that right?"

Dr. Richards frowned. "I'm sorry, Barbara. I can't help you, especially with that."

Even though I didn't have the money either, I had paid for her bus ticket back to Michigan. I gave her one of the laminated poems. She had cried at the bus terminal, and I cried along with her.

"That can never happen again," Dr. Richards later said. "Sometimes people expect us to drop everything and find their loved ones. Give them one of the cards and end it with that. It can't work any other way. We only gather information, take careful notes—"

"If all we're doing is gathering facts, how does this ever help anyone?"

"Because it might not now. Might not in ten years, twenty years. But one day, we'll have enough cases to show that this can't be ignored."

"Why was she asking about Argentum? Who is that? What is that?"

"I'm going to have a long talk with my esteemed colleague in Michigan about that. He knows better. It's a theory about extraterrestrials that we are all instructed to dismiss outright. I've heard some talk that it's about aliens inhabiting human form, or that it refers to interdimensional travel. It's our Loch Ness monster—everyone has heard of it, and no one has any proof." Dr. Richards didn't bother to hide his irritation.

"Perhaps I should refer her to some of the other organizations. I've read quite a bit about UFO theorists—"

"For God's sake, don't do that. Me and my . . . peers . . . we aren't like the others in those other groups. I mean, I appreciate the work APRO and NICAP are doing—"

"But you don't belong to them. The Aerial Phenomena Research Organization and the National Investigations Committee on Aerial Phenomena are quite open with their mission. Why not join them?"

When he raised his eyebrows, I shrugged. "I do research. I pay attention."

"Good organizations, good people, their focus is just different than ours."

"How?"

"We have a primary mission of trying to connect people who have gone missing to abductions. APRO and NICAP are doing admirable work on people who are returned quickly from abductions. My theory, and the theory that I share with my peers, is that unexplained disappearances of people all over the world can be tied to the abductions."

"Where's your proof, besides the stories told by people they leave behind?"

He chewed on the end of his pencil. "I wonder what you think . . ."

"What I think?"

He jotted down something on the paper in front of him. "You have a brilliant mind, Lynn." He looked once more, intently, at his writing.

I pulled my cardigan tighter around me.

I left work early, taking Barbara's file home with me. At home, I read through it five more times. Then I grabbed my coat. Tom had come home at that exact moment, and I told him I'd be back later. When he asked about dinner, I pretended I didn't hear.

Dr. Richards had already left his office, but he recently had given me a key, for emergencies. I figured this counted.

Three hours later, I found what I was looking for. I cleared off the battered couch in his office and lay down to read. At midnight, I'd meant to only close my eyes for a moment.

I awoke to Dr. Richards standing over me. "Your husband is banging on the doors outside the Curry Hall entrance. You better go."

"What time is it?"

"Seven A.M. Did you sleep here all night?"

"I have to tell you what I found."

"No, you have to go."

"It's the weather. That's the commonality. It's the weather."

"We can talk about this later. Go home. Take the day off and get some rest—"

"I have to tell you about this."

"Not a good time. Not only is your husband outside, but I have a faculty review today. I will have no time today."

"Then I will be here at the end of the day. Wait for me."

Tom and I had fought all day. I called him a stranger, he called me disconnected. I cried, he paced. I was grateful at dusk when he announced he needed to go out for a run. I lied about going to a coffee shop to work on my book.

I didn't even knock when I reached Dr. Richards's office. He put on his glasses as I sat down.

"You may not remember the Soothe case in Alaska; we don't have much on it," I began. "But something jogged my memory about the date. I realized why when I studied Barbara's case. A man went missing there, exactly two years to the day Barbara's brother went missing. In a snowstorm."

"There's always a snowstorm in Alaska in winter."

"His wife told police she saw lights in the snowstorm. You mentioned the abductions in Arkansas and on that Greek island. But you failed to mention it was during blistering nights of temperatures in the upper nineties—ninety-eight degrees to be precise—with scattered storms producing heavy downpours that lasted mere minutes. Same dates, almost exact same weather pattern. What if that's what happens? If we started to piece together all those dates, and match them up with the weather . . ."

I then slowly shook my head in realization. "That's what

you've been having me do, isn't it? You're not putting them in some kind of chronological order. You're matching the dates of the missing and comparing the weather."

Dr. Richards slid back his chair and walked around the desk, clearly uncomfortable in his proximity to me. "I think they come on the same days, in different years, but in the same weather. And I think they return to the same places, too, over and over again. But the abductions can come years, even decades apart. I don't know why. But that's the key, I think. Lynn, it took me my whole life to figure this out. You put it together in a few months. I hoped you would help me get organized. But I never expected you'd become a colleague."

When I smiled, he did too. I was surprised at how his entire face lit up, his usual downtrodden eyes forming crescent moons.

I've found that life has no tolerance for dwelling in memories. I may have wanted to stay in bed, examining those thrilling and confusing times to seek clues that could help find William. But my recollection was ended by an exhausted sleep, and then the cat pawing at my face, ready to be fed. Since school hadn't let out for fall break yet, I had to rush to get Greg to school and check in on Brian, followed by a complete collapse by Anne, in which she sobbed on the couch for an hour, and then a call from Tom that we needed to have dinner together tonight to discuss some important things. I'd put some salmon in the oven, but when we sat down to dinner, I quickly lost my appetite over what my husband had to say.

As he started scraping his fork to gather the last remnants of the angel hair pasta, I rubbed my temples. When the base of his wineglass caught the edge of his plate and made a sharp clang, I scooted my chair back, walked over to the sink, and began to rinse the plates before putting them in the dishwasher.

"I guess you don't think we should do it," he muttered under his breath.

"Of course I think you should do it. *We* aren't doing it."

"It's Diane Sawyer, Lynn. She's giving us an hour in prime time."

"I know who she is, Tom. And I think it's the right decision. For you to do."

"Lynn, you need to take part in it. People are going to be more sympathetic to someone like you than some perceived beltway insider. You or Anne—"

"No," I laid the dishrag down on the countertop. "Not Anne. Not Chris. No one but you. This family is hanging on by a thread. I won't put Anne through it—"

The knock came at the door, and he checked his watch. "Deanna said she'd be here at seven. Listen to what she has to say, Lynn. She's a communications expert; she's been a valuable asset. And the FBI has already signed on to this."

I dried my hands, then put on too much lotion. The October air was already wreaking havoc on my skin. When I turned back around, Deanna Ruck, Tom's communication manager, who I'd met on the porch the day of the news conference, was setting down her briefcase.

"Hi Mrs. Roseworth. Nice to see you again."

"Hi Deanna. Can I offer you some coffee?"

"No, thank you, I've smoked too much for one evening, and I don't think my nervous system can handle caffeine too."

"Have a seat," Tom said quickly, knowing I refused to clean his clothes when he'd been smoking.

Deanna produced a thick folder. "So here are the talking

points, all approved by the FBI. ABC is giving you an hour, so they will need a lot; enough to keep the story line moving along until the last quarter hour—"

"Story line?" I winced.

"Lynn . . ." Tom gave me a weary glance. "She means we want to keep viewers tuned in until the end of the hour, when I reveal the increase in the reward."

"We're not a TV drama," I replied softly.

"Please go on," he said to Deanna.

"As we discussed, you'll take Diane and the crew through the woods. You'll provide all of the new photos of William approved by your daughter. ABC is asking again if Anne or Chris—"

"No," I insisted. "They will not be doing an interview. No other member of the family."

"Have you given any thought . . ." she began.

"I won't. I'm sorry, I can't."

She nodded. "Here's where we have to have a tough discussion. Senator, Mrs. Roseworth, forgive me, but I have to ask: Is there anything—anything at all—that could be considered controversial about your family that you haven't already disclosed? No pattern of runaway behavior by William? No affairs by Anne or her husband? Drug use? Nothing that would make the tabloids?"

"We've gone over this repeatedly with the FBI. We're terribly boring," Tom said.

"Because if there's one single bit of information that's outrageous, anything that casts doubt on the family or your sensibilities, you will lose the public's sympathy in a heartbeat. A sideshow will disrupt what really matters. I'm sorry to be so crass. The producers have made it clear: The information about Brian is a nonnegotiable."

"Nonnegotiable?" I asked.

"Lynn, they have to have something to tease," he said.

"Tease?" I was gripping the side of the table now.

"We have a daughter who works in television news, Lynn, who has spoken to us at length about this. Kate has spoken to you about this. The more the producers can tease that they have obtained new information, the more people will watch, and the more people will be on the lookout for William. I will discuss briefly that Brian may have witnessed it and has been in a traumatized state ever since. End of discussion, Lynn. Deanna, do we have a list of questions?"

I envisioned walking over to the cake plate, calmly taking the last piece of iced banana bread, and throwing it in Tom's direction. But instead I sat with my hands on the table.

"The network won't provide questions, but we know the ballpark. You need to be prepared. That's what's in the talking points—"

"I need to assume questions about the VP offer. And if William was a troubled kid; if we acted quickly enough in contacting police; domestic terrorism—"

"Does it have to go there?" I asked.

"It can go there and it will, Lynn." Tom was getting angry now. "You don't get it: ISIS is converting suburban high school kids into extremists and teaching them through social media to shoot up military institutions and attack the government any way they can. I've read the files. You couldn't stomach them. Of course, they could have staked out our family and waited for just the right moment. You think kidnapping a family member of the only Democratic senator who led the charge to increase military presence in Iran to bomb those fuckers is out of the question?"

"It could have been any of you, truly," Deanna said. "But after the magazine came out . . ."

I stood up and walked to the stairs.

"I'm sorry, but that question will certainly be asked." She sounded more irritated than apologetic.

Tom was on his feet. "Lynn! Come on, Lynn. God dammit!"

I hurried up the stairs, my hand on my mouth. I went through the bedroom and into the bathroom, closing the door. I ran the water to mask my sobbing.

Nothing outrageous, Deanna warned. Nothing salacious or controversial should come out about any of us.

I roughly wiped the tears from my face. The small amount of mascara I'd earlier applied streamed down my cheeks. I grabbed a Kleenex and leaned into the mirror.

I stopped. A flushed face with weepy eyes and smudges of black beneath reflected back.

The desire to smash the mirror was so strong that I actually began to step back, to contain myself. But instead, I leaned in closer, looking at every detail of my pathetic face.

I would burn that image in my memory to use as ammunition, should I begin to doubt what I had to do.

The bells above the door to the Peddler announced my arrival, and I could see Barry Manilow's face on the computer screen reflected in Roxy's glasses. She was obviously so engrossed in her online research into his denials of plastic surgeries that she only held up her finger. "Be with you in a minute."

"Don't keep the customers waiting too long," I responded.

"Well, good morning. What a nice surprise."

I rubbed my shoulders. "It's cold this morning. You've done a nice job with the Thanksgiving decorations. I can't thank you enough for tending to the shop during all this. And I've been such a terrible friend, I haven't even asked about how Ed was doing this month."

"A few more rounds of chemo and he's done for a while, I hope."

"I am so sorry, Roxy. I should be checking on him at least once a week."

"Ed's tough. He'll beat it, like he's beat it twice before. In fact, he practically shoves me out the door every day. Imagine if the two of us were pecking on him all the time—he barely survived being around us every day of high school. He doesn't even the let the boys do work around the house for him."

I bit my lip. "I hate to ask you this, but do you think that Ed is well enough for you to go visit your brother in Little Rock?"

"Excuse me? You know I hate my brother's wife."

"I was hoping you'd like to go. And that you'd insist I come with you."

Roxy tried to hide in the pity in her smile. "Honey, say the word and we'll be out the door in two shakes. Tom stopped by and told me about the interview with ABC tomorrow. I know you don't want to be here when they come. You need a break from all this. But I do think we should screw Little Rock, let's go to Tunica—"

I shook my head. "No one would believe that. Certainly not the girls. They have to believe I'm going to Little Rock. And you have to go—for a week, that's all. Then you can come back. We'll schedule it that we arrive back at the same time."

"You've lost me. I'm going to Little Rock . . . but you aren't coming with me?"

"I'm not done. I need you to rent a car for me. I don't want to use my debit card for Tom to see. Of course, I'll pay you back immediately. I also hope you can drive me to the Enterprise over on Charlotte Avenue. And then when we both get back, you can pick me up there. It will look like we've been together the entire time."

"Where are you actually going?"

"I need to go somewhere alone. And the girls would be too worried if they knew."

"If you're going to have me lie, which I only do under the most important of occasions—such as telling Ruth Boster last week that the bleach is really hiding the hair on her upper lip—then the tradeoff is that I'm going with you. I don't know where you're going or why, but I *will* be going. I lie, I travel. *Comprende?*"

I slowly opened the door to the room Brian had shared with William. Two twin beds were tucked into the corners, one with Spider-Man sheets and the other with Batman. The red sheets with webs had remained untouched since summer.

As he did each day, Brian sat in a chair facing a bay window overlooking his backyard. The books that Stephanie, the tutor, had read aloud, trying to get him to respond, were stacked near his ankles. I gave Stephanie two more weeks, tops.

"Brian bear, it's Nanna."

He continued to stare, motionless. Even his blinking seemed mechanical.

"Honey, Nanna has to take a trip. I really wish you would talk to me before I leave."

A strand of hair drifted across his eye. When he made no effort to remove it, I gently brushed it back. *I've never just come out and asked him. I have to do it.*

"Brian. Brian, honey, did William . . . disappear into lights? Lights from the sky?"

When Brian failed to respond, I closed my eyes. I might as well have been talking to a statue. I looked out the window at the trees beyond.

Not wanting to look again at his vacant face, I leaned down

and kissed his cheek, and started to walk out, when I stopped at the door.

I tasted his tear on my lips.

West Side Story took us from Tennessee to Paducah, Kentucky. *Camelot* blared as we blew through Southern Illinois. After a dramatic accompaniment to "If Ever I Would Leave You," Roxy frowned at the construction off Interstate 57 onto Route 13. "Glad we got to avoid that mess. I suppose you'll tell me when I actually need to get off the interstate?"

I nodded.

"Thinking about the girls?"

"Kate—and Tom, for that matter—seemed relieved I was leaving. They're both practical thinkers and know the TV shoot will go easier without me acting like an old guard dog. Stella was suspicious; she knows it's not like me to leave in a crisis. Anne looked so panicked when I told her I was going with you to Little Rock. I know she won't take part in the interview, but I feel like I'm abandoning her. It was like seeing her again at six years old, after I took her to the first day of kindergarten. I promised to call her twice a day, and I told her I would only be about five or six hours away, which really isn't that untrue."

"Ah-ha! At last, a clue. So we're going five hours away, then. Took us three and a half to get here, so . . ."

"You know we're going to Champaign, Roxy. You've known since I first told you I had to go to Illinois."

"Well, I guessed it, but I thought maybe you needed to go to Chicago. Or maybe Springfield. I still don't understand why, though."

I closed my eyes and leaned back. Roxy took a swig of her Diet Pepsi and pointed to the console. "If you're still going to be evasive you're going to have to listen to *Evita*. And not that Madonna crap, I'm talking Patti LuPone."

After *Evita* came *Phantom of the Opera*, and then *Chicago*. Roxy was about to launch into "All that Jazz" when she spied a Cracker Barrel and announced her bladder was full.

After lunch, as Roxy puttered around the souvenir shop, I sat in the booth and stared out at the leafless trees. We were nearing Mattoon now, which meant I was close to breaking the vow I'd made to myself all those years ago, whispering to the baby inside me, promising to never return to this desolate part of the world. It was spring then, and I felt with every mile the world was getting greener. I was escaping, I had my baby girl with me, and Tom could join us once he graduated. If I had had to walk home to Tennessee, I would have. More likely, I would have run.

"OK, I've overloaded myself with crap, including those peg puzzles no one can ever figure out but that still get passed on to grandchildren," Roxy announced as she returned to the table. "I bought one for each of your brood, they were on sale. Of course, my sons are depriving me of grandchildren, only giving me tattooed girlfriends. I've paid. Thelma, it's time to tell Louise what exactly we're doing."

I slid out from the booth and swept Roxy's hand. "Not yet."

When we at last arrived in Champaign, I repeatedly blinked; a bad habit that surfaced when I was surprised at something. Logic suggested that a college town I hadn't seen in forty years would of course look very different. But I had seen towns in Tennessee sit unaltered for longer than that.

As Roxy gassed up her pickup truck, I marveled at the sprawl of neighborhoods and gas stations, feeling a surprising twinge of fondness for the brick buildings. It was what I remembered the most about Champaign: the red brick, as if the founders of the university and the town knew that if the people were to survive the blistering winds and mounds of snow of winter, wooden structures weren't going to cut it. The buildings on campus were brick, the restaurants were brick, even many of the new gas stations were brick.

"OK, sister, where to now?" Roxy tapped on the window.

I gave the directions, relying mostly on Google Maps on my iPhone, which was one of only two apps I had mastered. I had no choice but to conquer texting or else Stella would have driven me insane, and Tom insisted I understand the map app in case I got lost in Atlanta or Savannah. Though the streets surrounding the university had multiplied and the campus expanded, I was able to rest the phone on my thigh as we entered the school and give directions by memory. When I directed Roxy into the parking lot of the mostly plain (brick) building, my throat started to tighten.

Roxy threw the truck into park. "Says I need a sticker to park here, but maybe the truck looks beat up enough that they'll assume I'm a student. Are we going in?"

I swallowed. "Give me a minute. Keep the truck running."

Roxy looked out the window. "Having done this now, I feel like a moron that I never came to visit you here. Six hours away in Illinois seemed like driving to Canada to me when I was twenty-two. Now, I know I should have gassed up that Chevy and headed up here all the time. It may have eased the pain."

"The pain?"

"It was the worst time in my life when you came here. We'd been together every day since the second grade. I felt like I'd lost you to the north, like some pining widow of the Confederacy. Do you remember how we cried when you moved? I think Tom had to pry us apart."

"The feeling was mutual."

"I don't remember much about all those years you were away. Did we not talk on the phone? Why do I have so few letters from you? Do I need to be taking gingko for memory loss?"

"I made a firm decision not to talk about my life here. It wasn't a happy time."

"Then why are we back here?"

I sighed and pivoted in the truck to face her. "Remember when I worked for the astronomy department here, while Tom was in school? I ended up doing extra work for a professor on a project. He was involved . . . in researching missing people. Now . . . I just want to see if maybe his research could help us."

"For God's sake, Lynnie. It's completely against your nature to do anything irrational, and I know that grief can cause a lot of smart people to do a lot of stupid things, but this isn't ridiculous at all. Why wouldn't you tell me from the beginning? And why would an astronomy professor do research into missing people?"

"Let's go in before I lose my nerve."

We walked across the lawn, brown grass crunching beneath our shoes. Roxie bemoaned her lack of scarf and hat. "Good God, this wind is so strong! And cold! Does it blow down all the way from Chicago? How can anyone stand this?"

"There's nothing to block the wind," I replied, turning up the collar on my coat.

While the astronomy building too had been remodeled over the decades, it still clung to its original boxy shape. I was so taken back by the familiar silence of the building, and the smells of coffee and old paper, that I stopped, my hands fidgeting.

"What time are they expecting you?" Roxy asked.

"I didn't make an appointment," I said, turning away from

what I knew would be a look of exasperation on her face. I led her down the main halls, past the grandiose photographs of the former deans of the department, to the office where I began my new life as a wife. The door was closed and a yellowed sign read, "Supply closet."

A female student passed by and I quietly asked where we could find the office manager for the professors. The girl shrugged and mentioned there was a student worker at the front desk, around the corner.

We headed in that direction and found a room with a long desk and a very bored-looking young woman checking her cell phone. She smiled at our approach and set the phone to vibrate. I appreciated the gesture.

"Hello. Are the professors' offices still that way?" I asked.

"I think so, but I've only had this job for a few days. Can I help you with something?"

"I wanted to see Dr. Steven Richards."

The girl's smile altered, and she looked quickly at her computer. "Uh, yes. He's actually unavailable right now."

"We should have called ahead—" Roxy began.

"I'm happy to take a message. I don't know how soon he'll be back."

"Will he be back today?"

The girl's face paled a bit. "I don't think so."

"That's all right. Thank you, though." I smiled pleasantly, took Roxy's arm, and walked away.

She could feel me trembling. "That's it? That's all we're doing?"

"I . . . thought he would be here."

"Did you ever think to even call and see if he was still teaching? That was forty years ago, Lynn. He's probably dead."

"He was only twenty-nine when I was here. That would

put him in his early seventies. And, the college's website stated that he was here. The course schedule online even showed him teaching three classes this fall."

"Well, clearly he's not here, and that student is acting a little spooky about it. Maybe she's failing his class. Maybe she has the hots for him. Was he good-looking? More importantly, what do you want to do now?"

"I want to go home. That's what I really want to do. But I can't just sit around that house, that big empty house, anymore. Every room feels empty. Everything feels empty without him."

"Maybe we should find this professor's office. See if maybe he's in there, and the student didn't see him come in."

I looked around. "If I still remember the layout of the building, and I doubt that's changed, he should be right around this corner—if he hasn't moved in forty years."

"Can't hurt to check."

We passed a row of nondescript doors with the names of the professors on the outside. I noted all the names had changed. All the professors I had worked for, except for Dr. Richards, were old when I was a young worker.

"He was handsome, in a messy kind of way," I murmured.

I turned another corner, not surprised in the least to see the last door on the hall still marked with the name "Dr. Steve Richards, Astronomy." He wouldn't have ever wanted to move all his belongings and maps.

What was a surprise, however, was the note on the door, signed in flourishing cursive with the name of the dean. The message was typed and concise: "This office is closed. Any questions, please see your guidance counselor."

"Strike two," Roxy said. "Well, shall we see the guidance counselor? Perhaps ask her about some continuing adult education for two old chicks while we're at it?"

I reached out and turned the door handle, but it was locked.

"Lynn, are you going to let yourself in?"

"I want to see his office."

"Why?"

"He kept his information on the missing people in that office. I can't have come all this way without seeing if any of my old work is still here. But what are we going to do? That girl won't let us in, and I don't think the dean will let us borrow a key."

Roxy looked up and down the hallway. "Move aside." She reached in her hand-quilted purse and dug around. She pulled out a hairpin. "When your hair is as ridiculous as mine, these things are a lifesaver."

"What are you doing?" I whispered. "You just scolded me for trying to get in."

"Yin and yang, kid. Only one of us is allowed to be the bad seed. If you do something wrong, the earth might break from its axis. Remember when we snuck into my dad's locked liquor cabinet? I sampled it all, and all you did was fret and watch for his car to pull into the drive. I haven't done this for years, but locks don't change."

After Roxy swore for a minute or two, I heard the click of the door, and the office opened. We shuffled inside and closed the door quickly.

"Jesus, Mary, and Joseph," Roxy said.

The campus street lamps were starting to come on outside, offering faint light to the rapidly darkening office. We didn't dare turn on the overhead lights for fear of drawing attention from anyone walking outside. Roxy did a lot of huffing and sighing as I combed through drawers and file cabinets.

"Again I ask: Do you care to give me an idea of what we're looking for?"

"Keep looking for anything that might explain where Dr. Richards might be. I went over his desk, and it's a typical man desk: coffee stains, no organization, and dry pens. His calendar is blank, so clearly he does everything on his computer. And, as I found, it's password protected, so I've come up with squat."

Roxy leaned back in his chair and stretched out her legs, only to bang them harshly against something under the desk. I sighed, closing another cabinet. Every file, every drawer was filled with articles and research. Clearly, he had moved all his private research to his computer, and that was inaccessible. I slowly looked up at the maps that still covered the ceiling and walls, practically untouched over the decades. Apparently, he still needed that kind of visual reference—

"Care to explain this?"

Roxy was holding up a photograph, black-and-white and badly faded, of two people sitting together at a table. They were not touching, but they leaned in towards each other. I walked over and stared at the picture of myself and Dr. Richards

"Where did you find that?"

"Stuck on top of the safe under this desk. Which is locked, I might add. But that's you, Lynn Roseworth. And I assume that's Dr. Richards. So the question is—why does he have a minisafe with your picture stuck on top?"

"Are you sure it won't open?"

"Yes, I'm sure, I tried it. And please answer my question."

I looked around. The light was fading rapidly, and I began to run my fingers over the maps on the walls. I looked up and grabbed a chair to stand on.

"What are you doing?"

"Try this," I gave her a key tied to a pushpin on the ceiling. She took it and knelt under the desk. "Did it open?"

"I think so."

"Can we lift it?"

Roxy peered out. "We're stealing now?"

"I have to see what's in it, and we're out of light."

"It's not heavy. It's made out of that plastic stuff that won't burn."

"Stick your head out the door, see if anyone is out there."

"Fine. But I want to know how you knew where that key was."

I pointed up.

"Yes, I see it, it's a star system. The fool has them all over this wacked-out office."

"See the red pushpin?"

"Yes."

"That's where the key was hanging."

"How did you guess it would be up there?"

"Because the pin marks my star."

"What?"

"He named a star after me," I said. "Let me carry the safe."

At our room at the Hilton Garden Inn, on a table usually reserved for brochures on Champaign's historic sites and loose change, sat takeout food from P.F. Chang's and the safe. Roxy devoured her General Tso's Chicken while I mostly played with my vegetable rice.

She at last put down her plastic fork. "Well, we've committed breaking and entering and burglary. If that's my last meal before jail, I'll be happy."

"We'll return all this tomorrow. No one will know."

"Are you sure he won't come back to his office tonight? Or first thing in the morning?"

"You saw the look on that girl's face. I don't think he'll be coming back anytime soon."

"What's in this safe, Lynn?"

"I don't know."

"I think you have your suspicions. Why was your picture taped to it?"

"Open it, Roxy. Tell me what's in it."

She stood up and slid the key into the safe. I continued to look out the window.

"Lynn."

At the tone in her voice, I closed my eyes, afraid to turn around.

"Lynn, look at this."

Roxy slowly slid a map out of a folder. It had yellowed and weathered, a relic now of a time before satellite mapping. The map was on a grid, with latitude and longitude markings. There were faded pencil marks, with arrows pointing to a forested area near a small square.

I recognized my home immediately.

Roxy was already sifting through dozens of newspaper clippings, all of which featured pictures of my family on election nights. The pile included the *Southern Living* magazine with William on the cover.

She reached out and took my trembling hand. "We need to go to the police with this."

"We can't."

"We most certainly are."

"I didn't come here . . . because I suspected he might have taken William. I came because of his research into missing people. He's spent his whole adult life dedicated to it. But when we showed up at that office and I saw that girl's expression, I knew something bad had happened. I had to get into his office to see if I could find his research—or, more importantly, my own. But when you found that picture, and now this . . . I'm afraid he's been gone from this university since William disappeared."

"How did this happen, Lynn? When did this happen? You have to go to the FBI."

"With what? A hunch? And destroy my marriage and what's left of my family?"

"Why would it destroy your marriage and your family? This guy is obsessed with you, obviously—but that's not your fault."

I placed the *Southern Living* cover on the old photo of Dr. Richards and me, covering up my face. Side by side, Dr. Richards and William had the same dimples, the thick hair, the soft chin.

"Because it is my fault," I said softly. "Dr. Richards is William's grandfather."

NINE

We sat in silence in the cab of Roxy's pickup, nursing coffee and fogging up the windows. The safe sat on the floor by my feet. Roxy turned on the defroster to once again clear the windshield, revealing the astronomy building in the blue morning light.

"I hate to ask again, but are you absolutely sure . . ."

I nodded. "I'd always hoped Anne was Tom's. But seeing that picture of Steven and that cover photo of William . . ."

"Lynn, I'm going to say it again: We should be taking that safe to the FBI, or at the very least the local police. I watch enough *Dateline*. And we should go now."

"We have no idea what we're doing, let's not pretend otherwise. How are we going to explain that we broke into his office and found it?"

"You had a hunch. And you proved to be right. And once the police see it, they'll agree. So we need to leave this parking lot. The professionals need to see it. We don't need to put it back."

"The police aren't going to buy this. Neither would the FBI."

"Are you nuts? This seems to me to be the most tangible evidence anyone has come upon since William went missing."

"But why? Why would he take William? It doesn't make sense. I know something is wrong, but I can't believe he would do it. Why he would do it? Steven researches missing people. He wouldn't do anything to put a family through this."

"Now we're calling him Steven? And that's the other thing," Roxy huffed. "I don't get how an astronomy professor is somehow this expert on missing people. If he taught criminal justice or something, I would get it."

"I had hoped at this point you would figure it out, so I wouldn't have to say it."

"Well I'm old and I'm tired, so my usual razor-sharp mind is dulled a bit. He has a map of your property, Lynn. He has pictures of you and your family. He has the magazine with William's picture. He's obsessed with missing people. And while it's hard for me to even say it, he's likely William's grandfather. But I get it; I get why you're afraid to go to police with this, because of the can of worms it's going to open—"

"You don't get it. The reason I feel like I need more proof is because if I go to the police now, they will roll their eyes. Because of what Steven does."

"He's a professor—"

"He investigates alien abductions."

Roxy choked on her coffee, then wiped her lips with the Starbucks napkin. "Pardon my French, but what the hell, Lynn."

"I thought the same thing too, at the beginning. I couldn't believe it. Who could believe it? Now do you understand? If I go to police and say, 'I had an affair with a guy forty years ago, who believes in aliens, and I stole a safe out of his office, and he happens to have a lot of articles about me and my family, and I think that's proof that he abducted my grandson,' then you can see the problem. Because I don't think he has my grandson, Roxy. But what if he knows . . . what happened to William?"

Roxy leaned back in her seat. "I should have gone to Little Rock."

"Do you know what I remember so vividly about all those cases of missing people? That sometimes there was a phrase repeated over and over again by the people who either claim to have witnessed the abductions, or were the last to see the missing people: 'The lights took them.' Or some variation of that. And you know that's the last thing Brian ever said. Yes, I know I'm desperate. Yes, I know this is hard to believe. It's still hard for me to believe all the stupid things I did in this town. But I have to do something. . . ." I inhaled sharply, to stifle the tears.

"Oh, sweet girl." Roxy reached over to place her hand on my knee. "I'm sorry for being such an ass. I know admitting all this has to be hard."

" 'It's the lies that undo us,' that's what I tell the girls, what I've always told the girls. And look what I've done. It all sounds so ridiculous, and I know it sounds crazy. But I thought if I came here and found Steven and begged him to tell me anything he'd uncovered in the last forty years about these missing people, maybe I could feel like I was doing something to help."

"Lynn," Roxy said, taking my hand. "Forty years ago you believed this junk—I mean this . . . research. And that's OK. Lots of people believe in dumb stuff when they're kids. Hell, until I was twenty-six, I believed that if I sent Elvis enough mental messages, that he would seek me out and find me on the strength of my love. May I ask, though, what in God's name were you doing having an affair with some nutty professor who believes in little green men? I mean, all those maps and files? About alien abductions? Come on, Lynn."

"This is why I wanted to come alone." I opened up the truck door. "Stay in the truck, I'll be back."

"Oh, for God's sake," Roxy muttered, lifting the hem of her denim dress and sliding out her door.

I carried the safe, with a sweater draped over it, into the building, Roxy shuffling behind. The hallway of the professors' offices was silent, and I set the safe down outside Steven's door. Roxy grumbled to herself as she once again picked the lock.

I went in and slid the safe under the desk. Roxy looked around with renewed disdain at the maps. "What do we do now?"

"I need to find out where he may have gone—"

"Excuse me, but how did you get in here?"

A young man stood in the door. He wore dark-rimmed glasses and a flannel with a Morrissey T-shirt underneath.

"We're housekeeping," Roxy said with a smile.

"This office is supposed to be locked."

"Perhaps you should mind your own business." She smiled wider.

"This is my business. I'm Professor Richards's graduate student. No one is supposed to be in here."

Roxy sighed. "It is too early to be this annoying—"

"I'm an old friend of Professor Richards," I said. "I'm trying to find him."

"He's not here."

"Do you know when you expect him back?"

"I think you read the sign on the door before you broke in. He's on leave."

"It's important that we find him. Does he have a cell phone? Or could you give me his address?"

"He keeps an unlisted number and doesn't give out his address."

"Are you his student or the head of his security detail?" Roxy asked.

"Could I give you my number? Perhaps you could pass it along to him?" I reached into my purse and quickly wrote it down on an old receipt.

"I suppose. But I need to know how you got in here."

"Oh, for God's sake," Roxy snatched the paper out of my hands and thumped it against the chest of the student. "Here, take it and stick it in your Velcro wallet. Come on, Lynnie."

I gave him a soft thanks as Roxy walked me down the hall. "We need to get the move on. Mr. Personality back there seems the type to call campus police. Tell me you didn't write your full name or phone number on that sheet."

"I most certainly did."

"Really, Lynn," she said, pressing her key fob to open the truck doors. "Why not give them all the proof they need to bust us for breaking in."

"I don't care at this point. I need to find Steven."

"The police can take care of that."

"I can't go to police with this yet. You know why now."

"Well, Google Agent Mulder, then. See where he lives. I'm going to that Shell station we passed to get us farther away from the scene of the crime."

As she drove down the street, I pulled out my iPhone and stared helplessly at its shining screen. "I know how to use Google, of course, but where's the symbol—"

"They're called apps. Jesus, Lynn." She took my phone. "Don't go getting all senior citizen on me."

"We are senior citizens. And thus, you cannot look at that phone and drive. There's the gas station."

Roxy parked, took off her glasses, and spent the next several minutes holding the phone a good one to two inches from her face, rapidly punching on the screen until she swore and put her glasses back on. "Well, nothing pops. Not in Google, not in whitepages.com. Mr. Keeper of the Gates back there was right about the unlisted address and all."

My phone vibrated with the ring tone of chimes. "It's Stella."

"You better answer. The texts you sent the girls were uncharacteristically brief."

I answered the call. "Hi, hon. Yes, I'm fine. We're having a nice time."

I responded with genuine interest to the mundane, adding here and there brief statements of where we were supposedly eating in Little Rock's River Market district.

"Tell Anne that I'll call her later—"

"Give me the phone for a minute." Roxy reached for the phone.

"Uh, well, Roxy wants to say hi." I gave her a warning glance.

"Hi, sweet girl. Listen, when you do all that snooping to find people for your stories, how do you find them? Uh-huh. Well, my brother's trashy ex-wife owes him some money, and we think she's invested it in a tanning booth franchise in Hot Springs, but she has an unlisted number. Uh-huh. Really? You have to pay for that? No, you don't have to do it." Roxy waved away my gesture to hang up. "Isn't there another way? Uh-huh. Uh-huh. Good tip! Property deeds. Public record. We'll try that. Thanks darlin', love you."

Roxy handed the phone back but covered up the speaker, "Wrap this up, sister."

•   •   •

"I'm going to say 1910," Roxy said, staring up at the Victorian. "See the columns? Gauging by those and that tired old foundation, I'd say early 1900s."

I hugged my arms, looking at the empty windows and the snow drifting on the stairs. A few neglected newspapers lay on the front porch, still in plastic bags. The county's home-ownership records indicated Steven lived here. Strange that I felt bold enough to waltz into his office, the very place where it all began, but I was hesitant to even approach the house.

"Well, shall we?" Roxy said, taking the cracked concrete pathway up to the stairs. I hovered behind.

She repeatedly knocked. No lights came on. No one peered through the blinds. "Let's try the back door."

I followed her from the porch and around the house. *What if he's here? What am I going to say?* I thought of the magazine with William's picture on the cover in the safe in Steven's office. My cheeks flushed in anger.

The door under a weary overhang in the back gently opened with the rapping of Roxy's knuckles.

"Well, someone isn't too concerned about the crime rate in Champaign-Urbana. You can't commit breaking and entering if the door is unlocked, right? Hello? Hello?"

"Roxy . . ." I cautioned as she walked inside.

The mudroom was dark. I blinked, waiting for my eyes to adjust, scanning the glass fronts of a stackable washing machine and dryer, seeing no clothes inside.

Roxy continued to call out as we moved down a hall into the kitchen. Vinyl floors first laid down three decades ago matched outdated appliances and countertops. Mismatched furniture and newspapers littered the house. In the living room, a vintage refrigerator for Coke bottles stood right next to a sixty-inch-screen television.

I looked for photographs, any indication that Steven had a family, maybe even grandchildren of his own. The bachelor-pad vibe was too overwhelming to think he did.

"Well, I'm going whole hog. I'm looking around," Roxy said. "He's clearly not here, but I want to see if there's any other fan mail waiting for you."

A quick walk-through of the first floor revealed empty drawers left open, paperless file cabinets, and bare closets.

"I would like to sit down, but you know Stanley Steemer has never cleaned that couch." Roxy pulled up one of the dining room chairs instead, watching me cover my lips with a balled-up fist.

"What are we doing, Lynnie? Do you think he's crazy? I mean, obsessive compulsive, bipolar, schizophrenic? I mean, he'd have to be—to a degree—to believe that alien stuff—"

"You don't know what you're talking about."

Her eyebrows rose.

"I'm sorry."

"Don't apologize, just explain this to me: In the last twenty four hours, I've learned my best friend, who I say affectionately is the most normal, least-controversial person on earth, had an affair forty years ago, and maybe a love child, with a UFO hunter. So give me a minute to let all this sink in."

"I believed him. I believed in what he was doing. I reviewed his research, I studied the cases, I talked to the families. I knew all about them, every one of them. I wasn't just the office manager, Roxy. I was one of them."

"One of whom?"

"They weren't the people you see on TV now, talking about alien sightings and conspiracies. Back then, they worked quietly, communicated between universities all over the world."

"So you're telling me you were a UFO researcher too? Come on, Lynn."

"I believed in it as much as I believed in anything."

"And yet when you came back to Nashville, you decided to never, not even once, share all this with me?"

"Things got bad at the end. The work got too . . . intense. And when I found out I was pregnant, I knew I didn't want that kind of life for my child. I knew I had to make a clean break. It's why I never even went back for Tom's graduation, why I've never back here at all. Over time, with the kids and Tom's work and then his political career . . . it's been a long time, Roxy. I had no desire to go back to all that—"

My phone began to chime in my purse, and I sighed. "It's probably Tom, he's called three times." I dug it out, my eyes growing wide at the screen. "It's a 217 area code—I think that's Springfield. And Champaign."

"Well, answer it."

"Hello?"

"Yes, is this Lynn? Lynn Roseworth?"

"Yes."

"This is Doug Ellis. We met earlier today in Dr. Richards's office. I knew you looked familiar. You're married to Senator Roseworth. I also know you're Lynn Stanson, Steve's office manager from a long time ago."

That surprised me. "How do you . . . ?"

"I've been Dr. Richards's grad assistant for five years, and before that I was one of his students."

"It's very important that I find Steven. Can you please tell me what happened to him?"

"I had to give you the company line back there at school. I'm not sure if I can trust you."

"I promise you that you can."

He paused. "Can you meet to talk?"

"Of course. I have to find Steven. I thought he was still teaching, that's why I came all this way. I didn't even know he was gone until I arrived. We haven't spoken in decades."

"I'll have to talk to the others and see if they're willing to brief you about what they know. But I won't be able to reach them until tonight, and then they'll have to travel. How long are you in town?"

"Only for a few more days."

"Let me make some calls, but I think I can get everyone together tomorrow night. Can you meet at seven o'clock? I'll text you the address where to meet."

"Yes, I can meet you. Thank you, and please thank the others. If you need me before then, please call again."

He hung up without saying good-bye.

"What the hell was that, Lynn? Are we meeting Mr. McCreep? And who are the others?"

"I'm sure they're academics as well."

"Academics," Roxy grunted. "So we're going to stay in this Midwestern freak show for another day to meet more UFO hunters?"

"They're called Researchers," I said softly. "At least that's what we used to call ourselves. Let's go, OK?"

"Fine by me. All this tragic bachelorhoodness is making me crave a burger and a milk shake. Maybe I'll chase it with a Budweiser to complete the image."

As she walked out, I paused for a moment, looking around. The loneliness of the house was heavy, almost oppressive, as if it were waiting to sigh.

When I stepped out into the sun, my phone dinged. The text came from the 217 number Doug had called me from earlier. It simply read the address where to meet.

I put my phone in my purse, deciding not to tell Roxy yet that we would be returning to Steven's home.

Roxy was grumpy most of the next day. I let her stew as we flitted among antiques shops and bookstores. I texted with the girls and had a brief conversation with Tom, who said the interview had gone well, with no surprises. Roxy made little to no comment about anything, which meant she was about to blow. I'd learned over the years to give her space but remain close by when the clouds burst. We ate lunch and then dinner in a kind of understood silence, until she polished off her glass of red wine and narrowed her eyes at me. "So was this some kind of cult?"

"No."

"Because it sounds like a cult. And we're here for the reunion. And you said you were one of them? Really, Lynn, you believed in UFOs?"

I twisted my spaghetti with my fork. "I believed in Steven."

"You speak so calmly about it now. A day ago you nearly had a nervous breakdown even admitting it."

"It's freeing, in a way, to talk about it. It hung over me for a long time when I came back to Nashville, but then Anne came, and then Kate, and Tom and I got into a routine. Just as his political career was taking off we had Stella, and our lives were so hectic and full, it became easier and easier not to think about that time in my life. Now, speaking only to you, of course, I feel like I'm recalling some wild phase. Like when someone dyed her hair purple."

"That was not intentional, and it does haunt me to this day."

"It was like I was in on a secret, and all these really brilliant and strange and weird and daring people accepted me."

Roxy began to chew the last piece of garlic bread. "And Tom really doesn't know anything about it."

"No, he doesn't. He never had a clue. He was so wrapped up in his studies that I think he was happy that I had found something to occupy myself, and that brought in some extra money. But that's Tom; he never means to offend anyone when he's more interested in his work than he is in them, and I've come to accept that. I could blame the troubles in our marriage then on two young people who weren't ready to play house, but honestly, it was just a precursor to what would be the rest of our lives: him wrapped up in his career and satisfied if I appeared happy in whatever I was doing. It's only when he knows I'm frustrated or mad about something that he takes a break from whatever he's working on. If I'm happy, he's completely detached. I think after the girls were in college, he was more than ready for me to attempt, once more, to write a novel or start my own business. He couldn't be burdened with having to spend more time with his wife, who suddenly was without a purpose."

Roxy looked down at her plate.

"Please don't think I'm complaining," I said. "I'm certainly not. That's just how our marriage is, and most of the time I'm fine with it. In fact, I would have never come back here—ever—if William hadn't gone missing. Can you imagine if I revealed that I used to investigate missing people who we believed were abducted? Everyone would have thought I was having a nervous breakdown. No one would have believed me. And I would have created another problem for my family during the worst crisis of our lives. So I tried to push it aside. Now I can't seem to stop thinking about it."

"How could you have ever *not* thought of it?"

"I had to bury those years. That's the best way I can describe it. I had to smother them to make my marriage work, first of all. And when the girls came and Tom's career took off, I had to close the door on that feeling of . . . purpose? Is that the right word? First, I became a mother. Then a lawyer's wife. Then a state representative's wife, then a US senator's wife, and any ambitions I ever had to do something with my own life were gone. And once you've been given that taste of . . . professional acceptance, it's hard to douse. It took me years, Roxy, to get past it. But like all things, in time, I did."

Roxy took off her glasses. "I never knew. Here I am, your best friend, and I assumed you loved the whole mom-and-wife thing. That is, until we opened the shop."

"I do love it, don't get me wrong. But I got lost all those years ago, and it's reminded me that sometimes only by being lost do we find the path to who we are supposed to be. But . . . instead of staying on that path, I ran. I ran back home and away from everything here. So I never knew . . . what, or who, I could have been."

"Why did you run?" she asked quietly.

I looked out the window. "I was scared. I stood on the edge of a cliff to a wild and uncertain life and opted not to jump."

"And yet, here we are. Are you hoping to find out where this professor is, so you can track him down and make sure he's not involved with William's disappearance? Ask him why he had those maps of your property? Or do you honestly think . . . you'll find out something to explain where William has gone? If he has been . . . abducted . . . that these people will know how to call back the mother ship that took him?"

"I know sitting around Nashville putting Band-Aids on widely gaping wounds wasn't working. Maybe I'm doing it to convince myself I'm not useless. I can only explain what it feels like to have William missing. . . . It's like there's an elephant on my chest, and I can't breathe when I think about him being somewhere away from us. And being here, doing this, it's easier to breathe."

Roxy reached across the table and took my hand. "I promise to keep my mouth shut. Well, scratch that, we know that's not going to happen."

We took our leftovers, uncertain if they would ever be eaten, but knowing it was cold enough for them to remain in the backseat without going bad.

"So where are we having this Tupperware party?" Roxy asked as we slid into the truck.

I exhaled. "Steven's house."

"What? But he's not there and clearly hasn't been for a while. This is weird, Lynn."

"Maybe we were wrong. Maybe he actually lives somewhere else and he'll be there when we arrive. Maybe that's who Doug intended to be there all along."

"I'm biting my tongue, I'm biting my tongue," Roxy said, putting the truck in drive.

The old Victorian looked even drearier at night. No lights were on, but there were several cars parked outside.

"This is the part in the horror movie when the best friend advises the beautiful heroine not to go inside the haunted house. And do you know what happens to the friend in all those movies? She's the first to get her head cut off," Roxy said.

"Should we go around to the back again?" I asked, my heart in my throat.

"Nope. If no one answers at the front, we're not going in."

We approached the dark house and I knocked on the door. Within seconds, Doug opened the door, his cell phone illuminating his face.

"Come on in."

"Maybe you should turn on a few lights first," Roxy said, holding fast to the back of the sleeve of my coat.

"Everyone is downstairs," he said.

Roxy grunted. "There is no downstairs."

She rubbed her own forehead head as I turned to her in incredulity.

"I already knew you'd been here, I saw you on the security cameras." Doug motioned us in.

"You leave the back door open and you have hidden security cameras?" Roxy asked, still clinging to my sleeve. "And FYI, sir. I have 911 on speed dial."

"Just because a house looks like it has lousy security doesn't mean it actually does. Steven had to make it look like he left and never intended to return. And when he's out of town, he turns over the monitoring of his security to me."

"Is he here?" I asked.

Doug shook his head. "I wish he was, it would make this easier. Come on, I'll show you how to get downstairs."

He used the flashlight on his phone to lead us once more through the weary furniture towards the television. His light flashed over the monitor and then settled on the horizontal silver handle of the retro Coke-bottle refrigerator that had screamed bachelor pad to us when we first snuck in.

He pulled out his wallet and flashed what looked like a white credit card in front of the handle. We heard a soft beep, and he opened the door.

Instead of rows of Coke, there was nothing but faint light. Through the hollowed-out fridge was a staircase leading down.

"Clever. Creepy, but clever," Roxy noted.

"Steven had it custom built and the keyless entry added. We needed to have our meetings in private. I'd say ladies first, but I assume you want me to go down first."

"Sounds good to me," Roxy said, waving him on.

We followed him through the repurposed refrigerator and down the stairs that had clearly been reinforced over the years, for they failed to creak as we passed wood paneling dating back to the seventies.

We descended into an unfinished basement with enough patchwork to allow for gatherings for those unconcerned with comfort. Roxy said she felt like she was attending an AA meeting, but the looks on the faces of the people milling below kept her from saying anything more.

We slowed our descent as all the conversations stopped. Most of the people wore glasses and appeared to be roughly around our age. Several were in suits. Doug certainly stood out, and he beckoned for us to come all the way down.

"Let's everyone find a seat." He motioned to the scattered chairs and a battered couch, but everyone remained standing, staring at me.

"It really is you," one man said, taking a handkerchief out of his tweed jacket to clean his glasses. "I guess it's true: You believe in the little green men just like the rest of us. You look just like you do on TV."

I bristled at that. A woman walked forward, her long silver hair tied back in a braid. "Rupert, you prove yet again your impeccable skill for saying the wrong thing at the wrong time. It's been a long time, Lynn. You may not recognize the few of us who were here back in the day."

I cleared my throat. "I doubt you would have recognized me, or even remembered my name, if it hadn't been for my husband."

"Oh, I would have remembered," the woman said, smiling warmly. "I would remember the nice girl with the pretty blond curls who listened—didn't laugh at me, didn't judge—actually listened to me talk about my brother. Didn't think less of me when I twisted my hair like a little girl." She reached up and twirled a strand. "I still do it."

I tilted my head. "Barbara?"

The woman nodded. "And do you remember my brother's name?"

Don Rush. Of course I remember. But I don't know any of you. I could barely tell my best friend about my past. I'm not about to discuss my memories with strangers.

I forced a grimace. "I'm sorry, I don't."

"But I bet you remember his story."

"I remember wishing I could have helped you more."

"You did help." She reached out and laid a hand on my arm. "You made me feel like I wasn't crazy. You and Steven both. And you gave me this."

She handed me a small laminated card, frayed and yellowed over time. I smiled at one of the prayer cards Steven gave me to hand out to the families of the missing.

"Do you remember this? It got me through a lot of hard times. I whispered it like a prayer: 'You are with me. You are in the rain. You are in my tears. You are where the water falls,'" she recited.

I ran my fingers over the words, and Barbara closed my fingers around the card. "You keep it. Maybe it will bring you comfort now."

"How about me?" asked a morbidly obese man who was leaning on a chair. My heart skipped a beat as I instantly remembered him.

Marcus Burg. You were there for one of the most frightening moments of my life. "I'm sorry, it's been so long—"

"I wasn't this fat back then. I was fat, just not megasized. Marcus, the guy with the telescope? Ham radio operator? Trying to pick up the little green men on the radio? We met in a cornfield once."

"Oh yes, of course, Marcus."

"Again, let's everybody have a seat," Doug repeated. "We've got a lot to discuss."

A man in an expensive-looking Brooks Brothers suit frowned at Roxy. "No offense, ma'am, but this is highly sensitive information. I've never even seen you before. And I've only ever seen the politician's wife on television."

"Robert, at one time, this woman knew more about being a Researcher than you do," Barbara said.

"Prove it," the man insisted. "What's the Arthur Crowning incident?"

He disappeared while fishing after a rainstorm, his gear and lunchbox left inside the boat.

I shifted my eyes.

"What about the Doyle Robinson disappearance?"

Doyle Robinson went hiking on a trail in Giant City in downstate Illinois. Hiked the trail all his life. Was never seen again. But if I tell you everything I remember, you'll assume I'm still one of you. I have no idea what you intend to do with my memories.

I bit my lip. "I'm sorry, I don't remember."

"Those are only the most famous abduction cases in Illinois, and you don't remember them? So, again, we're here to make a deal with Steve's old girlfriend, and she doesn't even remember anything—"

"What about my brother Don?" Barbara asked quietly. "What do you remember about him?"

I will not, however, come off as a flake. "I remember he was your twin, and you were living in . . . Michigan. You awoke one night to lights in your bedroom. You went downstairs and found the door open, and you went to the window to see your brother standing out in a snowstorm. There were suddenly lights, and your brother was gone."

The room was silent. Barbara nodded slowly. "Yes, that's all true. You see, Robert, Lynn didn't investigate the Crowning or Robinson cases. But she did mine. And she cared, too."

I cared about all of them. I remember them all.

Doug cleared his throat. "We're here to talk about Steven."

"Yes," I said. "Why isn't he at the university?"

"The official word is that he was suspended for using university equipment, on university time, for personal use," he responded. "That's what Dean Fulton said. The only reason the dean even kept Steven around was because of his expertise. His articles about the gases on Mars alone have given this department a gold-star reputation in the academic world. But, as you may recall, Ms. Stanson—"

"It's Roseworth."

"Yes, as in Senator Roseworth, of course. You may recall, Mrs. Roseworth, that Steven is also terrible at playing the academic poker needed to stay ahead at this college. So I wasn't surprised when I showed up a few months ago and saw his office locked. I was surprised, however, that he left me no message. Nothing. All I had was the official word from the university's communications department that they severed ties with him, and that information was only supposed to be shared internally, not with anyone else."

"When did this happen?" I asked.

"End of the summer semester."

Roxy flashed me a look.

"Has there been no sign of him at all?" asked a woman in a long skirt, pulling her glasses up to rest on her crown of gray hair.

Barbara shook her head. "No, Mary."

"I don't understand," the woman continued. "Steven was so excited this summer. The last I talked to him, he felt like he was making some breakthroughs, especially on the Abel and Notish cases. And then, suddenly, he was gone. We still have no idea why, Doug?"

"As I've told you, I came to work to find that the dean had his office locked up. So I came here, and everything had been cleaned out, practically. And that's it."

"So he just skipped town? And no one has had any word from him? I know this drips with irony, but should you have filed a missing-persons report?" Mary asked.

The room grew quiet, and Doug shifted uncomfortably. "Can you imagine the questions police would have asked? Once I told them that the dean suspected he was using university equipment for personal reasons, and that all his belongings were gone, they would have assumed he was just lying low."

"Maybe he is," Robert said, loosening his expensive tie. "Listen, Steven is a great colleague. An even better Researcher. But there might be some truth to what the university suspects—"

"Bullshit," Doug interjected.

"—and Steven is trying to sort out his next move. But it's been three months. Even if he had a reason to disappear like this, we need to find him. Just to make sure he's OK."

"Which brings us to why we wanted to meet with you, Lynn," Doug said. "To see if we could help each other."

"I'm not sure how I could help. I came here for help myself."

Doug looked briefly to Robert. "We're willing to share everything with you. All of the records we've stored on thumb drives, or on the cloud, on every case. And, course, the video."

The room grew quiet and everyone looked at me, waiting.

"I'm sorry, what video?" I asked.

"Of course, you never saw it. It came to us years after you were gone," Barbara said. "Show her, Doug. Pull it up on your laptop."

Doug frowned. "Maybe we should finish talking about what we need her to do, first. I don't know about sharing—"

"Just show her, Doug," she insisted. "She was a Researcher long before you were even born."

In a move that was so dramatic that I knew Roxy was rolling her eyes, Doug reached into his shirt and pulled out a simple chain on which a thumb drive was attached. He slid a laptop out of a beat-up satchel alongside of his chair and opened it. After plugging in the memory stick, he huddled over the screen, keeping the keyboard close, so no one could see the passwords he was furiously typing.

After a few moments, he placed the laptop on a coffee table and swiveled it around towards me. "This is part of what we're prepared to share with you, if we can come to an agreement. But I must strongly warn you—"

"Doug, play it," Barbara said wearily. "And turn up the volume. It's hard to hear."

He reached over the screen to punch the volume key several times, and then hit the space bar. The blue video screen turned black, then the grayish-white image of a man sitting in a chair came into view.

Converted from film on which it was first recorded, the video occasionally flickered, showing the man dressed in all black, his hair slicked over, with the kind of hard part that was so popular when I was a little girl.

"I can't hear anything," Roxy said.

"It's coming, give it a second," Doug scowled.

"Are you comfortable?" the man in the video said, his voice

hollow, recorded on a microphone that was too far away from its subject.

The man leaned forward. "Can you tell me about what you saw?"

The film quality was so poor that I could barely make out that he was beginning to take notes.

"What do you remember about the ship in the sky?"

Doug reached over and snapped the computer closed. He stared at me, holding his chin high.

"What you've just seen is the first proof ever recorded of a government operative questioning someone who'd been abducted."

"*That's* your proof?" Roxy asked. "How does that prove anything—?"

"Where did that come from?" I asked softly.

"I wish I knew. Steven obtained it. But there's much more. And while we only have footage of the operative asking the questions, at the end, the camera moves a bit, and for a second you see whom he is talking to. I'm willing to show it to you, as well as all Steven's latest findings and research about the missing. It might help you too, because I know you think your grandson's been abducted too. There's one thing I'd ask for in return."

He leaned forward. "Go public. All out. Press conference and everything. Admit your past as a Researcher and how you feel your grandson has been abducted. Say that you're working with us to find him. The hope is that Steven will see it, wherever he is, and get back in touch with us. Or maybe even you."

I put my hand to my chest. "I can't . . . do that."

"Why?" Doug asked sharply.

"I can't."

"Then we tell you nothing." He waved his hand. "You once supported our efforts. You believed in it; Steven told me everything. Everything. Now your own grandson has gone missing, and you won't come forward with support for us? Do you care that much more about your husband's image than finding your grandson?"

I grabbed my purse. "It was a mistake coming here."

"Lynn," Barbara pleaded.

"I won't be forced into anything." I stood. Roxy joined me, chewing her cheek.

"Then you leave here with nothing."

"Doug!" Barbara said.

"Trust me, you want to see this entire film. But not without a guarantee."

"You are terrible people," I said, hurrying towards the stairs. Barbara stood, but Roxy held up a warning hand.

"You should be ashamed," Roxy scolded, wagging her finger. "Giving a grandmother false hope and all that. You're nut jobs, every last one of you. And don't think I won't call the cops on you all."

"You won't," Doug said. "Because it will all be traced back to Lynn, and apparently her public persona is more important than her grandson."

"Eat shit, you little punk," Roxy said, catching up with me at the top of the stairs as I stepped through the shell of the fridge.

We hustled through the house and out the door, Roxy's hand on the small of my back. I heard the truck unlock and practically ran around to get inside the cab.

My face was buried in my hands when she turned the key. "Oh, Lynnie."

"Drive, Roxy. Drive to the hotel and get our things, and then drive all the way home. Don't stop."

"Honey, let's think about this—"

"No, I want to go home."

"Of course."

I heard a rap at my window and turned to see Doug standing outside, shivering. He'd clearly run out after us, for he wasn't wearing a coat.

"Lynn, this isn't only about William." He was practically yelling.

"Back away from the car, you asshole," Roxy said.

"You'll never know. You'll never know the truth—"

Roxy threw the truck in reverse with such force that Doug stumbled back.

Outside, a bit of ice began to fall. It had been spring when I last left Champaign. It was fitting that it was winter now, and the air smelled like a snow. I was right to leave here and never come back. I prayed for the kind of whopper where snow covers the entire town. I could leave knowing everything here would be buried.

TEN

The silence in the truck was interrupted occasionally with my sharp intake of breath. When Roxy tried to comfort me, I shook my head. When we got into Nashville and neared the house, I proclaimed my stupidity for even suggesting the journey to Illinois. I insisted that I wouldn't put my family through any more agony, that we were never again to discuss what we had seen or learned. Roxy implored me to reconsider, said we should, at the very least, go to the police with the information that Steven had a map of the property and vanished at roughly the same time William disappeared.

"No," I said simply. "We'd be wasting their time."

Thus I perfected the art of denial.

The smells were my greatest ally. The earthy pine, the cinnamon candles, the burning of dry wood. Baking pumpkin bread, tangy oranges in bowls, and brewing flavored coffee were more powerful now than the things that once soothed the anxiety I routinely felt with the approach of the holidays. The idea of all those gifts to buy, all that wrapping, all that traffic, used to be balanced out by the white lights wrapping the trunks of the trees outside the house and Johnny Mathis holiday music. All those worries were petty and meaningless now, and no amount of music or decorations could lift my spirits.

So I relied on the scents of the season to smother my sadness. When I practically moved into the Rose Peddler, which we transitioned into its seasonal holiday phase, I inhaled deeply as I thoroughly checked each tree brought in from McMinnville for any traces of blight. When I was in the house, amidst the Christmas trees I couldn't bear to give more than a passing glance to, I put spices in a pot on the stove to simmer. My tall coffee mug was always in hand at the Green Hills mall, my nose kept close to the rim as I tried not to cry purchasing gifts for the grandkids, knowing who wouldn't be there on Christmas morning. When he was home on the weekends, Tom occasionally complained his allergies were kicking up because a candle seemed to be burning in every room.

Roxy kept the festive music at a lull in the store, but flooded the place with candies and freshly baked cookies to give to children as their parents fretted over finding the perfect tree. When Roxy caught me glazing over while looking at the small children, she rushed to the house and grabbed a bunch of buckeyes out of the fridge, returning as quickly as possible to fill the shop with peanut butter and chocolate.

I approached my daily tasks with a ferocity, finding if I baked twice as much gingerbread, vacuumed twice as often, the days passed instead of limping by. I sat in with Tom during the weekly updates with investigators, listening as he peppered them with questions, pretending to buy into their theories. My bottom lip developed a sore because I bit it so often.

When the second Friday of December arrived, and the discount prices on the Christmas trees began, I welcomed the crowd at the store as yet another blessed distraction.

It was nearly nine o'clock when the last family left and

Roxy declared it a night. We were sitting at the table behind the counter going over the receipts when Stella came in, her cheeks rosy from the chill. She'd come right from work to help with the Christmas crowds. "Mom, do you feel like one more customer? Some lady said you helped her out earlier, and she had a quick question for you."

"Sure, hon." I said, passing the receipts to Roxy.

"Oh, let me personally thank this woman for enabling me now to do all the closing by myself," Roxy said.

I patted her on the shoulder and grabbed my coat and scarf. The night was lit by rows of white lights strung above the trees. I slipped on my gloves and walked into the rows of pine, seeing no one.

"Hello?" I called out. "Did someone need help?"

Someone called out my name from the far end of the trees, and I hustled over. I peered out in the darkness beyond.

"Hello?" I said.

"Were there ladybugs swarming when your grandson disappeared?" a voice said from the trees.

I froze. A female shape stood between two trees, her long silver hair pulled back in a ponytail. She wore a long dark-blue overcoat, too thick and heavy for the southern winters.

"Barbara?"

It had only been a few weeks since I'd seen her, but she seemed thinner, even in her bulky winter coat.

"Did they, Lynn? Did they swarm?" Barbara asked.

I looked around for a moment before replying. "You know they did."

"It's been documented in so many cases. Sometimes the beetles cover entire walls, crawling like they've been driven insane. When I see ladybugs now, sweet as they are, it stops my heart."

She exhaled, her breath white in the icy night. "They have your grandson. They've taken him. Steven said he thinks he can help you find him. If your boy's been returned."

"Who has William? And where is Steven? I thought no one knew where he was."

"Steven is here now, Lynn. That's why I'm here tonight, to take you to him."

I looked past her to make sure neither Roxy nor Stella had come out to see where I was.

"How could you come here, after what happened?" I asked.

"I'm not happy about it either. Doug can be a first-class jerk, and can't see past his own ambition in order to do the right thing. The others think he's the Messiah, with his grand talk of taking all this public. He sees you as the key to do that, to finally get validation for all our work. And he is genuinely concerned about Steven. But he doesn't know how it feels to lose someone, like we do. You have to remember, Lynn, my brother was my twin. When he vanished, half of me vanished too. And you don't care if people believe you or not. You want to find him. My brother is long gone, but your grandson may not be. That's what Steven thinks. He thinks there's still a chance to find him."

A chill ran through me so severely that I tightened the scarf around my neck. "What do you expect me to do?"

"Come with me. Hear Steven out. That's all. You can walk away again if you want. It's just me and Steven this time, none of the others even know we're here."

"All this time, you've known where Steven has been? And you say he's here?"

"No. I hadn't spoken to him until he contacted me a few days ago. We only met here yesterday. I'll let him tell you where he's been; that's for him to say. I'm the only one who knows how to even contact him now. That was his decision when he decided to run."

"Run?"

"He can explain." Barbara looked back at the shop.

"He won't have to. I'm not going with you. I don't want anything to do with you or the others. Not after what happened. And I won't put my family through the scrutiny that Doug would require for this information."

"Doug isn't a part of this."

"I don't know that. For all I know, you could take me to him again. I'm sorry, but no. I can't do it. I won't do it."

"Steven thought you might feel that way." Barbara reached into her pocket. She brought out an envelope and offered it.

"What is that?"

"The names of two people Steven said for you to research. He said to look up their names at the local library, and you might change your mind."

I cautiously reached out and took the envelope. "I don't understand."

"Steven says you will, if you look into them. I'll give you all day tomorrow to inquire if you choose. Tomorrow night, if you want to see Steven, I'll wait for you at Chevron gas around the corner. I'll be there at nine o'clock. I'll wait thirty minutes. If you come, I'll take you to Steven. If you don't, then I'll take that as your decision. I won't fault you either way. I felt horrible about what happened, and I told Steven that you deserved better. That's why he came. That's why I'm here."

She buried her hands in her pockets. "It's colder here than I would have thought," she said, walking back once more into the pine trees.

●   ●   ●

I'd immediately gotten online after we'd closed the shop and Roxy and Stella had gone home, checking for anything about the two names typed on a single piece of white paper, along with corresponding dates. The fact that it wasn't written in Steven's all-caps handwriting seemed dubious, for anyone could have typed the names. But I looked anyway, and could find nothing about a Josh Stone, August 5, 1945, or an Amelia Shrank, August 2, 1934.

Amelia Shrank. I somehow knew the name. But like the answer to a Trivial Pursuit question that remained on the tip of your tongue and would not come until the other side of the card was read aloud, the explanation of how I recognized a name from the early 1930s would not surface.

I was at the downtown library as soon as it opened the next morning, and made my way to the microfilm room. It was as visually impressive as the rest of the library, with its light fixtures and paint colors straight out of Restoration Hardware, but it did not have the lure of the popular fiction section or the civil-rights collection. The emptiness of the room was disquieting; I feared any moment there would be some kind of whispered ambush from Doug in full entitled-Researcher mode, working alongside Barbara to get me alone to try and browbeat me into submission.

I cautiously sought out microfilm, peering down every aisle. I'd hoped the *Nashville Banner* published as far back as I needed to go. Before *The Tennessean* became the only newspaper in town, the *Banner* was its worthy competitor. Once I understood the catalog system, I found the archives of the paper for the entire year of 1934 and started sliding through the months.

The ancient technology still hummed as I remembered, but

I quickly grew frustrated with having to press the button to advance. I chastised myself, thinking of how I urged the grand-kids to develop patience as they whined about a video taking too long to load on YouTube.

At last came August 2, and I immediately started reading the obituaries. It was the only way to search by name. When I finished the last obituary, and found no Amelia Shrank.

Was this just another way for Doug to try and wear me down? Was he watching from somewhere, maybe an adjoin-ing room, to see how desperate I had become? Was he wait-ing, hoping I would break down in tears, when he would reveal himself, ready once again to make a deal? And what did he mean, that this wasn't only about William?

Barbara promised to take me to Steven, but if it were truly him, what would he want in return?

I thought of what Deanna, Tom's press secretary, had said: *Is there anything controversial about your family that we don't know about?*

Holding information for ransom wasn't the way of the Re-searchers I'd known. Intimidation, ultimatums, threats weren't how they operated. They were misfits, outsiders, even reclu-sive about what they knew, what they had seen. They wanted no attention.

In my time among them, I'd certainly learned they had reason to be afraid.

I leaned back and rubbed my eyes. A late night spent star-ing at a computer screen followed up by hours fixated on mi-crofilm made my eyes as dry as the winter air. They'd felt that way so many times as I sat at my desk in the astronomy depart-ment, reading case after case, only finding relief when my tears moistened my bloodshot eyes.

●   ●   ●

I'd been so thrilled to escape that desk and all those tragic stories when Steven had come to me, almost in desperation, asking if I was able to meet one of his colleagues in a remote rural
area outside Springfield.

"It should be me going, but every spare second has to go
to my course review. I suppose I failed too many students last
semester. Dr. Roberts says it's something important and he
needs me to come tomorrow, and he doesn't come down from
Chicago very often."

"Dr. Roberts?"

"Mathematics professor at Loyola University. Chair of the
department. Rhodes Scholar. And one of us."

I had calmly, almost indifferently, agreed to go, but under
the desk clasped my hands together. I'd done my best to stay
aloof ever since Steven kneeled dangerously close to me in his
office the day I revealed the weather commonality of the disappearances. I didn't like how I left his office feeling flushed.

I told Tom the truth—at least the part that I had to go to
Springfield the next day for some research at the state capital.
When he had failed to even ask why an astronomy project
would require a trip to the home of the legislature, I knew he
wasn't paying attention and abruptly left the apartment.

I'd passed Decatur, rolling up the window at the smell of
the cornstarch plant, and headed down I-72, finally getting off
on exit 23. Cornfields flanked me on both sides as I traveled
down a paved road.

About twenty miles north of the interstate, I saw the lights
from police cars. Two squad cars were at the end of a dirt road,
and three more were parked around a white farmhouse tucked
on the edge of a tree line. An ambulance was rolling up to the
house. I'd slowed, and one of the officers waved me on past.
I'd hoped someone elderly hadn't died in the heat.

Five minutes later, on that same road, I found the address I was looking for. As Steven had explained, there was the heavily faded navy-blue stripe on the mailbox, the number thirty-five, and the dirt drive.

Yet as I stepped out of the car, I saw the house clearly hadn't been lived in for years. The windowpanes were cracked in several places and the roof sagged; it most likely was abandoned following one of the tornadoes that so plagued this area of the world.

"Mrs. Roseworth?"

I'd missed the pickup truck parked behind the house. A man leaned up against the bed. He was dressed in pressed pants and short-sleeved dress shirt.

"Dr. Roberts?

He walked out across the road, looking down in the direction I'd driven. His close-cropped white hair revealed skin splotchy with age spots, but he moved with a young person's urgency.

"So you're her," he extended his hand. "You're the one he talks so much about. Shall we be on our way?"

I was glad I wore a head scarf, or he would have seen that my ears flared an alarming shade of red.

"It's nice to meet you. I thought we were meeting in someone's house. . . ."

"That's the closest address that I could give to show Steven what I'd found. Apparently, no one lives there. Where we need to go is actually in the corn. You have on pretty shoes, but the ground is as dry as bone. They'll get dusty but not ruined. I'd pull your car back beside mine; we don't want to draw any attention from the road."

I did as he suggested and then joined him in the corn. Once

again, I was thankful for the scarf. I could already feel beads of sweat on my neck.

"Did you bring a camera?" he asked.

"A Hawkeye Instamatic."

"Good. Steven will need to see on the ground what I saw from the sky."

"Pardon?"

"I took some pictures from a friend's crop duster this morning. He's a photographer, too, and brought with him one of the photos we processed. But he can't print all of them in time for you to take with you tonight, so it's good you can snap some pictures while you're here. I'll send the aerial photo back with you, though."

"Photos of what?"

"We're almost there. I am surprised, though, that he sent a woman." He turned around with a sheepish grin. "Forgive me. There's not many of us of the female gender. But he obviously finds you capable, otherwise he wouldn't have sent you. I should have known he wouldn't have come."

"Why?"

"Because of the cornfield."

"I'm sorry, what's wrong with the cornfield?"

Dr. Roberts took out a handkerchief and wiped his forehead. "His sister, obviously. He still hasn't gotten over it."

He continued walking, and I hurried to catch up. "I don't understand what a cornfield and Steven's—I mean Dr. Richards's—sister, has anything to do with anything."

"You'll see."

We walked for another ten minutes, until the corn gave way to a clearing. The sunlight was blinding without the shade of the stalks. When I shielded my eyes, I realized it was no barren field.

Whoever farmed this land would soon come upon the bent stalks and ruined corn and most likely utter a litany of curses. The green stems and husks were pummeled to the ground for several yards in all directions. I knelt down, examining one of the stalks, seeing it was bent at a perfect ninety-degree angle.

"They're all like that."

I looked over to see a man sitting on an overturned bucket. The sight was almost comical, due to his immense size and how he somehow balanced himself on the pail.

"Lynn, this is Marcus Burg: pilot, ham-radio expert, and photographer. He's the one who first heard about the missing boy. He's also the one who found the circles."

"Circles?" I asked.

"Crop circles." Marcus held out his sagging arms. "You're in the middle of one now. Points right to where—"

"Let's let her look at the picture first, so she understands."

"Steven told me a two-year-old boy was missing, but that's all I know. How long ago did he disappear?"

"Two nights ago," Dr. Roberts answered.

"Two nights?" I looked out towards the police lights at the farmhouse. "He could still be alive, just not found yet. He went missing not far from here, correct? Why would you think he's been . . . ?"

Dr. Roberts gave me a pitying smile. "It took me a long time to say it out loud as well. And I'll admit, it's even strange to say it now. Abducted. By extraterrestrials. The longer you're at this, the easier it becomes to verbalize it. As you know, we typically don't get involved until much later, when the cops are gone and families get desperate. But when Marcus told me what he heard on the radio and what he saw from the sky, I came down. And summoned Steven here, figuring he wouldn't come. But I hoped, regardless."

"Why wouldn't he come?" I asked, frustrated at having to repeatedly ask for clarification of everything this man said.

"I probably shouldn't be the one telling you this, but if you're going to work with Steven, you need to know. Maybe sending you here is his way of letting you find out. He's strange, that one, but brilliant, and a good man."

"Steven's sister was abducted by aliens," Marcus said, rubbing his neck.

"Dr. Richards's sister is missing?"

"Abducted. It's the truth as he sees it, and it set him on this path, that's for certain," Dr. Roberts said. "I don't want to gloss over the details, and perhaps one day he will tell you all about it. He was eight, maybe nine. Steven, his parents, and younger sister, Elise, went to spend a weekend at their family farm in northern Iowa. I think it was his uncle's place. Anyway, there had been a terrible storm, and Elise and Steven were trapped in the house all day. When it let up a bit, they'd thrown on their boots to go play in the corn at dusk. Steven said his boots got stuck in the mud, and he was separated from Elise. He knew he would get in trouble for losing her, so he kept searching, until night. He was found by his parents, thanks to the farmers who saw his flashlight. A strong beam of light. Except that Steven wasn't carrying a flashlight."

Despite the heat, goose bumps rose on my arms. "His sister was never found," Dr. Roberts continued. "His mother later committed suicide, and his father blamed Steven for all of it. I don't know if Steven was a strange kid before that, but he certainly was afterwards, he even admits it. He became obsessed with trying to find Elise. It was only when he became a young man that he was able to get the police reports from that night. There was absolutely nothing to explain what happened. The assumption was that some kind of bobcat or something got her. The fields were even cleared to try and find her body. There was no sign of her. All the police report noted was that Steven's uncle didn't care if that particular stretch of land was cleared, because it was useless anyway. And it was useless, because something had flattened the crops in large circles."

Dr. Roberts motioned around them. "Obviously, no one took pictures back then, but when Marcus heard about the missing kid, and that the farmer of this land reported someone had ruined large swaths of his crops—"

"I took my plane up, and I saw the circles, but I couldn't take pictures while I had the controls. I had to get Max down here from Chicago, and when we went up, he took some pictures with my camera," Marcus said. "Want to see?"

When he didn't bother to stand, we walked over. He reached into the front of his bib overalls and took out a black-and-white photo and handed it to me. "I've only had time to print one of them."

The photo clearly showed a series of large circles—ten in all—in a single row among the corn. At closer inspection, I could see they varied in size, the first much larger, gradually diminishing to a tiny circle.

"We're standing in the middle of that row now," Dr. Roberts said. "You keep following the circles, and they end at the farmhouse where the boy is missing."

I looked closer at the photo. "It's like they're marking where they do it." Marcus pointed. "An arrow straight to their target—"

"That's my bucket."

The voice caused us to turn around. In the row we had walked now stood a thin man.

He was filthy, with tattered, dusty clothes and hair that clearly hadn't been washed for days. I couldn't tell if it was the angle of the sun or his complexion that enhanced the dark circles around his eyes, which had caused me to misjudge his age. He couldn't have been more than sixteen.

"Mama says we can take an ear or two," the teenager said. "I need my bucket."

"You live near here?" Dr. Roberts asked.

The boy flicked his thumb back down the row. "You done parked at my house. Why you'ins out here? You wit' the cops? They ain't gonna find that boy. Not them men in suits neither."

"Shit," Marcus said. "Max—"

"Why won't they find him?" Dr. Roberts took a step forward. "Where is the boy?"

"You got money to pay me to tell you what I seen? Them suits had money."

Dr. Roberts dug into his back pocket and pulled out a worn wallet. He slid out a few singles, handing them over.

The boy smiled, exposing rows of crooked teeth and squinting in the sunlight. "Mama says I'm lyin', but I seen it. I seem 'em get dragged right up into them clouds. He gone. Straight up to heaven. That's what I told them suits too."

"When did you talk to these men in suits?" Dr. Roberts demanded.

" 'Bout two hours ago."

"Shit!" Marcus said, looking around wildly. "Shit!"

"Go," Dr. Roberts ordered, motioning for me. "We've got to go."

"But I haven't taken a single picture," I said, watching Marcus practically bulldoze into the corn after brushing past the teen.

"It doesn't matter." Dr. Roberts took me by the arm. I looked back one last time at the boy, who stared after us with dull eyes.

"They could be anywhere!" Marcus cried out.

"For Christ sake, keep it down, Marcus!" Dr. Roberts whispered.

"What is going on?" I asked.

Dr. Roberts didn't answer. When we at last emerged at the house, Marcus was already in the truck, firing up the engine.

"Come on, Max!"

Dr. Roberts ushered me to my car. "Drive until you hit the interstate and don't stop. Drive the speed limit. If anyone in a black suit tries to pull you over or talk to you, remember my sexist comment about Steven sending a woman. If you can, don't stop, keep driving. Do you have enough gas to make it back to Champaign?"

"I filled up when I got off the interstate—"

"Then go. Right now. And take this," he said, giving me the photo.

"Max, let's go!" Marcus yelled.

"Give it to Steven, tell him what we saw." Dr. Roberts ran over to the truck. As he got in, he leaned over Marcus. "Hide that photo in your purse, Lynn! Go now!"

I'd slid the photo beside my wallet, turned the keys, pressed the gas, and the car lurched forward. The engine died immediately. Even with Marcus's truck gunning past and Dr. Roberts motioning at me wildly to drive on, I forced myself to calmly turn on the car once more, and drifted out onto the dirt drive.

I turned left, even used the blinker, and was once more on the road. In the rearview mirror, just as the corn hid the house from view, I saw the boy from the field point in my direction to a large woman with similar dark circles under her eyes who came out to stand on the dilapidated front porch.

As Dr. Roberts had instructed, I kept my speed at the limit. *What is it, exactly, we're running from?*

As my pulse started to slow, I saw the lights from the police cruisers. I tapped the brakes to go at an even more casual pace, even giving a friendly, gentle wave to one of the officers stationed at the perimeter of the missing boy's property. He tilted his hat.

I almost didn't see the man in the black suit until he was right in front of me.

He stepped out so casually from beside the squad car, it was as if he was perturbed that a car had chosen to drive in his path. I hit the brakes, but I was already going so slowly that the car only took a moment to stop. The man rounded the hood and came over to the window. I rolled it down slowly.

"Sorry if I startled you there, ma'am."

Everything on him, except for his crisp white shirt, was black. I imagined his eyes black as well, hidden beneath his dark sunglasses.

"I saw you drive down the road here a bit ago, I wanted to make sure you were all right," he said, leaning his arm on the door. "There's a boy missing around here."

I saw another shadow. Another man in a black suit was even more jarring, given the contrast to his white-blond hair. He leaned on the driver's side door, peering in.

"That's terrible." I felt the sweat on my upper lip. "I'm actually such a fool; I think I took the wrong turn to my aunt's house. I have to take the next exit on the interstate, apparently."

"You're quite a ways from the interstate," the blond-haired man's voice was muffled through the glass. "You've taken quite the wrong turn."

I knew they could see me sweating now. "How long has the boy been missing?" I blurted out. "His poor parents must be devastated—"

"They are," the first black suit said, looking out down the

road from which I came. "Not sure what happened to him. You didn't see anyone strange on your wrong turn, did you?"

"Nothing but a lot of corn." I attempted to laugh.

"Not much to take pictures of."

I glanced at the camera in the passenger seat.

"Because the last thing the boy's family needs is to make this situation worse, with anyone trying to document all this," he said, still looking down the road. His hand, however, had drifted into the car, his long fingertips brushing the handle of the purse I'd hurriedly sandwiched between my hip and the door. "Doesn't feel right . . . a woman by herself driving around with all this . . . strangeness going on. Maybe you should step out of the car."

The blond-haired man rapped on the window. "Why don't you step on out, ma'am."

If you encounter anyone in a black suit, remember my sexist comment about Steven sending a woman, Dr. Roberts had warned. I heard the door handle lift.

"Oh, you're right about that," I leaned back casually in the seat. "I do wish my husband was here to drive, he knows I can't find my way around anywhere except for my kitchen. And my sister can't even make pancakes to save her life! If I don't get there soon, my little niece Amy, who's turning three this month—I can't believe how big she's getting—won't even have a birthday cake! I don't understand why we couldn't have the party at my sister's house—"

"Just be careful," the man quickly withdrew his hand, continuing to walk across the road. The blond stared at me for a good minute before slowly walking away.

I lazily rolled up the window and gently eased the car forward.

When I finally approached the interstate entrance, I took off the head scarf and rolled down the window. The hot wind on my face was hardly refreshing, but I needed as much air as I could take. I wished desperately for some water or a Coke, something to quench my desperately dry throat.

The dark car pulled up on the shoulder of the road so quickly that I almost gasped in surprise. Theirs was a rolling stop, just enough time for me to see another man in a black suit and sunglasses at the wheel. I caught a glimpse of the teenager from the cornfield in the backseat, and a heavyset woman with her arm around him. Even though she had been far away when I saw her at the ruined house, I knew she was the teenager's mother. Were those tears on her cheeks?

When she slammed her hand against the glass and cried out something to me, and the car sped away up onto the entrance ramp towards Springfield, all I could do was watch in horror. I saw her turn around, and then the car was gone.

I was on the interstate a moment later, breathing in and out as if I had finished a marathon. Even though it had never happened to me, I knew I was close to hyperventilating. *Where were they taking them? If they'd looked at that photo, would I ever have been seen again? Should I call the police?*

I knew I wouldn't, and I hated myself a little bit more every mile I sped away. What could I do for them? I didn't even know why the black suits had them. *Of course you do. They took her because of what her son saw, and what he told her of how the missing boy went into the sky. The black suits paid her son money, and in return came and collected them all.*

I'd spent the next two hours in a fog, repeatedly replaying the entire encounter in my mind. I was surprised when the sign with the population of Champaign came into view, and how near my tank was to empty. I exited the highway, gassed up, and headed straight for the university.

I wanted to rush into Steven's office and breathlessly describe what had happened. But I knew there was no room in his world for anyone who couldn't emotionally handle the work. So I sat in the parking lot, collected myself, and reapplied my lipstick.

Steven answered the door to his office, and I did my best to walk in calmly. I sat, smoothed out the wrinkles in my skirt, and produced the photograph.

"Dr. Roberts and his friend explained to me the theory of the crop circles."

Steven had stared for a long time at the photograph without speaking.

"I'm very sorry to hear about your sister."

He looked up. "He told you?"

"You should have told me."

"Yes." He looked back at the photograph. "I should have."

"You know, if you shared your sister's story with more people, then all this," I motioned around the room, "wouldn't seem as . . ."

"You know I'm not a great communicator. Thank you, Lynn. I'll put in a call to Dr. Roberts tomorrow."

"Tell him I did encounter a man in a black suit. Actually two. But I got away without them realizing anything."

His astonished reaction was exactly what I'd hoped for. I crossed my legs.

"Jesus!" he said, dropping the photograph on his desk. "Lynn, what happened?"

"Who are they? The mention of these black suits by a boy in the field made both your colleagues run off like the corn was on fire. And then I saw the mother of that boy being driven away, and she looked terrified."

THE DARKEST TIME OF NIGHT   131

"Wait, what happened?" Steven kneeled before me. "Start from the beginning."

I'm certain he rubbed his forehead seventeen times before I finished.

"You . . . actually encountered men in a black suits? You're certain?" he said.

"I'm quite sure I know the color black."

"If I had any idea, I would have never sent you. I would never, ever have sent you." He then took my hand in his. "I'd never forgive myself if something had happened to you."

Somehow I remained calm, although I wanted to profess how terrified I was as well. "What would have happened to me? What happened to that mother and her son? Who are these men?"

Steven took off his glasses. "We aren't exactly sure. They show up sometimes when people go missing. The arrival of the men in black is a clear indication that an abduction has occurred. They are the reason we have to be so secretive about our files, our findings. We know . . . they know about us."

"How can you be certain?"

"Because when people vanish, sometimes our investigators go missing, too."

"Miss?"

I looked up from the microfilm machine to see a college-age girl with a Bettie Page haircut and a polka-dot shirt smiling at me. "Are you finding everything you need? I'm assigned to archives and a few other sections, and I didn't know anyone was in here."

"I'm fine, thank you."

"Most people don't even know how to operate these anymore," she said with a smile. "They think Google can find everything. One day, hopefully, we'll even have these old papers online."

"I used to do a lot of research." *I used to be brave, too.* "I'm a bit rusty on the microfilm, but it's slowly coming back."

"Holler if you need anything."

I smiled back and returned my attention to the glowing square screen. I read once more through the death notices of the day, the next day's obits, and then the day prior. As I prepared to fast forward to read the rest for the entire week, the black-and-white face of a girl whirled by.

I slowly rewound, finding the girl's photo on the front page of the August 2 issue. She was smiling, with a left front tooth missing and straight-cut bangs. It was obviously her family's picture, provided to the newspaper.

GIRL GOES MISSING IN MILLER'S WOODS
By Clark Bass Sr.

The search continues for a three-year-old West Nashville girl missing since early Friday morning.

The parents of Amelia Shrank report they fear she had somehow wandered out of the house.

"They think she went looking for the family's missing dog in the middle of the night," said detective Ralph Fulton.

Shrank is the daughter of Dr. and Mrs. Mark Shrank, who described their daughter as being three feet five inches, wearing a black-and-white nightgown and her hair in a long braid.

The Shranks' home backs up to the woods off Woodmont Avenue.

Woodmont Avenue was just a few streets away from my home. And just like that, I remembered how I knew Amelia Shrank.

I knew I was starting to sweat. I popped out the canister, making sure to keep it close by, and inserted August 5, 1945. Instead of going directly to the obituaries, I slid to the front page. But it was page three news that told of missing hunter, Josh Stone.

HUNTER PRESUMED DEAD IN CREEK

By William Buck

A 32-year-old father of twins is believed to be dead some- where in Richland Creek, Nashville police report.

Josh Stone was last seen by his wife, Janet, heading out to squirrel hunt in the early morning hours Friday.

Janet Stone found her husband's shotgun several yards away from Richland Creek late yesterday evening, according to police.

"We can only surmise that he walked too close to the edge and fell into the creek," said Captain Kris Kemper.

Police said Stone wasn't a good swimmer, and are focus- ing on searching the waters for his body.

The location of the gun is well known to locals in that area, due to the grave marker placed there by the Shrank family ten years ago, to mark the last spot their daughter, Amelia, was seen.

"He may have stopped to pay his respects, and that's why he left the gun there—because he thought he'd be right back," Kemper said.

Police said they will resume their search of the banks of river Sunday morning.

"Because of all that rain we've been having, we've had a lot of erosion, and on top of that, the creek is fast-moving and swollen," Kemper said. "If somebody who couldn't swim good fell in, it could be a real bad deal. It's been so hot this August, maybe he thought he could get a quick drink and the ground collapsed under him."

Next to a photo of Stone and his wife was another picture of a child-sized gravestone with Amelia Shrank's name engraved upon it. A gravestone I had discovered as a child, when I followed my father and those strange men into the woods.

I sat forward. Amelia Shrank had disappeared in August, as had Josh Stone.

Eighty years later, in the same month, William would vanish from the same woods.

ELEVEN

I could see the yellow from the edge of the trees. In those first terrible weeks, the crime-scene tape, marking the spot where Chris found Brian in a state of shock, had been hidden by the dense foliage. Now, with the leaves fallen and the branches covered in a thin layer of snow, the garish yellow was easily seen.

The realization of what afforded me the view brought bile to the back of my throat. I stood under the bell on the back of the shop, and I could feel its weight bearing down on me like a wicked headache. It was here, nearly fifty-five years ago, that I watched my father and those men enter the woods. From here, the place where William disappeared was only a short walk away.

Moving through the burr oaks was easier now than in the summer; low hanging branches easily snapped away in the gray afternoon light. The winter winds, or perhaps a confused and panicked deer, had torn one section of the tape apart.

Chris could be out here. He was known to wander with everything from rakes to hoes, clawing at the ground, desperate to find some sign of his youngest son, something to indicate what had happened to him.

I'd also seen Detective Strombino a few times in the woods. Once, I had gone out to ask him for an update. He only shook his head.

I doubted either would be out here today, for the conditions were miserable. Sleet spit from the sky, and the thin layer of icy snow crunched beneath my feet. I felt confident no one would see what I was about to do.

I set the cloth grocery bag on a flat stone and lifted out the glass terrarium. I had several of them in the house and in the shop. Even in the deepest of winter, I could have moss and ferns growing inside with just a little water and maintenance. The empty terrarium I carried was my smallest, but what it contained needed little space.

Taking one more look around, I walked through the cordoned-off area, holding the terrarium over my head. I looked up through the bottom to see the ten or so ladybugs I'd collected from inside the house crawling erratically.

I'd fully understood, then, why Daddy had dropped his glass lantern when he saw that his little girl had discovered him and those other men. If anyone now came up on me suddenly, I would be unable to explain what I was doing. The glass container certainly would have slipped from my fingers as well.

You'd warned—no, threatened—me not to come in these woods. What did you know? Were those strange men some of the first Researchers, who had come to these trees investigating the disappearance of Amelia Shrank and Josh Stone? Had they needed your permission to come out here? Had they explained what they were doing with those ladybugs? You weren't a suspicious person, and you always wanted to help people. Did you think they were a bit eccentric? Why did you help them? What did you think you would find—

The popping sound came from above.

I lifted the terrarium even higher, and the beetles inside responded with even more ferocious swarming, slamming against the glass like little rocks, just as the ladybugs had done in the sconces on the front porch the night William disappeared.

I lowered the terrarium to my waist, and almost immediately, the ladybugs stopped their furious dance. I thought of Barbara's words the night before: *"That's what ladybugs do when they arrive. We don't know why. But it's been documented in so many cases. Sometimes the beetles cover entire walls, crawling, like they've been driven insane."*

The terrarium was out of my hands and smashed against the ground before I could even comprehend what I'd done. The sound of the shattering echoed for a moment through the lonely trees. The anger and the irrationality felt addictive and I wished for more things to break. I thought, for a wild moment, I might run into the house to gather more of the glass canisters and then return to break them all around the site, like a christening of a cursed ship.

I wanted to scream to the heavens, curse whatever crossed the skies to hover here, taking my William and leaving behind some kind of lingering force that enraged the beetles. A ruthless calling card that no one would ever understand. I imagined trying to explain it to the police, to the FBI, to my husband, to Anne and Chris. *You see, they obviously come close to the earth, and whatever they use to entrap people leaves behind an aura that also happens to aggravate beetles at a certain height, like a radio frequency that only insects can pick up. What's that? No, I don't take antipsychotics.*

Instead, I knelt and started to pick up the glass. What would happen if Chris came back out here and wondered why the glass was everywhere? He might call the police—

The police.

I ran then to the house, not caring at that moment if any-one found the glass. I rushed into house, rummaging through the utility drawer to find the business card.

I dialed, brought my cell to my ear, and listened to four rings before Detective Strombino answered.

"Mrs. Roseworth? Is everything all right?" he asked in his thick Boston accent.

"I'm really sorry to bother you. I have a quick question."

"Of course. I wish I had some new news for you."

I took a deep breath. "Detective, do you know if anything was found in the woods where William went missing?"

"No, ma'am. Nothing. As I've told you, there is no trace of who took him."

"I'm not talking about something someone left behind. I mean something on the ground."

His silence told me everything I suspected. "I'm not sure—"

"I want to know if you found a gravestone. A small marker for a girl named Amelia Shrank."

More silence until he cleared his throat. "Yes, Mrs. Roseworth, we did find that, but it was of no consequence—"

"Then why was it taken into evidence?" I asked.

"Ma'am, I would have certainly shared it with you if it had pertained at all to your grandson's disappearance—"

"A child's gravestone was found in the same location where my grandson went missing and you don't find that strange?"

"That girl disappeared almost eighty years ago, Mrs. Roseworth. There is no connection—"

"Thank you, Detective, that's all I needed to know," I man-aged to say before sinking down into a chair at the table as I disconnected the call. I could picture them, the detectives or police or even the FBI, finding the grave marker, wrapping it in protective plastic, and thinking they had been to first to find some bizarre remnant of history, like an ancient piece of crockery. They'd done the research into Amelia, of course, and dismissed it. A weird coincidence, nothing more.

They didn't know a grown man had vanished there as well.

The headlights from my Volvo flashed over the Honda Accord parked in the corner of the Chevron. Barbara's hair was momentarily illuminated, and she squinted. I pulled up next to her and lowered my passenger-side window.

"You're welcome to ride with me," Barbara offered.

"My friends and family use this gas station all the time, and if my car was left here unattended, it would raise some eyebrows."

Barbara nodded. "I'm not a fast driver, and I'm unfamiliar with these roads, so stay with me. We're going to the Holiday Inn in a town named Murfreesboro. Sound familiar?"

"It's right off the interstate not far from the square. I know where it is."

"If we get separated, I'll wait for you in the parking lot, and we can go in together."

"I won't lose you. In fact, why don't you follow me? The interstate's the quickest way, and we can pick it up a few miles down Harding."

Barbara appeared grateful. I took a deep breath and turned the wheel.

Anne seemed fine to watch the boys tonight, even if it meant she slouched with Greg on the couch while Brian sat in his room alone and Chris was in his study. No one would think it was strange I'd chosen to stay home alone on Saturday night. Tom would be in on the eleven o'clock flight, and a car would bring him home. As long as I was home by then, no questions would be asked.

It would take thirty minutes to get to the hotel, and thirty minutes to get back. I wouldn't have long to spend with Steven.

This is stupid to do alone. Roxy would throw a fit if she found out. But I'd already dragged her six hours away on a fruitless endeavor and then refused to even discuss what happened.

My cell rang as I got onto the interstate. I briefly looked to see that it was Tom calling, and I silenced the phone. I looked in the rearview mirror to make sure Barbara was still behind. The Accord was keeping up.

I thought of picking up the phone to call him back. *What would you say if you knew?* I pictured his jawline jutting out when he paced while on the phone with his staff, dealing with either a domestic or foreign crisis. *Or would you walk around for hours with your hands behind your head, as you did when Stella left for college or when Anne nearly married that set designer? Or, worse, would you stare off out the window with tears in your eyes that you could somehow keep from running down your cheeks, as you did all those nights when William first disappeared? What version of your heartbreak, your anger, would surface if you knew what I did then?*

The first time Steven kissed me, after I'd returned from the cornfield and the encounter with the men in the black suits, I was surprised at his intensity. Given that he often seemed nervous when we came in close physical contact, I expected soft brushes of lips. Instead, he was unbuttoning my shirt within seconds of our lips touching for the first time. Our clothes were soon tossed onto the floor of his office.

I should have felt incredible guilt afterwards. Instead, I lay in his arms on the couch and smiled as he pointed out the star on the map above us that he had secretly named after me.

From then on, he didn't give me assignments. The calls that came in often asked for me first, because I'd become the point person. *Lynn Roseworth, please,* they said.

Steven began to introduce me to the other Researchers who visited from universities in Illinois and other states such as Indiana and Missouri. The Researchers had potlucks, and some expected me to stay in the kitchen. Instead, I would sit next to them on the couch and point out there was no common shape of the ships as described, and that even though the descriptions of the beings were similar, that could just be the brain's reaction to such a traumatic experience.

I remembered how they cocked their heads at me, cleaning off their glasses, wondering how the young woman in the floral swing dress knew so much about the reported height differences in the aliens known as the Greys.

When Steven led their meetings, I didn't sit at his side and certainly didn't serve appetizers. Instead, I often leaned on the doorframe, clarifying the data. He would gesture to me in those rare moments of emotional expression. "That's right! Listen to her, fellas. Listen to her," he would say.

Sometimes I found them staring at me, and I chalked that up to the lack of exposure to the opposite sex. In time, they didn't just ask for my input—they bombarded me with questions. Did I think the aliens could communicate telepathically? What about inbreeding with humans? Did the creatures even have genders?

"OK, boys, that's enough," Steven would say, placing his hand on the small of my back. He was always touching me. At the end of the day, he rubbed my shoulders. As we sat at his desk in the office, with the door firmly locked, one hand would be writing and the other would rest on my knee. When we went to his apartment to make love on our lunch break, he wrapped his arms around me until the very last moment before we had to get dressed. I could see the pride in his eyes when he introduced me. My wedding ring felt heavy on my finger.

I awoke one fall afternoon in his bed and found Steven looking at me from where he lay on his pillow. I scrambled to get dressed, fumbling with the clock to see the time.

"It's only two-thirty," he said. "You fell asleep at one. It's OK. I have no classes, and it's Friday, so no one's in the office. Come back to bed."

I snuggled up to him, and he brushed a curl from my forehead.

"I've been thinking about something. Do you remember that once you told me that the missing come back?" I said. "I have yet to find a single case of that happening."

He brushed my cheek with his fingers. "I'd rather talk about you. I wonder, who do you more look like—your father or your mother?"

"I don't remember my mother, but from the pictures Daddy kept of her, she had curly blond hair like mine. Otherwise, I'm all Stanson."

"How old were you when she died?"

"Daddy says it was right before the discovery of my tumor that I've told you about. I can't imagine how my Dad handled it: the death of his wife and then a terrible diagnosis for his only child. He couldn't talk about her without tearing up."

"If you are anything like her, I can see why he was so devastated. It's awful to lose someone you love. But . . . to have someone you love vanish, without an explanation, never knowing what happened to them . . . that's a different kind of torture."

I kissed him again. He never discussed his sister. It was clearly too painful.

"Have you ever actually met one of the missing who returned? What did they remember? All those horrible stories about being probed and violated . . ."

His response was to pull me closer. It was the last time we made love.

It rained heavily the next day, and my passenger seat was stacked with files. I didn't know why Steven had insisted I bring them out of the office and to the motel on the outskirts of campus.

A fierce humidity forced me to constantly wipe the windshield with my hand. I saw Steven's car as I pulled into the parking lot. The red sheen of his hair stood out in the haze. A man with a beard stood near him, smoking. I pulled in quickly, behind a bread van.

I peered over the steering wheel, trying to identify the stranger. It wasn't Dr. Roberts, as I had hoped. I hadn't seen him, or Marcus, again, after that day in the cornfield. Steven explained that Marcus didn't play well with others, and Dr. Roberts's wife's cancer had advanced so he wasn't able to travel. I suspected it was actually something more, remembering that look of fear in both Marcus and Dr. Roberts's eyes. Maybe they'd had enough.

The man talking to Steven hadn't attended any of the Researchers meetings, and his face didn't look familiar from any of the scientific journals I'd reviewed at the bequest of the astronomy professors. I unconsciously reached over and put my hand on the files protectively. All Steven had said was to bring the files on the Allen, Bristoff, and Carson cases. I assumed we were meeting another out-of-town Researcher, and it wasn't strange he was staying at a discount motel. None of them was in it for the money.

I watched the man toss the butt of the cigarette aside as he and Steven stepped into the room, leaving the door ajar.

Not wanting to risk the files getting wet, and frankly feeling that I needed to know more about this man with whom we were sharing data, I opened my umbrella and dashed to the end of the overhang.

I didn't know if the water on my forehead was sweat or rain. Why was I acting so possessive? Why did I feel so off kilter? Yes, I worked hard on these cases, but it certainly wasn't only my work. It was Steven who helped me become a Researcher. He could show the files to anyone he pleased.

I thought for a moment of how it would look if, by some terrible coincidence, Tom drove by and saw his wife enter a motel room with two men. Usually, my resentment towards him helped justify my indiscretions, but at this moment, I felt ashamed. I tried to brush it off, hurrying past the other motel doors. The curtains were drawn in the room that Steven and the other Researcher had entered. Smoke was drifting from the room, explaining why the door remained open.

"These wingtips are killing me," I heard the stranger say.

"Pretty high end for someone in our circle," Steven said.

Just another professor. I reached to open the door. *Probably from Chicago—*

"What does she know?" the man asked. I withdrew my hand.

"More than I do, at times. She's whip smart."

They must be sitting just inside the door, maybe on the edge of the bed.

"I mean, how much does she know? About the weather? About the other theories? Even Argentum?"

I bit my lip, remembering Barbara asking for an explanation of Argentum, and how Steven refused to even discuss it with me.

"Why would I waste her time with that?" Steven replied. "We don't even know what it is. It's a glorified urban legend about aliens, without any details. We've all been told to dismiss it anyway. Why do we keep asking what it is if we don't even have a shred of information?"

"Is this smart, Steven? She's not even a scientist, or a professor."

"Not all of us are in academia. It does us good to have others."

"If we go underground, will she do it?"

"I think she would, especially if I decide to as well. She's seen a lot, enough to understand why this is so important."

"It's necessary, Steven. Not everyone agrees, but we have to become more militant about things."

"Militant isn't the word I would use. I think it's important for those of us in academia to continue gathering information from the families of the missing. I know you say that you've been contacted by some . . . parent organization over the Researchers. But come on. I've been doing this for nearly ten years, and I haven't heard of such a group."

"The Researchers aren't calling the shots. Don't you realize someone . . . something. . . . is driving all our work? Sure, we Researchers share information, but something is connecting us, beyond a shared passion. All I know is that the call I received came from someone with the Corcillium, which, if you remember from Latin class, derives from *corcillum*, meaning 'heart,' as in 'heart of the organization.' This is a chance, Steven, to join the true mission. To go so far under the radar that no one can find us, especially not the Suits. They say it's the only way we can move around the country without being recognized. And they said if you were interested, that you should come meet with them. I didn't anticipate you insisting that your girlfriend come too."

I shook off a surge of nausea, leaning into the door.

"You really think they're monitoring us? The Suits?"

"Of course they are." The man sounded weary. "They're not stupid. They know we're asking questions. They can dismiss us for only so long. This remote research is important, but it's only scratching the surface. We would live among these people, spend time in their communities. Understand the commonalities that we have theories about. Live in all these places for a while, spending weeks, maybe months, in the locations of the disappearances. You said she can cook? That might be helpful."

I was really fighting the urge to vomit. *What is wrong with me? Is today the thirtieth? It is. I should have started last week.*

I stepped back, my hand on my stomach. *It's been more than that. It's been two weeks. I'm two weeks late.*

"I'll have to think hard about it. How do we know this isn't a setup by the Suits? You think they may even have information . . . about what happened to my sister?"

"I think they've got information beyond anything we've ever known. Steven, they say there is more to the Argentum theory than what we know. But they made it clear over the phone: Once you're in, you don't get out. I'm ready for it."

"I'm not sure. I know I want to be with her, and I think she's more than ready to move on with her life."

Navigating what I would later realize was my first bout of morning sickness, I teetered back to my car in the rain, not bothering to even pick up the umbrella. Steven was carrying it when he returned to his apartment, where I had gathered the few belongings I had recklessly left there.

"I found your umbrella outside the hotel door," he said. "How much did you hear?"

Having already thrown up twice before his arrival, my tone was as cold as a January morning. I explained that no one would be taking me underground or anywhere away from my family and friends. I wasn't going to live my life skulking from one remote location to the next. And how dare he talk about me like some kind of trophy girlfriend? And I certainly wasn't going to cook for him or anyone in that underground world. This was goodbye.

He practically got down on his knees, begging for forgiveness; he said all he wanted to do was to protect me. That without me, he wouldn't join whatever this secret organization within the Researchers was.

I leaned in close and said I never needed anyone's protection in my life. From this moment on, he was no longer part of it. He'd helped me realize whom I needed to be with, and that was my husband.

He chased me down to my car, grabbing my arm and imploring me to listen. I snatched my arm away and slammed the door.

I drove away, and only allowed the tears to come when the sight of him standing in the rain and holding my unopened umbrella had vanished from my rearview mirror. *I just can't, Steven,* I remember thinking. *I just can't raise a child in that world.*

More than forty years later, I was coming back to him.

I flicked on my blinker in a startled realization that we had reached the exit. I swerved to make it, and saw with relief that Barbara was far enough behind that the sudden jerking of my car didn't throw her.

I followed the ramp and crossed over the interstate, looking for the glowing Holiday Inn logo.

The green-and-white sign with the cursive capital H beamed in the dark, and I pulled into the circle drive. My heart was beating faster than I would have liked.

Barbara parked and stepped out of her car, looking tired. "He already has a room. 404. He's waiting inside."

Glass doors opened at our approach. The smell of steam-cleaned carpet and soap wafted through the lobby and stayed with us in the elevator, up to the fourth floor, and down the hallway. I didn't have to ask if Barbara had a key.

A quick swipe, a beep, and Barbara motioned me in. "I'll be down in the lobby," she said, shutting the door. "I'll give the two of you some privacy."

I slowly walked in, past the bathroom and into the bedroom. The man sitting on the edge of the bed stood.

He wore a tan jacket of a style popular in the late 1990s, with a button-over collar and slightly too short sleeves. His jeans were from the same era as well, though his Reeboks were of this decade. His hair had gone completely gray, and he was shorter than I remembered. But he had become more handsome as he aged.

He pushed up his glasses from the side, not in the middle as he had done throughout our time together.

"Hello, Lynn."

I breathed through the slight purse of my lips. "Hello, Steven."

"You look good. Great, actually."

"What do you know about the disappearance of my grandson?" I clutched my purse in both hands.

Steven blinked. "He . . . has my hair, or the color, at least, which didn't last long after you left. And your oldest daughter looks just like my mother, from what I've seen in the papers and on TV—"

"My husband, Tom, is the father of my children and grandfather to our grandchildren."

"I never had a chance to be Anne's father."

"Is that what this is about? Because if I need to beg for forgiveness, I'll beg—if it means getting information about what happened to William." I hated that my voice was cracking. "I want him back."

"I wish I had him to give to you, Lynn. But I don't."

"Then why am I here?"

"Because I failed to keep a promise to your father, and now our grandson is gone because of it."

"What are you talking about? My father? You didn't know my father."

He reached inside his coat and pulled out a yellowed envelope. "I never met your father. But I did know him."

"You know nothing about my father."

"You think it was by chance that your father, this land-scaper, could pull strings at a university two states away and get you a job in the astronomy department, of all places? I got a call from a colleague in St. Louis who said he knew of a young woman looking for a job at the university, and that her father *supported our work*. What do you think that meant?"

"This is insane."

"Read this." He held out the envelope. "He only had one request of me, and I failed him. Please, Lynn."

He held up the envelope to show the handwriting on the front. In Daddy's bold, decisive letters, were Steven's name and the address of the astronomy building.

I took the envelope and slowly opened it. The pages inside were rigid with age and still smelled faintly of pipe smoke.

Dear Dr. Richards,

I want to thank you for bringing Lynn into your fold. I am not at all surprised to hear that she is exceeding all of your expectations. My girl has always been remarkable.

I also want to thank you for so readily taking my phone call all those months ago. I didn't know if you would, given that I had to limit my interactions with your peers for many years now.

I simply couldn't risk what happened to my wife happening to Lynn.

Daddy's words began to blur, and I blinked, holding the paper closer.

As I told you on the phone, Lynn doesn't know the truth, and I honestly hoped she never would know. Yet I've always been plagued with guilt that she doesn't know her own true story. When you become a father, all you ever want to do is protect your children. I thought that when she moved to Illinois, she would finally be safe. But I fear that one day she will return to our land, and I beg you, sir, to do everything in your power to keep that from happening. I am not a well man, and if it comes to it, you must explain to her why she must never move back. In order for her to understand why, you have to know what happened.

Lynn was five when they took her. There had been a wicked storm, and she and I were on the porch, watching the fireflies come out, late on an August evening. She wanted so desperately to chase them. I must have dozed off, and the next thing I knew, I awoke to a terrible light in the trees and ladybugs swarming everywhere. I couldn't find Lynn, and when I went to look in the woods, I found her shoe. My wife, Freda, and I looked through the night. You have to remember how remote our home was then—we barely have neighbors now, almost twenty years later. There was no one to call for help that late.

My wife and I didn't sleep, and I was preparing to head into town to find help the next morning when this man shows up. Dr. Rex Martin. He said he was a professor who lived in St. Louis and had received several reports from the area of power outages and lights coming from the heavens. I told him that all I cared about was finding my missing daughter. He calmly put his hand on my arm and said that my daughter was gone. But he thought he knew where she would be.

Those words would change my life. I would regain my daughter and lose my Freda.

What happened over the next six months is something that I still cannot fully comprehend. Where Dr. Martin led us, and what we found. Freda kept pushing us until we found Lynn. My brave, brave wife would never would stop. She sacrificed herself in the end so we could escape.

It is a story perhaps for another time. It's still too painful for me to think about. In the end, I returned home with only my little girl.

I had to concoct two stories: that Lynn had gotten sick with a brain tumor and we took her to have it removed in St. Louis, and that Freda died of a sudden heart attack and was buried in her home state of Missouri. Of course, there was no surgery; nothing was ever removed from Lynn, but it was all I could come up with to explain our absence and Lynn's lack of memory when we finally found her. And thanks to Dr. Martin, I was even able to produce forged medical records for Lynn and a death certificate for Freda. We were private country people with almost no family, so there weren't many who even knew us well enough to mourn.

By the Grace of God, Lynn finally began to accept me as her father and relearned everything. If you didn't know, you'd have thought she had a normal life. I've done every-thing in my power to give her one.

Even when Dr. Martin and others in your profession needed to come and study the woods and the location where all the people have vanished, I was hesitant. I let them come once and only once. I could not risk more. It cost Freda her life having to enter your world of secrets and shadows.

And now, the most important person in my world is in your care. I fear I will not live long enough to explain all this to her, and it's why I felt better about deceiving her into thinking she was getting a job in the agriculture department. I need you to teach her what you know about the missing, and if I don't survive, explain to her why she cannot return to our home.

She will fight you on this. This is our land, and Lynn is a homebody. She sees Illinois as a temporary location, but it must become more than that. Dr. Martin believes the devils come back from time to time, and I cannot risk the possibil-ity that she could be taken again.

She will be stubborn. Her husband, Tom, is a good boy, but he too will have difficulty believing all this, so you must start with her. She is deeply rooted in reality, as am I. I wish I could go back to the beliefs I had before this, where the only purpose of the stars was to bring us light in the dark. Now I cannot look too long into the heavens for fear of what I might see.

Sincerely,
Bud Stanson

I read the letter twice. I wanted to find a chair and collapse into it.

It couldn't be. Not me. That happened to all those other people whose disappearances I'd researched.

Not me.

But it explained the bell. The day he entered the woods with the strangers. Why he could never speak of my mother. His last words to me not to raise my children near the woods. I tried to fold the letter up and place it back in the envelope, but my hands were shaking too hard.

"How could you have kept this from me?"

"Because I was angry. You broke my heart. I realize now that I was a self-involved, self-important jerk. Your father wanted you to know about what happened to you on your own terms. I intended for you to learn it either from him or, in time, from me. And when you left me and I found out you returned home, I assumed your father would tell you, and you would come back to me. When you didn't, I thought you had made your choice."

"My choice?" I held up the letter. "My father couldn't speak when I moved back home. He couldn't explain this to me. I settled there. I raised my family there. And they were all in danger! You let this happen!"

"I know that." He took a step towards me. "It's all my fault. I even tried telling you, so many times. All those years ago, you asked me how we could keep encouraging families, telling them that sometimes the abducted come back. But how do you explain to the woman you love that of all the missing we were researching, she was the only one who ever did?"

"That's what I was, wasn't I? A test case," I said, my eyes narrowing. "The Researchers who constantly peppered me with questions—they just really wanted to ask if I remembered anything about being abducted. You all were studying me. I was a glorified test subject—"

"No. You were never that. We all had fallen in love with you—"

I placed Daddy's letter in my purse. "I should have never trusted you."

"It's why I had to go into hiding. *They* know that I know."

"I don't even care to know who *they* are."

"Your husband's employer."

He took off his glasses and rubbed between his eyes. "When I first heard that your—our—grandson had vanished, I immediately feared the worst. I knew if I suddenly showed up, after all these years, with a wild story of you being abducted as well, it would have made an already bad situation worse. But I had to do something. I started with downloading the maps of your property, so I could know where to start searching. That was my first mistake. Not two hours later, I was summoned to the office of our esteemed dean, who promptly fired me for using university equipment for personal use. An anonymous tipster, he said, had alerted him. I was escorted out and blocked from all my work. I rushed home to find FBI agents carrying all my belongings out of my house.

"It was no coincidence. I should have known they would be monitoring any outside internet searches. Especially from any-one who worked in astronomy. So I had to run, with only the shirt on my back. And when you're my age, that's not easy. I couldn't contact you or anyone. Even getting cash out of an ATM was out of the question, since they were monitoring that too."

"Steven, please—"

"It's vital that you know how far they'll go, Lynn, because of what I'm about to tell you. If it hadn't been for the Corcillium, I wouldn't have been able to even find out about the other miss-ing people from your property."

"Corcillium—?" I asked, and then stopped. I knew the

name. I'd heard it, all those years ago, when that Researcher had tried to convince Steven to take me deep into what he had called the underground.

"Consider them . . . a board, of sorts, that governs the Researchers' work. I knew someone was distributing information to us, but I never knew who. I was so destitute that I was living in a homeless shelter when they found me. They not only rescued me, but their resources allowed me to find out about the others abducted from your woods. It took me some time, but once I had the information, I immediately headed for Nashville. When I reached out to Barbara, she told me that you'd come searching for me first. As soon as I heard about William, I wanted to come to you. But you know the danger. There was a time when you came face-to-face with the Suits yourself."

"I don't live in that world anymore. I was young and naïve and, frankly, desperate for anything that would have saved me from my marriage at the time. You could have been doing research into chimpanzees and empowered me like you did, and I would have thrown myself into that too."

"I don't believe that. It took you a few months to figure out the climate patterns and the commonalities in these cases when it took me years to realize them. You could have done anything with your life."

"You know nothing about my life."

"Listen: I think I know where William is."

"He's still alive?" I asked, a twinge of hope swelling in my chest.

He nodded. "What I've learned from the Corcillium in just the past few months makes me believe we can find him. But Lynn, there are risks—"

"Steven, please. You owe it to my father to tell me. Tell me
what you know—"

"We go together, then. I'll tell you everything when we get
in the car," he responded, looking around the room. "I don't
dare say much more here, as I've come to learn they have ways
to monitor everything—"

"Tell me now. Right now."

"I'm not talking about losing a job and having all your
property seized by the government. No one has returned
alive from where we're going. But I want to find William
too—"

The door suddenly beeped and Barbara pushed through.
"Jesus, Steven, they're here! They're all wearing FBI jackets,
coming up the stairs."

"What?" he asked, now angrily scanning the room.
"Dammit, I knew it!"

"They're coming now!"

"Go out the back stairs and take your car, like we talked
about. Take it and run. Now, Barbara!" Steven ordered.

"Come with me," she pleaded.

"I'll be right behind you,"

She gave us one last, fleeting look before running out.

"What's going on?"

Steven rummaged through his duffel bag and brought out
a folded-over envelope. He leaned in close and whispered
softly, "Put this in your purse."

"What is this?"

"Look for your star."

"What are you talking about? I don't understand—"

"Lynn, the Argentum theory—"

The door thudded. A second later, it smashed open, and

agents dressed in SWAT jackets swarmed in. Steven moved past me, holding up his hands.

"You got me, OK? You got me. Don't hurt her."

"We have no intention of hurting her," one of the agents said, seizing Steven and cuffing him.

"Dr. Richards, you are under arrest on a charge of domestic terrorism and kidnapping," declared another agent, her voice muffled under the full protective mask she and the others wore. "Where is William Chance?"

"This won't silence me," Steven grunted, grimacing in pain. "Don't believe them, Lynn!"

They turned him around, and he twisted back to me. "Remember what I told you!"

The agents forced him out the door and into the hall. He stumbled, and they yanked him around the corner.

I started to follow. "Please, don't—"

"Mrs. Roseworth, I'm so sorry," said the female agent, her ponytail now loose from where it was tucked into her shirt. "Are you all right?"

I nodded once. "I'm sorry it came to this. We had to follow you until Dr. Richards could be found. We knew he would, at some point, reach out to you. Senator Roseworth said you used to work for him."

"My husband knows?" I asked, dazed.

"He does as of tonight, when we told him we were moving in. I want you to know we're going to find that woman, his accomplice. We're tracking her now. She may know the location of your grandson. Let's go, your family is anxious to see you."

She took off her mask, and slipped a cigarette between her lips. I blinked in recognition.

"I know you don't like cigarette smoke."

"But you're Tom's press person," I stammered, thinking that it wasn't that long ago when she sat at my kitchen table. "Why are you wearing an FBI jacket?"

"Let's get you home," she said, sneaking a quick drag and gently taking my arm.

TWELVE

"I'm sure you are more than capable of driving," Deanna said, the red and blue lights of the police escort flickering on her face, "But after what you just went through, I thought it might be best for you to rest a bit. I know I've asked you already, but do you need anything? I have an extra water in my backpack."

"Where are you taking him?"

"Likely the Davidson County jail. He'll be booked there."

I kept watching the snow that was starting to fall. "May I ask your actual name?"

"It's Deanna. Deanna Ruck. I used my real name when I was assigned. There was no need to tell your husband otherwise. He thought I was a specialist in crisis communications."

"Why did you have to lie to him?"

She tapped on the steering wheel. "Your husband will understand. Sometimes the FBI does things in order to protect and serve important people in Washington."

"Why not come clean from the beginning that you were an agent assigned to him?"

"Because I wasn't assigned to him. I was assigned to you."

I looked at her. "What do you mean?"

"We identified Dr. Richards as a possible suspect pretty quickly. We've seen the map of your property he kept in his safe, along with the articles about your family. I know you've seen them too. We thought he might reach out to you."

"You followed me to Champaign?"

"We found William's jacket in the basement of Dr. Richards's house. We have a team there now, looking for any trace of him."

"Why would he leave William's jacket there?"

"Because he was on the run, Mrs. Roseworth. Our intelligence shows he's been involved in this antigovernment group linked to domestic terrorism. He obviously has some sort of obsession with you and your family, and he harbored some kind of vendetta towards your husband. He thought if he kidnapped William, he could hurt the senator."

"What you're saying doesn't make sense."

"It makes perfect sense." She looked at me briefly. "It needs to make sense."

I let that one sink in. "What does that mean?"

"No one has to know that you went in search of him. No one has to know about your relationship. It's really going to be in the best interest of everyone involved that you have a long talk with your friend Roxy and decide that keeping all this quiet will allow your family to move on. Questioning our investigation would only force us to disclose everything."

I sank back into the seat. "You all really think this is going to work?"

"What do you mean?"

"You get your suspect, and I get my family back? The problem is that it isn't true, and I'll never know what happened to my grandson."

"Dr. Richards kidnapped your grandson, Mrs. Roseworth.

We have William's jacket and enough evidence to convince any jury. If he starts to blather on about his alien abduction theories, everyone will think he's insane."

"William wasn't wearing a jacket."

"Did I say jacket? I meant pajama top."

I turned back towards the window, closing my eyes.

"I'm glad we could ride together, Mrs. Roseworth. Your family has already been briefed on all this: How one of Dr. Richards's operatives contacted you and insisted you come alone to get information on his whereabouts. How you bravely went, hoping to get information, and how we trailed you without your knowledge. You're a real heroine in all this. You might even get a profile in *People* magazine."

"I don't read that magazine."

"I know you'll do the right thing, Mrs. Roseworth. Your husband is home from Washington, and your entire family now knows. They'll be waiting for you. After you catch up with them, you'll encourage your friend Roxy to sit up with you until you fall asleep. The two of you can use that time to get on the same page."

"Or what?"

"It's not even pleasant to talk about that."

"You can really save the pleasantries at this point."

Deanna turned up the heat a bit. "It's a shame she isn't better about hiding all those plants her husband grows in their garden."

"He has cancer," I said quickly.

"And there's all those people to whom she sells the weed—"

"She doesn't sell. She gives it away, for medicinal purposes." My chest was now tight.

"Drug trafficking is serious business in Tennessee. She'll go to prison. Think about it, OK? Let's all get on the same page.

Plus we've been watching Dr. Richards for some time, and we have recording devices in that hotel room. You know what was said between you, and what a disaster that would be for your family to hear. You want to spare them that kind of embarrassment."

"He didn't tell me anything. You and your agents came just as he was about to tell me where he thought William was."

"He would have lied to you, Lynn, to keep you hoping, to throw you off his track."

I stared hard at the young woman's face. "Will you keep looking for William? Or did you ever really look?"

"We did the best we could. I'm fairly sure William . . . what we believe to be William . . . will be found in Dr. Richards's basement. It will be difficult to identify, but even badly burned . . . it will be enough to convict. What's important is that your family can move on, once and for all. Do this for them, Mrs. Roseworth. Close this sad chapter."

We sat in silence for the rest of the drive. As the police escort pulled onto our street, and I could see the girls' cars in the driveway alongside several others with government plates. The house beamed as if every light and lamp were turned on.

Deanna put the car in park. "Let me come around and help, it might have turned icy—"

"I'm fine," I said, opening the door and walking briskly through the cold.

Tom was waiting at the back door, and he embraced me with such fierceness it took the wind out of me for a moment. "You should have told me, Lynnie. You shouldn't have put yourself in any danger."

"I was never in any danger—"

"Mom." Stella pulled back Tom to hug me. "Jesus, Mom, what made you think this was a good idea?"

"Going off on your own, Mom?" Kate said, her hands raised. "We were worried sick—"

"Let's give your mom some breathing room," Deanna said, closing the door. She met my husband's disapproving gaze. "I'm sorry, Senator. I wish I could have been more upfront from the beginning."

"I have a lot to discuss with your boss. But for now, I want to know everything. And these fellas haven't told us much." He motioned to the men in suits standing uncomfortably, near the pie safe. He leaned in to me. "Is it true, Lynn? That this is all because of that professor? Steven Richards?"

"Mama?" Anne slowly crossed the room, her eyes bloodshot and her voice breaking. "What did this man do with William?"

"Where is my son," Chris demanded, his hands behind his head. "Who is Steven Richards?"

"Everyone, please, I know you have lots of questions," Deanna said. "Let me fill in the holes my partners here couldn't. Mrs. Roseworth, please have a seat."

"I don't need to sit," I said, but Stella sat me down at the kitchen table, squeezing my hand.

My ears starting to ring as Kate poured another cup of coffee. I watched her fumble with the coffee maker while vaguely hearing the words "obsessed with your mother," and "domestic terrorism."

I don't need to pay attention. I've already been given the presentation.

"Your mother led us right to him," Deanna said.

"Where is my boy?" Anne shrieked.

I started to stand, but Stella held me back. "Mom," she whispered, "She needs to hear this."

"We're combing Dr. Richards's house in Champaign right

now," Deanna said, and then exhaled. "Mrs. Chance, I'm sorry, but we've already found his pajama shirt."

The family eruption sounded hollow to me. I stared numbly at the wooden table, reaching out to run my finger over a carving, done either by a child, or a nick from a fork or knife.

"I'm going there right now," Chris said.

Deanna raised one hand. "Mr. Chance—"

"I don't care if you are with the FBI, lady, we're going there now," Chris said, striding from the room. Sobbing, Anne stood and stumbled after him, with Kate helping her to the door.

"Mama!" Anne stopped, looking back wildly.

"Go, Sis," Stella said. "We'll take care of the boys."

"Lynn." Tom knelt beside me. "I'm going too. I'll call you from the car. Are you OK? I'll stay here if you need me—"

"Just go," I said softly.

"Why would he do this, Lynn?" he asked.

I shook my head and closed my eyes. I could feel him looking at me, but when he heard the sounds of the cars engines turning on, he hurried out.

Deanna walked across the room to stand on the other side of the table. "I hope we're wrong about William, that he's still alive. Whatever happens, know your mother is pretty remarkable. It's amazing what she did for this family."

"Thank you, Agent," Stella said.

"We'll leave a team outside if you have any other questions, and we'll brief you on any new developments," she said. "Take care of your family, Mrs. Roseworth."

I did not look at her as she and the other agents walked out.

"Mom, don't worry about Brian and Greg. The neighbors are watching them, and I'll head over there later," Stella said.

Kate was already on her cell. "Trevor? I know it's late, but things are moving faster since our last briefing. Here's the deal:

Deanna Ruck is no longer working press for us, that's got to be you for a bit. It will be very clear quite soon. . . . I know you don't know what's going on, but have a bag ready, you might be going to Champaign, Illinois. I'll explain in a minute. I'm calling both the Nashville office and the Washington office with strict instructions: All network calls go to me, all local press calls go to you. But here's what you need to know: No one, I repeat, no member of the media is to approach my mother or my family. Repeat that in your head. . . ."

"Mama." Stella pulled up a chair, taking my hand. "You heard the agent. They could be wrong. William could still be alive—"

"It's a lie," I whispered.

"What?"

"Nothing." I pushed away from the table and walked to the sink. My hands were shaking so badly that I dropped the cup into the sink, where it clanged jarringly.

"Mom?" Kate asked, and briefly turned back to the phone. "Marcus, I'll need to call you back."

"What is a lie, Mom?" Stella asked, slowly standing.

"Everything!" I cried out, startling both my daughters. "Everything is a lie."

"I knew there was more," Stella said, pointing her finger towards me. "I could tell it the minute you came in here. Did that bastard do something to you? Did he, Mom?"

"He didn't do anything. He didn't do anything to me or to William."

"What is it, Mom?" Kate asked.

"Tell us, Mom. That's how you raised us. No lies. Not ever, even if it's ugly," Stella said. "What happened—?"

The back door came flying open and a red-faced Roxy strode in, her gray-streaked hair wet from the snow. "Why in the hell wasn't I called? Some FBI agent called about twenty minutes ago and told me to hightail it over here, something about you leading them to Steven Richards."

"You know about him too?" Kate asked.

"Um, not really, that's just what the agent said," Roxy replied.

"You're a terrible liar, Roxy." Stella flicked a hair from her forehead.

"Well, somebody tell me what's going on," Roxy said.

"The FBI said this Steven Richards, who Mom worked for back when Dad was in law school, is obsessed and kidnapped William. Has some kind of vendetta against Dad. Some woman contacted Mom and led her to a Murfreesboro motel where he was waiting. That's when the FBI nabbed him," Kate explained. "They think they've found William's pajama shirt at his house."

Roxy stormed across the room. "This was tonight? Lynn, why didn't you tell me? I would have gone with you! Does the FBI really think he kidnapped William? Do they know—?"

I raised my hand ever so slightly, and Roxy bit her lip. Stella saw it all. "I don't know what you two aren't telling, but you better spill it. Mom says this Richards character didn't hurt her or William. Mom, for the last time, what is going on?"

"Tell her, Lynnie," Roxy said.

"You don't know what they'll do, Roxy. I do. They made it very clear that we all have to play along. They'll come after you too."

"No one is coming after anyone," Kate insisted. "I can guarantee you that."

"You can't guarantee this, Kate," I said.

"I can tell you one thing, Lynn Roseworth . . ." Roxy leaned on the table. "I'm not afraid."

"Well, I am."

"Tell them, Lynn."

I looked from Roxy to my girls and sighed. "I don't even know where to start."

"Oh hell," Roxy said, sitting down at the table. "Start with the damn aliens."

THIRTEEN

Complete silence was so rare in the house that I was surprised by the noises that surfaced in the sudden stillness of the room. I'd never noticed, even in the deep of night in Tom's frequent absences, how the pantry door slightly tapped against its wood frame when the heat kicked on; how the holly bush outside the east kitchen window flicked against the pane; even how the energy-efficient bulbs that were now so dramatically expensive at Target hummed in the black chandelier above the dining-room table. But I heard it all in that moment. The air even seemed unsure what to do, as if no one was bothering to breathe.

It was in the silence that sprung from my daughters' astonishment, hearing me tell of my work with Steven Richards, that I knew I would not share everything. That would be for Tom and Tom alone.

"You . . . were a UFO researcher?" Kate asked at last.

"I told you, I wasn't a Researcher, at first. I was only an office manager."

"It's going to take me a minute," Stella said. "The guy who kidnapped William studies UFOs? And you used to be his assistant? And you went to his motel room tonight? What did he tell you?"

"He said . . . he was going to tell me what really happened to William. He doesn't have William." *And what happened to William happened to me, as well.*

"What do you mean 'What really happened'?" Kate asked. "That William . . . was abducted by aliens?"

When I didn't respond, Kate shook her head. "Mom, come on. Mom, are you kidding me?"

"Give your Mom a break, Kate," Roxy scolded. "She's been through a lot."

"I know Steven isn't responsible."

"How could you possibly know that, Mom?" Kate walked to the edge of the table. "And do you care to elaborate on why he has such an obsession with you and this family?"

"Watch that East Coast tone when you talk to your mother, Kate Elizabeth," Roxy warned.

"I know we're not getting the whole story, Mom," Kate said.

"I had to do whatever I could to try to find William."

"Are we talking about getting answers from UFO researchers?" Kate asked.

"What if it helps us find William? And I can't live with someone being punished for something he didn't do—"

"Jesus Christ, Mom," Kate said. "Why do you want to protect this man so much? Are you even listening to what you're saying?"

"I saw the reports once, I knew them inside out. I worked hard on those cases, I made the connections. I wasn't just some housewife—"

"Is that what this is all about? Trying to reclaim some past independence?" Kate said. "My God, Mom, you will ruin Dad. You will ruin this family—"

"I will *not* let this family be ruined." A sob caught in my throat. "Don't you see why I had to do this? Losing William, and Brian in the state he's in now, will hang over us forever."

"Mom, this is over." Kate circled the table and knelt, unsuccessfully trying to get me to look at her. "You have to get it together. William . . . could be dead. We have to prepare for that. Listen to what the police are saying. To what the FBI is saying. I know you don't want to let go of William, none of us do. They said they found his clothes. . . ."

"It's not the truth. It's not the truth even if Steven is charged. Even if he's convicted. It's not the truth."

"Fine, Mom, fine. Buy into their crazy shit—"

"Kate, back off," Stella said.

"I won't back off. Good God, Mom, you aren't even crying! William is dead—"

"He's not dead! Steven said he knows where he is—"

"Don't you dare say that to Anne or anyone else. I will not let your delusions give her irrational hope or make us the laughingstock of the country. Do you know what they'll say? 'Oh, that poor wife of Senator Roseworth, she's so distraught she's lost her mind.'"

"Jesus, are you always in PR mode? Have you ever known this woman to be delusional? Ever? For one moment in our entire lives?" Stella asked.

"Did you ever know that our Mom believes in aliens?" Kate motioned to me. "Or that she had an affair on Dad?"

"Kate Elizabeth!" Roxy stood.

"It's so obvious. I'm done here." Kate walked across the room and grabbed her purse. "But know for damned sure I'm not letting you do this, Mom. No fucking way." She walked out and slammed the door.

"Go after her, Stella," I said softly. "Let her smoke a bit, but don't let her drive. She's too upset."

"I'm going to tell her where she can shove those cigarettes." Stella lifted her coat from where it hung on a chair. "I have to be honest with you, Mom—this is really . . . hard to understand."

She obviously wanted to say more, but instead walked out the door.

I stood and looked out the window. Stella chased after Kate, her hands rubbing her arms. "Clash of the Titans, there. Daddy's girl versus momma's girl," Roxy said, coming to stand beside me. She put her hand on my shoulder. "Lynnie, you have to rest," she whispered.

"I can't—"

"It's not a suggestion. Time to take an Ambien, or maybe one of Anne's Xanax, if she left one lying around. I'm not kidding, Lynn. Tomorrow is going to be tough when word comes out about Steven. You are going to have to get some sleep."

"How can I sleep? How can I sleep knowing what's about to happen?"

"You don't know what's about to happen."

"I have to tell Tom. He has to know."

"In time you can tell him everything."

"There isn't time, Roxy. Don't you see? They're going to *plant evidence* in Steven's house, to try to prove William is dead. How can I live with that?"

"Plant evidence? Really? Oh Lynn, why would they do that—?"

"They'll arrest you for drug trafficking. They know about your basement."

"What?" Roxy said in astonishment. Seeing my horrified

look, she forced a smile. "So I'll become a folk hero in East Nashville, big deal."

"They'll send you to prison!"

"Oh Christ, Lynn, I'm nearly seventy. They won't prosecute me. Plus, even if they do, I'll be out in a few days anyway. Some Colorado attorney will swoop in and save me."

"I can't live with that!"

"Well, I can't live with you having a heart attack or a nervous breakdown, which is where you're headed if you don't get some rest. It's been a terrible night, and there's nothing you can do now. I'll stay with you—"

"No, go home. I'll call you in the morning."

"I suppose I better go home and destroy the evidence." Roxy rubbed her eyes. "I'll go play referee with the girls. You, take some good *legal* drugs and knock out. Understand?"

I nodded, watching Roxy pull on her gloves, point towards my bedroom and then step out the door.

I slowly ascended the stairs to the dark bedroom. On the edge of the bed, green eyes flashed. The cat had all but vanished in the commotion, but Voodoo decided it was safe to resurface. As I laid down, he approached in the darkness and nuzzled my hand. I softly scratched his neck.

After several minutes, I heard Roxy's pickup drive away. I didn't hear the door to the house open, which meant the girls were still at it.

My lower back ached. My favorite flannel nightgown was still on the chair by my bed. Voodoo's nuzzling was already making me drowsy. *My eyes won't feel so dry when I shut them.* Kate was right; this is over. I will offer support. I will be stable. I will pick up the pieces of our family and put us back together in time. I will move us away from this property and fulfill Daddy's last wish.

I closed my eyes, ready to let the darkness lull me away. But instead, all I could think of was a little boy. Not William, but Brian, lying in this very bed on the night William disappeared, after he had whispered the last words he would ever speak.

We lost two children that night.

I was on the stairs a moment later, hurrying to where my coat lay limp on the table. I quickly buttoned it up and looked out the window, seeing the embers from Kate's cigarette flashing in the spitting snow as she and Stella argued near the back porch.

Keys in hand, I walked through the dining room and into the formal living room, exiting through the rarely used front door. I quietly locked it behind me and slowly walked down the front stairs, then rushed to the Volvo. I slipped in, fired it up, and tore down the driveway, embarrassed by the gravel I was kicking up.

In my rearview mirror, I saw the girls waving and calling out my name frantically. I hated that I would cause them to worry, on top of the news of William's supposed death.

I reached over to silence the phone as the first call came in from Stella. I pressed the gas, knowing I would be long gone before either could get to their cars and hope to follow.

The late-night patrons at the Waffle House near downtown appeared even bleaker under fluorescent lights. It was nearly midnight, and the crowd from the honky-tonks on Lower Broadway wouldn't start filing in until closer to three or four. I sat stirring my tepid coffee across the aisle from two drunk sorority girls and a furiously texting man wearing a cowboy hat. You can always spot the tourists, Tom always said, because they're the only ones in town wearing Stetsons.

There was no chance anyone I knew would come across me here.

I glanced at my dark phone, long since powered off, knowing Tom would be trying to reach me once Kate reported that I'd driven away. *Are you on the road still, insisting on driving so Anne or Chris could sleep, even though neither will? Have you repeatedly called, now that you've had the time to piece together the fact that some man from our far-flung past will be charged with our grandson's murder? Are you wondering why he would come after us? Are you surprised that you didn't even remember his name?*

Or, even worse, would you lean into the phone and ask quietly, "Did you love him back?"

Steven had actually been quite brave, standing in front of me as the agents burst into the room. I should have reached out to him, reminded him he was old and so was I, and it was an unnecessary gesture. I cannot bear to think of an old man in a jail cell because of me.

And had the agents found Barbara? Was she still on the run too?

It was all my fault, all of it. What I did decades ago was slowly taking down one life at a time. If I did tell people, even the local police, what I suspected, the story would eventually unfold in the papers, online, on television. The looks of pity I would get from customers, from friends. *It isn't your fault, Lynn,* they would say. *He was crazy.*

I reached for my purse to open the envelope Steven had given to me, smoothing out the two pieces of paper tucked inside. One was an enlarged section of a map of Colorado from an atlas in the *National Geographic* magazine. The upper left-hand corner revealed a copyright of September 1960.

The other was a map of the stars.

I remembered what I learned during my time in the astronomy department, so I knew the placement of the constellations was comical. The Big Dipper was in the wrong place. So was Andromeda. Whoever did the map had skills in graphic design, but the artist knew nothing of the heavens.

There was only one true accuracy: my star, right where it should be.

"Look for your star," he had whispered, softly enough that the recording devices in the room from the FBI couldn't pick up his words.

And then, he had said something about Argentum.

Another ghost from the past. That theory that Steven dismissed when Barbara first mentioned it all those years ago. He'd said he didn't even know what it was, and it was not worth discussing. I'd heard that again outside the motel room, when Steven and the Researcher had discussed going into hiding. Steven referred to it as an urban legend about aliens, without a shred of proof. He'd clearly been annoyed with it.

A quick Google search on my phone revealed only two explanations: that *argentum* meant silver in Latin and that a senior-living association had adopted the name.

I scanned the enlarged section of Colorado, dotted with the names of towns and counties. I'd have to dig out my reading glasses to attempt look at them all.

Again I returned to the star map. My star wasn't the only one of a different hue. While most were a brilliant white, a few others were larger in scale and gold.

My fingertips were smudged from ink. Both documents had been recently printed.

I felt a flare of anger. I didn't have time for this. Too much was happening, too much was at stake, to sit here and try to unravel a riddle. Just like those files, all those years ago, with all the blacked-out words that so infuriated me—

I stood so quickly I almost banged my knees on the table. I walked briskly to the counter.

"Excuse me," I asked a ponytailed young man scraping burnt leftovers on the stovetop. "Do you have any tape?"

He laughed. "When your menus are this old, something has to hold them together." He rummaged around under the counter. "Aha!"

I thanked him and hurried back to my table. Taking a deep breath, I placed the Colorado map on top of the celestial map, taping them together at the top and bottom so they would align and not slip.

The two fit nearly perfectly on top of each other.

An encryption. Just like all the blacked-out documents. The stars were in the wrong place because Steven had made the celestial map not for accuracy, but as a key.

I slowly raised both towards the light. The smaller stars didn't show through the state map, but I could see the larger gold ones.

My star was harder to find because it was nearly lost in the Rocky Mountains. I squinted, seeing it match up at the base of the range. The star appeared to be in a gap in the mountains in the Colorado map.

I tore off the tape and separated the two pages, madly scrambled to find my glasses in my purse, and looked closely at where the star had rested in the state. That area was completely barren, void of anything except for the tiny name of one town, deep in the mountains.

The town's name was Argentum.

FOURTEEN

I balled up my scarf, the only spare piece of clothing I had besides my coat, and tried to use it as a pillow. The few other passengers quietly chose their seats. I turned to the window and looked out on the blackness of the tarmac.

There would be snow when we landed. I would have to buy not only boots, but days' worth of clothes and all my toiletries. I would have to rent a car, drive in a strange city, and navigate a mountain range. I almost wished I were going to Washington; at least I knew where to catch the taxi at the airport.

There's still time to get off the plane and get home before anyone notices—

"I don't suppose this seat is taken."

I didn't dare open my eyes. I couldn't have fallen asleep and dreamed this—

"Seriously, Lynn, move your purse. This stupid coat is going to take up a seat in itself."

"How are you here?" I asked.

Roxy struggled to take off her long overcoat and unwrap her scarf before unceremoniously plopping down. "We have about two seconds to get off this plane. But we're going to raise some eyebrows if I start dragging you down the aisle. So, I'm here to yank you home if—for the first time in your life—you're drunk. Or perhaps overly medicated. But most importantly, I am here to find out what the hell you're doing."

"I don't know what I'm doing. How are you even here?"

"Here are the Cliffs Notes, as the attendants are circling. You didn't make it easy, sister. Stella called me after midnight, pretty frantic, even though you texted her to say you were all right. I figured you were driving around, maybe even got a hotel room to get some peace. You never carry cash, and you lost your debit card last week—as you will recall—so that meant you used your credit card. And for shits and giggles, I checked the Peddler charge card—thanks for putting me on that account, by the way—and it showed you'd bought a ticket to Denver. So I booked myself a ticket too and hustled my fat ass over here. I stopped to kiss Ed and tell him to burn the stash and pop a few extras to numb the pain. I told him I could be back this morning. Or it might be a few days, if you needed to meet Tom in Champaign."

"You can't leave Ed, not if he's having pain—"

"For Christ sake, Lynn, he has stage-four colon cancer. He's gonna have pain. But he's fine. I filled him in on what happened with Steven's arrest. Well, not everything—for God's sake, I don't want the man to have a stroke as well as cancer. Now, Lynn, what are you doing?"

"I'm so glad you're here." The words barely came out of my throat. "I can barely breathe, I'm so nervous."

"Lynn, you need to tell me right now if whatever it is you're doing—you are doing it of a sound mind and body. Or if you've been threatened and are in danger of some kind."

"At this second, I am lucid. But my stomach is doing backflips."

"Well, there's a convenient puke bag right here if things go south. But let's avoid that if we can. Do I need to order you a drink?"

I shook my head, and Roxy waved over a tired-looking flight attendant. "Can we get a cup of water? Thanks." Roxy then dropped her voice. "Why are you going to Denver?"

"I'm not going to Denver. I'm going to a town called Argentum, somewhere in the Rocky Mountains."

"And why, pray tell, are you going there?"

The flight attendant brought over a small cup and reminded Roxy to fasten her seatbelt, as they were preparing to take off.

"Time's up, Lynn. This is when you tell me if you need me to get you off this plane, or if we're about to make a cross-country flight."

"You can't go with me."

"I most certainly can and will. Case closed. Now, why Colorado?"

I set the cup down in the console. "I think it's where Steven thinks they've taken William."

Roxy's eyebrows rose. "That little nugget of information was not shared during our wonderful experience with the girls. And just who is it that's taken William? I can't believe I continue to say this, but—the aliens?"

"I don't know. I don't know anything. And I could be completely wrong about all of this. All I know is I have to try, because if I don't . . ."

"Here's what we're going to do. We're going to use this flight as good long nap when we take off. But first, you're gonna spill it all, friend. Everything. Got it? Start with telling me everything about going down to Murfreesboro and seeing Dr. Richards. OK?"

I took a long drink.

Roxy nodded and bit her lip a few times to keep herself from interrupting. I couldn't bring myself to talk about Daddy's letter to Steven, so I finished with the discovery of the celestial map fitting onto the road atlas. "There wasn't time to ask him if that's what he intended me to figure out. And God, Roxy, I could be wrong. Steven could be insane, he could be trying to confuse me to keep the investigation off himself. The FBI could be completely right, and I'll be in Colorado when my family needs me the most."

He couldn't have faked my father's handwriting, though.

Roxy settled into the chair. "I need some time to think this through. Of course I brought nothing useful, as I had no time to pack anything, but I happen to carry my sleeping mask during Ed's chemo. So it's yours. It will be daylight soon, and you need sleep."

"I can cry myself to sleep and now no one will see."

"You're due some tears. Now lower that window shade."

We slept the entire trip, waking groggily to a ding alerting us that we had landed at Denver International Airport. After the plane came to a halt, we walked down the connector onto a red carpet, standing amongst the sea of people at the gate.

"Well, I've been wearing these clothes for two days now; shall we buy ourselves some nice 'I love Legal Marijuana' sweatshirts? Speaking of love, I'd kill for a shower. Can we get a room and sleep some more?"

I powered up my phone. "I can only imagine how many calls I've missed."

"What do you want to do, Lynn?"

"If we're going, we'll need clothes and a car. And I did get a new debit card after I lost mine, thank you very much, and I took out a bunch of cash before I headed to the airport, so there's no way for anyone to know where we are now."

"You don't watch *Dateline* as much as I do. If Tom starts to suspect you're not in Nashville, it will take the FBI two seconds to get access to all your credit cards, and they'll see our flights. And I know Tom never balances your checkbook, but if he looks at your account, he'll see the money you took out. And if they want to know where you are, all they have to do is track your phone to the closest cell tower. Wherever we're going, we better get there fast. Or seriously convince your family you need time alone to grieve. I also clearly watch too much *Dateline*."

I pressed my phone to my forehead. "I've missed fifteen calls and there are ten voice mails. I have twenty-five texts. I can't even look at them."

Roxy pointed to the rental-car signs. "We can get a car. It's now or never. We either book a flight back home or head to Enterprise."

I sat down in an empty row of chairs. "Tell me doing this isn't crazy."

"Lynn, we are nearing seventy." Roxy sat down beside me. "Women our age are dyeing wool and wandering through yard sales. Instead, we have gone to Illinois, broken into an office *and* a house, met with UFO researchers, and you just witnessed an FBI raid. So I think we're already far along on the crazy train. Flying to Colorado on a hint from someone who could be a lunatic seems pretty par for the course."

"He's not a lunatic."

"Listen, I'm not going to tell you this isn't crazy. The last six months have been horrible. You're desperate to find your grandson, and I don't blame you for that. And I know what you're thinking: It's not only William you're trying to find. You're trying to bring Brian back from whatever dark place he's in. But you have to be prepared for all of this to be a hoax, and the possibility that right now the man who kidnapped your grandson is in police custody and William is gone. I won't judge you, whatever you decide to do. I've told you that before. Even if I don't believe in these alien abductions, I have always believed in your instincts. So tell me, what does your gut say—?"

"You're her."

We both looked across the aisle at a teenager with floppy bangs hanging over a forehead of acne. He pulled out his earbuds, the light from his iPad reflecting in his glasses. "You are. You're her," he said.

"I'm sorry?"

"You're the alien lady. The one who believes aliens took your grandson."

"What are you talking about?" Roxy demanded.

Taken aback by Roxy's tone, he pointed to his screen. "I just saw you online. Don't be offended. I agree with you. I think aliens are real—"

"Give me that." Roxy strode over and swooped up the iPad.

"Hey," he said, but her look froze him to his chair.

"Oh sweet Jesus," she said.

I hurried over. "What is it?"

Roxy scrolled up to the top of the NBC News home page, where a red headline screamed: "Professor arrested in U.S. Senator's grandson's disappearance."

Below the headline, a subhead read, "Video shows Senator's wife asking for help from UFO researchers."

I was suddenly so flush I thought I would break out in sweat. I wanted to sit down, but I forced myself to keep reading.

PROFESSOR ARRESTED IN U.S. SENATOR'S GRANDSON'S DISAPPEARANCE

VIDEO SHOWS SENATOR'S WIFE ASKING FOR HELP FROM UFO RESEARCHERS

By Dave Botcher

Champaign, Illinois—FBI agents raided the Champaign, Illinois, home of a former University of Illinois professor overnight and announced they have found clothing belonging to the missing grandson of U.S. Sen. Tom Roseworth, D-Tennessee.

Dr. Steven Richards was taken into custody late Thursday evening in Nashville, Tenn.

FBI spokesman Raymond Lewis said Richards had attempted to abduct Roseworth's wife, Lynn, at a hotel in Murfreesboro, Tenn.

Lewis said Richards lured Lynn Roseworth to the motel with the help of accomplice Barbara Rush, who is also now in custody.

"These two took advantage of a grieving grandmother in her most vulnerable moments to try and convince her of her grandson's whereabouts," Lewis said, "when all along it appears the boy's clothing had been in Richards' basement. We're searching the residence now."

Lewis would not elaborate as to the connection between Richards and the Roseworth family.

Hours after Richards' and Rush's arrest, a group of supporters of the professor released a video on YouTube, decrying the charges and posting video of what appears to be Lynn Roseworth meeting with Rush and others in a basement in Champaign late in October.

In the video, Doug Ellis, identified only as a researcher, talks about how Richards and Rush are innocent of any

*crimes and were only trying to assist Roseworth in finding
her grandson.*

*"The FBI has pushed our hand to release this video,"
Ellis said in the video. "But we have no choice but to show the
world that Lynn Roseworth herself met with us and acknowledged our work into the existence of extraterrestrials. Barbara sought to help her, nothing else. As did Steven Richards."*

*The video shows a brief interaction between Lynn Rose-
worth and Rush. Ellis can also be seen in the background.
You can watch the clip here:*

I raised a trembling finger and hit the link.

The video player that emerged showed a still frame of me
standing in the basement of Steven's house, surrounded by the
other Researchers.

"That bastard recorded us," Roxy said. "Little shit had one
of those GoPros or something set up."

I swallowed and hit the play button.

"It really is you," the researcher in the tweed jacket could
be heard saying. "I guess it's true: You believe in the little green
men like the rest of us. You look just like you do on TV."

Barbara could be seen walking up to me. "Rupert, you
prove yet again your impeccable skill for saying the wrong
thing at the wrong time. It's been a long time, Lynn. You may
not recognize the few of us who were here back in the day."

In the video, you could hear me clear my throat. "I doubt
you would have recognized me, or even remembered my name,
if it hadn't been for my husband."

The video then cut off, and Doug Ellis once again leaned
towards the camera. "Lynn Roseworth once was one of us and
came to us for help. To think Steven Richards or Barbara Rush
had anything to do with that boy's murder—"

I stepped away. "Put it away."

"Here." Roxy thrust the iPad back at the teenager.

"Can I take a selfie with you?" I could hear the teenage boy ask as I ran towards the nearest bathroom.

I barely made it to the toilet. Very little came up, as I'd eaten almost nothing in the last twenty-four hours. I wished for a heart attack or a stroke—any way I could die at that very moment.

Instead, I waited till my temperature dropped, sitting on the toilet. I then flushed and went out to wash my face and hands.

Roxy stood waiting for me. "Lynn, I'm so sorry."

I rinsed my shaking hands. "It's what the text messages and phone calls are about. It's everywhere now. Everyone has seen it."

"I'll go see about the latest flight back."

"No." I looked up at my haggard face. "Go buy me some sunglasses and a hat."

The four-wheel-drive Suburban was much too big for the meager clothing and basic toiletries that we carried in plastic bags from the shops in the airport, but when Roxy explained to the rental-car worker where we intended to go and that we needed a Mazda, he arched his eyebrows. "You realize it's December in Colorado. The mountain towns can easily be snowed in. That car won't make it."

Roxy asked for specific directions to Argentum. I stood behind her wearing dark circular sunglasses and a ridiculous sock hat. "I have to be honest with you, ma'am, I've never heard of it, and I'm from the mountains near Pueblo," the worker said.

I'd already worn out my phone's battery trying to find anything on a town named Argentum, but the search engines gave me nothing. Why the town showed up on the old road map but nowhere else was a nagging enigma.

I showed the guy behind the counter the page from the atlas Steven had given me. He raised his eyebrows.

"Huh. It would have to be San Juan or Hinsdale County. Pretty isolated. It's all national forest out there. I wonder if it's not even a town anymore. That map looks pretty old. Are you sure that's the right place? Do you plan to take a four-wheeler with you? 'Cause that's the only way you're going to get in. We've had a break from the snow for the last few days, but a whopper of a storm is coming. You'd have to take 160 and just ask around, as long as it stays open. But any roads leading off it won't be when the snow starts."

Roxy mumbled that she wouldn't be riding any four-wheeler, but she would be driving. When the worker explained that they only took credit cards, I mentioned how much he looked like my son, who was waiting tables in Fort Collins. I said that I always carry cash so I can tip people who work hard but don't make a lot of money. He accepted my cash, including the extra twenty dollars I counted out and gave him, and had me fill out paperwork, which I returned filled with blatant lies. I breathed a sigh of relief when we were safely in the SUV and on our way to the interstate.

From the airport we turned south on I-25. I nervously tapped my phone as it repeatedly dinged. "How easily can they track my cell signal?"

"Easily, but only if they ask the cops to look for you. And they're probably getting to that point. Say you're too upset to process what's happening and need some time alone."

"It just sounds so pathetic. The girls won't buy me disappearing like this. They know I wouldn't leave them under any circumstances. Tom won't believe it either. I have to convince them that I had to leave. No . . . *you* convinced me to leave."

"I have no problem being the bully."

"That's our story. I wanted to drive to Champaign. But I saw the YouTube video and am terribly embarrassed, and you said the last thing I needed was to show up there and have the attention focus on me. So you're driving me to a halfway point—let's say Paducah—and we will head to Champaign as soon as there's confirmation of anything."

Roxy nodded with appreciation.

"Give me your phone. The text is going to come from you."

"Throw in a few F-bombs to make it seem authentic," she suggested.

I sent a group text to Tom, Kate, and Stella.

It only took a minute for Roxy's phone to ring with my husband's number displayed in red.

"You have to answer it."

Roxy picked up the phone. "Hi, Tommy. Yes, we're fine. Yes, she's fine. She's right here with me. She's tired and scared and embarrassed and a little sick to her stomach. We're in Paducah. It was my call; it's a good place to wait. No, we're not going to Little Rock. No, we never went to Little Rock in the first place, but that's a conversation to have with your wife when she's feeling up to it."

I watched as Roxy listened for a while, her face finally wrinkling in annoyance. "Yes, we've seen the news. We had no idea we were being recorded in that basement. Lynn's taking it hard. Real hard. Uh-huh. Yes. Uh-huh. She wanted to come to Champaign this morning, but she doesn't need to be anywhere where there's going to be cameras. You tell Anne that her momma is close by and will be there in a heartbeat if you get confirmation— Yes, Tom, I am aware of how far Paducah is from Champaign, you're going to have to handle this until there comes a point when we need to get there. Uh-huh. She knows it, Tom. She hates to be away from Anne. Listen, I love you like a brother and I hate that this is happening, but you are getting on my nerves so I'm going to go."

Roxy hung up and sighed. "He is so used to everyone doing what he says, he can be a real pain."

"Did he buy it?"

"He actually said it was a good idea. He's used to you handling all the family drama stuff. He knows how to bark orders, not how to calm Anne when she's upset. So as long as there's no word on William, and Anne holds it together, we'll be OK."

"What did he say the FBI were doing?"

Roxy gave me a worried glance. "It's not pretty. The media is going nuts. That's why Tom thinks it's wise you're staying back for now. They caught the other woman, I can't remember her name. The one who brought you down to Murfreesboro."

"Barbara."

"She and Dr. Richards are being kept in complete isolation. His house in Illinois is blocked off with police tape, and the agents are scouring it. They're giving Tom and Chris and Anne hourly briefings, but they haven't come up with anything yet, besides the discovery of pajamas. Lynn, if they found what they think are William's clothes . . . ."

"They could be manufacturing all of it. You didn't ride in the car with the agent. She was very clear about how far they would go."

"But why, Lynn? Why do all this? What does the FBI gain? What does anyone gain by framing the wrong guy?"

"I don't know. I have no idea. Maybe they look bad because they haven't found the person responsible? Maybe . . . they're covering something up."

Roxy gave an exasperated sigh. "OK, sorry for that. But come on—"

"Let's not talk about it anymore." I leaned my head against the strap of the seatbelt while watching the bleak landscape rush by. "Look for Route 50 and take it west."

We expected the ease of the Smokies. Like many Tennesseans, we'd breezed past the goofy golf courses and Dollywood attractions of Gatlinburg in order to climb through the mountains to get to the Biltmore Estate on the other side. We'd laughed nervously when the air became crisper, and sighed with relief at the decline towards North Carolina, slightly embarrassed that we'd been anxious at all to travel through the mountain range.

The Rockies, however, were like arrogant giants, towering above in annoyance at the vehicles scurrying up the highways crisscrossing through the peaks, like ants crawling up their pants legs. I'd never seen such white, even having lived through the bitter winters of central Illinois and the occasional whiteouts in Tennessee. But here, everything was blanketed in it: the earth, the mountain peaks, the miles and miles of evergreens scouring the valleys. I was grateful for the sunglasses. If I didn't have them, even the deep crow's feet around my eyes would be weary from my squinting.

The further we drove, the whiter Roxy's knuckles became as she gripped the steering wheel, asking every five minutes if our exit was coming up. Even as we approached hour five, I didn't mind the repeated questions. I couldn't imagine making the harrowing drive alone.

I looked down at my phone, hovering my thumb back and forth over the voice mail icon. I finally touched it, and a row of messages appeared, most from Tom, several from Stella, and the most recent from Kate, from just a few moments ago. *I'll start with hers and work my way down.* I pressed the phone to my ear.

"Mom. We are all worried sick. Dad just told me that you were in Paducah with Roxy. Please just stay there for now. I'm really worried that you'll try to find those people. Those . . . Researchers, or whatever they're called.

"Mom, I hate to leave this on a voice message, but you *cannot* talk to them again. I know some part of you thinks they want to help you; that maybe this Steven Richards wants to help you. He does not. They do not. They are crazy. Steven Richards had maps of our property. The FBI says he hates Dad. Do not speak to these people. Do not promise them anything. We can handle the fallout from the video. We can say you were desperate. No one will judge you. But we have to make sure the story is about William from here on out. If you get in touch with these people again, all the public will ever hear about is how you believe in—I can't even say it. It's going to be plastered on every tabloid. It will be the top story on every website. But it's a twenty-four hour news cycle. The video story will pass as long as you never have anything to do with them again. Please, Mom. Whatever you've done, call me. Please, Mom, just call—"

I hit end and turned off the phone.

Roxy endured the silence for a few moments. "I keep telling myself, 'It will be easier going down. It will be easier going down.' We have to be close now. Tell me again what I'm looking for?"

"The man at the counter said it is either in San Juan or Hinsdale county—"

"The least populated counties in Colorado, according to that charming fact from Google. It has the fewest roads, the fewest people. It sounds delightful."

"Look, San Juan County. That exit," I pointed.

Roxy exhaled loudly as we veered onto an exit ramp and were immediately surrounded by pine trees. The suburban started crunching over hundreds of fallen pinecones. The ramp rambled down to a road without a sign. One way led back onto the highway, the other curved into the trees.

"When is this snowstorm supposed to start?" she asked.

"I'm trying not to think about that."

"We're going five miles—tops—and if there's no sign of where we are, we're turning around."

We surpassed five miles, then ten, then fifteen. I hoped Roxy wasn't watching the odometer as closely as I was.

"Thank you, Jesus, there's a gas station," she said. "And don't think I don't know we're well past five miles."

We parked next to an ancient pump and stepped out to the smell of fried chicken coming from a building covered in badly faded cigarette and beer ads. The smell was both nauseating and comforting, a reminder that the southern favorite was a staple of gas station fryers all over the country.

"We don't have much gas," a man called out, sucking his teeth. "Trucks won't be coming up for another two weeks."

"We'll take what you've got," I said. "Is this the exit for Argentum?"

The man leaned on a post. "Never heard of it. I'm not from around here."

I once more brought out the old map and approached him. He took a close look and nodded. "Well, how about that."

"Any idea where it is?"

He shook his head.

"Can you direct me to the next closest town? They might have heard of it."

"Only unincorporated towns around here. Little pockets of people. Old mining towns scattered here and there. Impossible to know all the names."

"I'm guessing if there's a gas station here, there must be a town nearby. I didn't pass any on the way from the interstate. I'm assuming they're farther up the road?"

He nodded and again sucked his teeth.

"All I can get is five dollars out of this," Roxy said.

"I told you we were low."

"Thanks for your help," I gave him a small wave.

"Do you want some chicken for the road?"

I waved Roxy into the Suburban, knowing if the man made the noise again, there might be a brawl.

"Better hurry," he called out. "Feels like a storm's coming."

After sixty-five miles of nothing, Roxy started driving at a crawl, looking for any sign of life. We passed no towns, not even a side street. It became abundantly clear why the gas station was low on fuel; there couldn't be enough people to justify frequent deliveries.

"Hon, I don't even want to think about what we'd do if this SUV broke down."

"Someone has to be out here. Just a bit more."

We both pointed at the same time when the barn and a side road appeared. Hoping a house would be nearby, we turned onto the road, potholes and other precarious dips causing us to bounce in our seats. The closer we got to the barn, the more our hopes teetered. As we pulled up in front, it was clear the wood slats were beyond dilapidated. The doors had long since fallen away, revealing an empty interior.

I began to suggest we get back on the road when I caught a glimpse of a large letter *A* painted in faded white on the edge of the barn's eastern side.

"Can you drive around there?"

"Please keep an eye out for sinkholes."

Next to the painted *A* there was an empty space, and following it were a faded *G* and an *E*.

"Pull back a bit," I said.

Roxy looped around and then stopped. "Well, shut my mouth."

From that view, we could see that a long time ago, someone had painted a single word with a stream flowing underneath. Time had erased two of the letters; now it only read *"A GEN UM."*

"Argentum," I said softly. The painted stream ended in the tip of an arrow, pointing down the crumbling road.

Roxy applied the gas. "Well, here we go."

We drove down the road, navigating more potholes, a fallen limb, and a perilous rise, finally stopping on a ridge.

"Well, this is . . ." Roxy said.

"Quaint."

"I was going more for bleak. Does this town only have one street?"

"I bet it was a silver-mining town."

"It looks like a ghost town."

It would have been easy to dismiss the town as abandoned. The road leading into Argentum was ruined from endless cycles of snow and ice eating away at the aging infrastructure. The pine trees cleared enough to reveal a town that had taken on the colors of winter; the wood of the weary buildings was the same shade as the dirt-caked snow that clung like moss on a fallen tree.

Roxy pulled up to the first structure, a whitewashed

building with two strong wooden posts holding up a front porch. A sign read, "The Argentum Inn," and smoke drifted from the chimney.

"At least someone is alive in there," Roxy observed.

Wincing in the icy wind, we scurried up the front steps and opened the door. The front room was cozy, with overstuffed chairs and a crackling fire. I suddenly felt very tired.

"Well, hello there," said a young woman with deep red hair, who came from a back room to sit behind the counter. "I thought I knew everybody in town. I'm Sarah."

"Just visiting for the day," Roxy said.

"Visiting? I'm not sure we've ever had an actual visitor! But you know about the storm, right? Once it hits, we may be shut off from the hard road for a while. I don't mean to be crass, but are you lost?"

Roxy shook her head. "We're two old spinsters who like to visit all the mountain towns. Do you have any vacancies?"

"When exactly is the storm supposed to hit?" I asked.

"Tomorrow, the radio says," she answered, and then blinked. "Oh, we're not an inn, despite what the sign reads outside. We're more of a boarding house for the locals who like having their beds made and not having to shovel steps."

"Do you have rooms we can rent for just the night?"

"Come to think of it, we do. Just one, though. Mr. Peterson died over the summer and no one has claimed the room yet."

"Charming. We'll take it," Roxy said. "Tell me it has two beds, though."

"Sorry. One queen."

"That's fine. So tell me, what do we need to see? And more importantly, where do we eat? Are you a local?"

"I've lived here and there. It won't take you long to see the town. You may be ready to go home in an hour."

•   •   •

"All right," Roxy said as we slid back into the Suburban. "Even if we knocked on every door in this town, we'll probably be done in twenty minutes."

"Sarah said that off Main Street, there are a few more streets."

"What's your plan, Lynnie?" Roxy wiped off her sunglasses with her scarf. "I mean, we are, absolutely, in the middle of nowhere. There are probably two hundred people in this town, tops. I know we've talked about this, but why in the world would Dr. Richards tell you this is where William was taken?"

"I don't know." I looked at the empty storefronts in the street that made up the entire downtown.

"And Lynn, who exactly took him? The government? Homegrown terrorists who hate Tom? Maybe some even more wacked-out version of the Researchers from Illinois? There's never been a ransom note. No one has ever asked for money in exchange for returning William. Nothing legit has come from the reward. Do you think maybe Steven knew he was about to be arrested and needed to come up with something to try to make you believe he's not guilty?"

"All I know is that when I worked for Steven, the word 'Argentum' came up more than once. He didn't even know anything about it—he called it an urban legend about aliens. So for him now to direct me here . . ."

"OK. So all you know is that people—who believe in alien abductions—mentioned a theory about something called Argentum, but Dr. Richards had no idea what it was?"

"I remember his frustration about it. That it was an unproven theory. I took it to be almost like a code word for something. He even mentioned once that it was a theory about other dimensions or something. He said several times that he and his fellow Researchers were told to outright dismiss it. So imagine my surprise when he whispered it to me in the hotel room. That and . . . other revelations."

"For Christ sake, Lynn, you hadn't kept a secret from me in sixty years, I thought. Now you keep popping them out, one after another."

"I'm sorry. Everything has been a blur since Barbara waited for me outside the shop two nights ago."

"Wait, what? That Barbara woman came to the shop?"

"She waited for me in the Christmas trees."

I told her of the two names Barbara had given me to research, and how I went to the library and found that the girl, Amelia Shrank, had vanished in 1935, and that the hunter, Josh Stone, disappeared a decade later.

"And they both went missing in the woods behind my house. In the same month William disappeared."

"We're talking nearly three missing people in a century's time, Lynn, how can there possibly be a connection. I mean, don't get me wrong. It sounds strange."

"It gets even stranger." I took a deep breath, and told her about seeing my father and the men in the woods. Then, I reached into my purse and brought out the letter Daddy had written to Steven.

When she was done reading it, Roxy looked at me in astonishment. "Is this real?"

I nodded. "It's Daddy's handwriting."

"Lynn . . . your father believed you were abducted as well? From the woods?"

"I still have trouble accepting it. But this is my father's letter. And . . . I believe him. That he and Mama found me once. I can only hope I can do what they did."

"Did they find you here?"

"I don't know."

"I still can't believe any of it." Roxy looked out the windshield. "I need a moment to wrap my head around all this. As long as you have no more revelations for the moment, I suppose we need to figure out where the hell we go now."

"I have no idea."

"Well, I'm old and cranky and scared and need caffeine. I don't suppose they have a Publix out here anywhere, so that charming country store sign must indicate our only option."

We rolled down the street to stop at the end of the businesses. A sign hung from the porch; it depicted a man waving from atop a mountain, with the word "Climbers" underneath.

"I'll go in," I offered. "If there are any customers, I'm going to show them William's picture while I get you a drink. It can't hurt to ask."

"That depends. You realize that everyone in the country knows William's picture. And if they have a TV, or a radio, or wifi, they've seen the video and may be talking—at this very moment—about the alien-obsessed wife of the senator."

"Oh God, you're right."

"Let's stick with me asking about William. You can't see me in that video. And if anyone makes a joke about it, I'll give them a fat lip. Just keep that sock hat and your sunglasses on if you run into anyone. And be quick with that Diet Pepsi. I'm dragging."

I slid out of the car and walked across the wooden porch, entering the building that smelled like pipe tobacco and cardboard. Three rows of boxed goods, limited produce, and random medical supplies made up the entire shop.

"Can I help you?" asked an older man sitting at the front counter, a pipe in his mouth. He had hair that curled like duck-tails around his ears.

I almost asked for the sodas, but all I could think about was that video released online. How dare those people use William's disappearance to try to shame me into supporting them? They only made it harder for me to find him.

"Yes, I'm actually looking for someone."

"By the ring on your finger, I'm sad to say it's probably not me," the man said, smiling kindly.

I brought out the picture of William. "Do you happen to recognize him?"

The man squinted and looked closely, then shook his head. "Sorry. Never seen the handsome devil. And I know every-body in this town. Let me guess: custody dispute? You the grandma? Your daughter won't let you see your grandson or something?"

"No, nothing like that. It's a long story. He's my grandson, and I'm trying to find him."

"His parents hippies or something? Come up here to take a stab at the marijuana trade? Can't think of any other reason someone would bring a little boy this far out here. We don't have many kids. All the ones I know are locals."

"I wish it were that simple. Well, thank you. Oh, do you happen to have any sodas?"

"Got a few Diet Cokes and some Mountain Dew from my quarterly trip to civilization for supplies. Can't get any of the delivery trucks to come here."

"I'll take a Diet Coke."

The man reached under the counter, and I heard the faint whoosh of a small refrigerator door. The man placed the bottle on the smooth wooden surface. "On the house for the pretty lady."

"Thank you."

"I have to be honest with you: If there was a new kid in town, I'd know. We only have a few hundred people anyway."

"I understand. But I have to try."

"Good luck!" He added a small wave.

I opened the door of the Suburban to Roxy's scowl. "Jesus, I hate Diet Coke."

"You'll survive. Let's start at the bar."

"OK, I'll go there. I carry a flyer with William's picture on it wherever I go, so I have something to show."

"I'll wander up and down the main drag, see if I run into anyone."

Ten minutes later, having only seen abandoned stores and no people, I found Roxy sitting in the Suburban. "Sorry, Sis, no luck. In the laundromat, there was only a stoned couple—thanks for that, Colorado. Apparently, TV—and the internet for that matter—isn't big around here, so they hadn't seen him. Nor had the three people inside the bar, and their TV was set to SportsCenter. Let's leave this booming metropolis and just start driving."

We got in and drove for an hour, up and down the few quiet streets, seeing no one. "It's getting dark now. And I'm beat. Let's find somewhere to eat."

I nodded. "I think that Scotty's bar is all that's open."

At Scotty's, we took a booth and ordered two small salads and grilled chicken sandwiches.

"What if he's not here?" I asked.

"Honey, all you could do was check it out. And you did. You have done everything you could for William. And Brian.

And Anne. You were supposed to call her tonight. I'm actually surprised there haven't been any calls or texts. But I guess no news is good news."

We ate our meal in silence. After a short drive back to the inn, we climbed the stairs to our room. Roxy opened the door and a small piece of paper fluttered to the floor.

"They didn't wait long to stick us with the bill," Roxy said.

I picked it up, realizing it was no bill. The old postcard had an artist's rendering of the Argentum Inn back in its prime, perhaps the early twenties, surrounded by images of small waterfalls landing in creeks. Written in flourishing cursive were the words: "Stay at beautiful Argentum! Where the Water Falls."

My arm immediately tingled in pinpricks.

"Where the Water Falls."

The poem on the cards that I, and untold numbers of Researchers, had given so many times to the families of the missing came whispering in my mind.

You are with me.
You are in the rain.
You are in my tears.
You are where the water falls.

All those years ago, Steven had dismissed the poem. He grumbled that he didn't even know why we handed it out. He'd only said one of his colleagues started doing it and insisted all Researchers follow his lead.

Steven hadn't realized the poem wasn't intended to comfort families. Whoever that colleague was, he had meant it as a guide.

You are where the water falls.

"Sweet God," I whispered. I looked again at the picture and quickly turned it over to show to Roxy when I saw the writing on the back.

In all capital letters, someone had scrawled: "LEAVE BEFORE THE STORM."

FIFTEEN

The wood complained with every step as Roxy thudded down the stairs. I stood at the top of the staircase, holding the banister to keep from swaying. I looked down to see her reach the counter and repeatedly hit the small gold bell until Sarah came out from the back.

"Hello ma'am—"

"Who's been up in our room?"

"No one. Joan won't even come until eleven tomorrow to start cleaning—"

"Then who, do you suppose, slipped this into the door?" Roxy slid the postcard across the counter.

Sarah scanned the card. "I have no idea—"

"Someone clearly intended for this to spook us, and I'd like to know who. Right now."

"Ma'am, I have no idea. I've been in the back all night, and only locals live here—"

"Then which of those locals would have done this? Would you like me to complain to the owner?"

"I'm really sorry this upset you. I would move you to another room, but there aren't any left."

Roxy leaned on the counter. "I'd like to speak with the owner."

"Ma'am, please, I need this job. . . ."

"And he's going to can your butt if he hears someone has been harassing one of your customers while you were on duty."

Even from my vantage point from above, I could see Sarah nervously brush back a strand of her hair. "Please, I'm so sorry. . . ."

"You're from around here. Tell me who lives here."

"I'm not local."

"When we checked in, you said you knew everybody in town."

"I do know most people in town. Or, at least, I've learned their names and faces over the past six months or so."

Even though I couldn't see her face, I knew Roxy's eyebrows were rising. "Then I suggest you tell me which of these faces went by our room tonight. I'm a lot meaner than I look, and I'm aware, right now, with these dark circles under my eyes, I look pretty frightening."

"I need this job," Sarah blurted out.

"Well, I'd like to speak with your boss, Sarah . . . whatever your last name is."

When the girl burst into tears, Roxy shook her head. "Oh, for God's sake, here. . . ." She reached into her purse, bringing out some Kleenex. "Why are *you* so worked up—?"

"You don't understand . . . if you go to the owner and he fires me, I have nowhere to go." She wiped her eyes. "And I can't tell you my last name because I don't know what it is. Who's going to hire someone who doesn't know their last name?"

"Listen, I'm full up with drama, trust me. Clearly, this is

getting me nowhere. But I'm serious. I will find out who left this postcard, and if I get another one, I will track down this owner and seriously chew some ass. *Comprende?*"

The girl nodded, and Roxy gave her the rest of her Kleenex packet. "I don't suppose you have surveillance video of the hallways or who's come in the front door?"

The girl shook her head.

"What does it mean, 'Where the Water Falls'?"

The sound of my voice surprised both of them. I must have come down the stairs so quietly they didn't hear.

Sarah exhaled in an attempt to compose herself. "I asked the same thing of the old timers when I first saw it. When the first settlers came here, they said the creeks were so shiny they looked like argentum, which I've since learned is Latin for silver. And when the snow melted, there were so many little waterfalls leading into the creeks that it became a way to try and lure others to visit in the spring."

"And how many of these old postcards are conveniently lying around town?" Roxy waved it in the air.

"I haven't seen one in a while. Listen, I'm really sorry—"

"We'll figure it out." Roxy took me by the arm. "But I'm dead bolting our door tonight!"

Roxy muttered all the way up the stairs and loudly shut the door as we entered our room. I went to stand before the window.

"Well, don't know if you heard her say it, but that girl says she doesn't know who left this," Roxy said. "She said they don't keep surveillance."

I stared into the dark. "Ten minutes ago, I was wondering if I was wrong about everything."

"Just to play devil's advocate, couldn't it be somebody

worried about two old broads who could be stuck here in a snowstorm?"

"I don't think anybody in this town is concerned about our welfare."

I thought about telling her about the connection I thought I'd made to the Researcher's poem. But the idea of explaining to Roxy the theory, and thinking about how she would certainly respond with sarcasm, made me very tired.

"Should you call Tom?" she asked, digging through her bag for the nightgown we bought at the airport.

"I tried as we were coming up the stairs. Couldn't get a signal out. Can't send a text either. Might be why there's been no calls or texts. Oh God, I hope nothing's happened that has Anne panicked. If she can't reach me, and Tom can't, it may prompt him to ask police for help tracking me down."

"Lynn, I have to tell you, this scares me a little. I don't like this note. Should we call the police? Go make a report?"

"And tell them what exactly? Anyone who hears what we're doing would think we're the crazy ones. Especially if they've seen the news."

"I thought we were crazy too," Roxy said, holding out the postcard. "Until this."

I took the postcard from her. "Even if they can't get ahold of me, and they try to trace us, I don't care. I'm not leaving until I know if William is here."

"I would say I'm hormonal, but that ship sailed long ago, so I guess I'm just hankering for some guilty pleasures," Roxy said as the Suburban rolled down the street. "I'm going to need some Doritos,"

"It's 8:15 in the morning," I replied, wincing. It was still bright outside, even with the endless gray skies. I looked down at my phone. No calls or texts, either to my phone or Roxy's. Clearly there was no service here. There was no doubt Tom would start worrying. We were running out of time.

"I don't want to go back into that bar, even for decent food. So when you can't have scrambled eggs, you have Doritos, and I saw some in the window of that general store. Climbers, was it? Why don't you bat your eyes at that old man and get us a free bag to go with my free Diet Coke from yesterday?"

"That old man is probably younger than us."

"Look, we're already here. One perk of this town is you can be anywhere in two seconds."

I slid out, feeling a bit ridiculous that we drove instead of walking. But from here on out, we would be driving the rest of the day, trying to map out a plan. As I once again stepped in the store, the tobacco smell reminded me of Daddy. Had he been in this town as well? Looking for me?

"Well, this is my lucky week," the man said with a smile, still perched at the counter.

"Good morning. I hope you have coffee."

"That, my dear, I have plenty of."

"This isn't for me." I slid the bag of Doritos across the counter.

"Hey, whatever gets you through the day."

"Can you make it two cups?"

"Don't break my heart and say that you're here with your husband."

"Just here with an old friend."

"Still on the search?" he asked, pouring the coffee.

"Back at it today."

"Like I said—don't get your hopes up. If the wind blows in a different direction, I'm usually the first to know."

I studied the man's face. "I don't suppose you tried to warn me of the storm with a postcard stuck in my door last night?"

"Somebody warn you about the storm in a note? Around here, warning about snowstorms is as common a greeting as good morning and good night.'"

"Something like that."

"You staying up at the boarding house? Pretty nice folk up there, doubt they'd do anything to scare somebody. When we get storms, it's no sweet Georgia rain. The snow comes in and it pounds us. Generators keep us alive; sometimes we go days without power. I doubt you have to deal with that down south."

"The accent gives me away?" I paused before signing my name.

"It's a beautiful accent." He held up the receipt. "Nice to meet you, Lynn . . . Stanson."

"What's your name?"

"Joseph, but I go by Joe." He reached out and shook my hand. "Please let me know if I can be any assistance to you."

"The coffee helps a lot. Are you from here?"

"Wish I knew," he grinned. "Now, don't you start thinking I'm one of those old guys with Parkinson's or dementia. I can tell you the names of the starting lineups in the bullpens for the Rockies since the early nineties and every song on Johnny Cash's first album. But anything from my childhood or teenage years . . . nothing."

"Nothing?"

"Woke up in our little medical center on the edge of town with absolutely no idea who I was. Can you believe it? Memory never came back. I assume I was some messed-up kid. Maybe some drugs fried my brain, or I got into some hell of a bar fight. No one ever came looking for me, so I must not have been a real charmer. Anyhow, people in this town were really good to me, so I stuck around. Started stocking shelves here, got friendly with the owner, Mr. Climbers. When he got sick, he asked me to run the place till he got better. That was fifty years ago! So here I am. Just me and Moses."

"Moses?"

Joe pointed out the side window at what appeared to be one of the largest pickup trucks in the world.

"That's something else," I said.

"Instead of parting the Red Sea, I part the snow. My other job is helping to clear the streets when the snow comes in. I'll have a busy next couple of days, if what the radio says is true."

"So," I started hesitantly, "do you listen to the radio a lot? Aren't there more accurate warnings on TV or online?"

"Spend about five minutes in Argentum and you'll see we're a bit behind the times. Internet service is for shit up here, and no company is going to invest in fiber lines for a small town with less than five hundred people. Plus, most folks here like living off the grid, it's why they're here. Our major news source is pretty much AM radio. We don't even get the Denver TV stations."

At least there's one town in America that doesn't think I'm insane, I thought.

"It's been nice talking to you, Joe, but I really have to go."

"You be careful Miss Lynn. You run into any problems, you know where to find me. Especially if you get stuck!"

I waved as I walked out.

"Jesus, did you give him your number?" Roxy said as I climbed in. "Give me that coffee and those Doritos, in that order. So, what did Mr. Handsome have to say?"

"I didn't realize you were watching that closely through the window."

"That's a fine-looking man, Lynn, like you didn't notice. I may be postmenopausal, but I'm not dead. Maybe he's the one who left you the note."

"I flat-out asked him." I sipped at the coffee.

"Well, someone left her shyness back in Tennessee."

"What are we going to do if we get snowed in?"

"We best get a move on and do whatever it is we're going to do, and maybe drive back towards the interstate for a bit to try and get a signal to call Tom. Did Romeo in there have any suggestions as where to start?"

"Poor man, he doesn't even know if he's from here. He doesn't remember—"

"I'm sorry, what did you say?" Roxy put down her coffee.

"He said he can't remember anything from his childhood, had amnesia of some sort—"

"He really said that?"

"Yes. Why does that matter?"

"Because if you were eavesdropping properly last night, you would have heard young Sarah at the front desk say she doesn't remember her last name. And she doesn't remember where she's from either. That's why she freaked out when I demanded to know who owned the inn. She said she was afraid she'd lose her job if he found out, because who would hire a girl who didn't even know her last name."

Roxy placed her hand on my leg. "Lynn, my God. My God."

"What?"

"You always thought that brain tumor caused you to lose your memory as a kid. You always said your first memory was waking up and not recognizing your father. You had to relearn everything. But your father's letter stated you never had a brain tumor. What if, Lynn, you were just like them?"

I remembered Daddy's words from his letter to Steven:

I've always been plagued with guilt that she doesn't know her own true story.

I felt hot all over, regretting the coffee. I tapped the power window to allow a crack, letting the icy air brush my face. Daddy had concocted the story. Faked the medical records. All to cover up the fact that his daughter had no memory and couldn't explain why to anyone.

I lowered the window even more, taking several deep breaths, the air stinging my lungs.

"Lynn?"

"Let's just drive."

"I could be wrong. Let me turn down the heat—"

"I just need some more air. I promise to roll it up in a minute."

We drove down the same few streets, seeing no one. Finally, we found one woman walking her corgi. She shook her head sadly at William's picture. "He's a handsome boy. A few of the kids play up at the old ball field around the corner; you might find someone there who has seen him."

"You should have asked her if she knew her last name," Roxy said as we drove away.

We arrived at the park and found it to be as deserted and neglected as the rest of the town. A tiny yellow bus was parked nearby, and a few kids ran and screamed on a weary-looking playground.

"Hang around here. I know you said Mr. Hot Stuff back at the store got all his news from crappy radio, and so far no one has recognized you or William, but let me take it from here. Looks like there are a few houses around the baseball diamond down there. I'll look for signs of life. I'll be right back."

"I need to walk a bit. But I'll stay close."

We both exited the Suburban, and I watched as Roxy

walked away. I huddled in my coat, wishing I had bought thicker gloves. I'd gone from hot to bitter cold quickly, and I shuffled along to keep up the circulation.

I brought out my phone to power it up. Maybe I could get cell reception out here. I needed to call Anne—

A laugh in the distance caused me to almost drop the phone.

Four boys on the other side of the park were playing a game of touch football. One of them had dropped his hat, exposing his red hair.

The boy turned around. For a split second, I saw his face.

William pulled his hat over his ears and laughed.

SIXTEEN

"William?"

I started at a jog, not daring to take my eyes off the boy chasing the others. "William! William!"

He was giggling, holding his sides at whatever joke someone had said. I had heard that laughter a hundred times before, at SpongeBob on television, when Chris tossed him over his shoulder, as Tom pretended to gnaw off his fingers when ice cream dripped on his little hands.

"William! Baby, it's Nanna! William!" I was sobbing as I reached him. I grabbed the sides of his face, seeing replicas of Anne's eyes, my own freckles on his cheeks, his dimpled chin.

"Oh, thank you God, thank you," I pulled him close. "Oh baby. . . ."

I felt his small hands push away as he stammered back. "Miss Cliff," he said, looking around, his eyes wide with confusion.

I reached out and took off his hat, running my fingers through the hair that I had combed for two summers, when he would take a bath at my house before Anne came to take him home, knowing he would fall asleep on the two-minute drive. "Oh, baby. It's me, it's Nanna."

"Miss Cliff!" William practically screamed.

The boys that had gathered around us began to part, making way for a slow-moving woman whose face was lined with wrinkles.

"What's going on here?"

"This is my grandson." I smiled through tears. "I've been looking for him. Oh William, I can't believe it—"

"Miss, I think you have the wrong boy," the woman said, placing a weathered but protective hand on William, who moved in closer to her.

"You don't understand. William, it's Nanna."

"Miss Cliff," he said anxiously.

"Your birthday is June 26." I kneeled down, flinching as he stepped farther away. "You hate peas. You love dinosaurs. If you pull up your pants leg, you'll see the birthmark you have on the back of your right thigh—"

"Miss, you're scaring the children. Boys, take Alan and go to the bus."

"No!" I cried out as William and the boys turned and ran.

Miss Cliff shuffled in front of me, her ancient voice lowering to a whisper. "You need to go. Right now. Whoever you are, get out of here *now*."

"No." I tried to step around her.

"I warned you," Miss Cliff said, looking back to the bus. "Security! I mean, officer, can you please come here?"

"William!" I screamed, seeing him look back once more before hurrying on the bus.

I easily sidestepped the woman and ran, seeing a figure emerge from a car that I hadn't noticed was parked behind the bus. A man, wearing a dark blue jacket and matching pants, put out his arms.

"What's going on here?" he said.

"That's my grandson!" I cried out, pointing to the bus. At the door, the hunched-over figure of Miss Cliff was herding the other children on, pointing one curved and bony finger to hasten their step.

"Please calm down, ma'am, and tell me what's going on," the man said, blocking me.

"My name is Lynn Roseworth, my husband is Senator Tom Roseworth. We've gone on television to say our grandson is missing. And he's right there!"

"OK, OK, calm down."

"Lynn!" Roxy waved as she hurried over. "Lynn, what's happening?"

"He's on the bus! He's in there! William's in there!"

The doors to the bus closed and the engine fired up.

"Lynn, are you sure?" Roxy was almost out of breath.

"Ma'am, just relax," the officer said.

"It's leaving!" I said as the wheels of the bus shuddered and turned. "No! Stop that bus!"

"Ma'am, that's enough. You're going to have to calm down—"

"And who the hell are you?" Roxy demanded.

"I'm police—"

"If my friend says her missing grandson is on that bus, then you better stop that bus."

The man murmured into the speaker on his shoulder. "Five-ninety, please send a car to the north end of the park."

"No!" I watched the bus drive way. "Roxy, no. . . ."

"What the hell is wrong with you?" Roxy squared off with the man. "Stop that bus!"

"You both have caused quite the scene out here. That bus is only going up to the day care, and once you've calmed down, we'll see about going up there and checking this out. But I saw that little boy, ma'am, and he didn't know you from Adam."

A white car pulled up, its red light lazily spinning on the dashboard. I turned to Roxy with frantic eyes. "He didn't recognize me, Roxy. He didn't know it was me. He didn't *remember*."

Roxy's hand went to her mouth. She reached into her purse and began to dig around for her phone.

"What's going on?" another officer, also dressed in dark blue, asked as he approached, looking intently at Roxy as she tore into her purse.

"I'm going to call her husband right now, who happens to be a US senator."

"What we're all going to do is calm down," the first officer said. "Let's take a ride and go over all this."

"Let's go." The second officer took Roxy gently by the arm.

"Get your hands off." She tried to jerk away, until she looked closely at his face.

He sucked his teeth loudly. Even I could smell fried chicken from where I was standing.

"Jesus," Roxy said softly.

"You have a good memory," the man said, opening the door to the squad car.

The front hallway of the building the officers called their police station was sparsely decorated with historic photographs of Argentum in cheap frames, including one of an old barbershop in which a mural was painted with a waterfall spilling into a creek. *Where the Water Falls* was written in decorative letters in the stream.

That photograph melted into my blur of panic. I knew I'd been wild-eyed in my demands for my phone to call Tom, practically screaming at the officers as I kept looking out the back window of the squad car for any sign of the bus. Even when they ushered us into the building, I took another glance before the door shut, hoping to catch a glimpse, to even know the direction William was going.

I had him. And I let him go.

The men took us to a back room, telling Roxy to try and calm me down. She responded with a colorful tirade of curse words interspersed with idle threats. They shut the door and said through the glass that they were getting in touch with the FBI.

"Google her, you assholes!" Roxy shook the locked handle. "Lynn Roseworth! Wife of Senator Tom Roseworth! Her grandson's disappearance has been announced all over the world! What kind of rock have you been living underneath?"

I paced the room, my fingers entangled in my hair. "What the hell is going on, Lynn? What is wrong with this place? That officer was the gas station creepo yesterday, now he's a cop?"

"She didn't call them officers at first," I said, my eyes darting.

"What?"

"The woman with William and the other children. She told me I needed to leave, and then said she tried to warn me. She called 'security,' and then quickly referred to him as officer."

"My God, now that I think about it, they weren't wearing any badges. . . ."

"I shouldn't have let that bus go. How can I ever tell Anne that I had him, and I let him go?"

"You could have hung on to the back of that bus and it

wouldn't have made a difference," Roxy said, then she added quietly. "Are you sure, Lynn? Are you sure it was him?"

"It was him."

"Dammit," Roxy stood, wincing. She had run too fast from the other end of the park when she saw the commotion. "Why didn't we call Tom, or Ed, or anyone for that matter, to tell them where we are?"

"Because I know what they would have said. I could blame the cell service, which doesn't seem to exist here. But I could have called from the road. I knew the second I called, I would hear Anne plead for me to come to Champaign, or Tom would remind me how reckless this is and all the damage I've caused."

"Speaking of Tom, and I know you hate to hear this, but you're both public figures, and they can't keep you locked up in here. One search online and they'll see everything they need to know. We're going to get William, Lynn."

"He didn't recognize me. Is that what's happening here? People who are kidnapped are brought to this town? Joe at the general store woke up in the hospital in this town without his memory. Sarah at the inn doesn't remember anything of her life, either. Roxy, is this is where Daddy found *me*? I didn't have a memory either."

"Well, we know two things: that Dr. Richards was both right and wrong about William being here. Your boy ended up in this town, but obviously wasn't abducted by aliens and isn't soaring around the cosmos in a spaceship."

"So what, then? He was taken by someone, maybe some sort of group, and the people they abduct end up with memory loss?"

"And it doesn't explain how Dr. Richards knew he would be here. If I had my phone . . ."

"They're not going to give us our phones."

"Well, my patience has officially run out. We've done nothing wrong, they can't lock us up in here when we haven't committed any crime—"

The door handle turned and a small man stepped in, quietly closing the door behind him. His thinning hair was parted to cover a sizable bald spot, his skin color an ashen gray. He fumbled in his suit coat to bring out a pack of cigarettes. Every bit of clothing on him, from his head to his shoes, was black.

"We have a pretty bad storm approaching, ladies. It's best that you get out of here before it hits."

"I don't think so," Roxy said. "I don't know who you are, but we have come here to find my friend's grandson, who she just saw at a park in this town. And I'm happy to remind you again who she is married to—"

"We will be pleased to arrange for transportation out of here." The man fired up a cigarette. "We'll make sure you get out safely."

"I will not leave my grandson."

"We want to return you to your family, Mrs. Roseworth," the man said, taking a deep drag. "We understand you must be very desperate. In light of what's on the news websites now, I know it must be hard to admit he's gone. No one is sure, though, why you thought he would end up here—"

"Because she saw him," Roxy interjected.

The man ignored her and kept looking at me. "Your family has gone through a great loss. Please don't make them go through another."

"I will not leave him—"

"Lynn, I want to go home." Roxy reached out and touched my arm. "I can't do this anymore. I need to get home to Ed.

My back hurts, I can't go through a storm like that without my pain meds, and I'm out. Let's do this. Obviously you were wrong. If it were William, he would have recognized you. You must be delirious or something. We have to admit that now. Let's take this ride out of town. I'm done."

She squeezed a bit harder. "I'm too tired to do this anymore."

I looked at her, and under her weepy eyes, Roxy flared her nostrils.

"Thank you, we'll take that ride," I said.

"Good," the man said, already finishing off the cigarette. "I have a car pulled around. We'll take you by the inn to get your things."

"We'll need our purses," Roxy said.

"Of course. It's all waiting for you in the car."

"Thank you," she said, wincing as she stepped. As the man walked out, Roxy mouthed words to me: "Act old."

"What are we doing?" I mouthed back.

We walked out of the building as slowly as possible. The white unmarked car waited outside, with the red light still spinning beneath the windshield. "Is it OK if I sit in the front?" Roxy asked. "I can never get comfortable in the back."

"Of course," the man in the black suit said, nodding.

"Welcome, ladies," said the teeth sucker as we got into the car.

Roxy slid into the front seat. "Lynnie, is my purse back there? I need to see if I have any of my OxyContin left. My hip is killing me."

"It's here."

"I have a bum leg too," Teeth Sucker said, pulling the gear into drive. "Tough living with the pain."

I looked out the window, making eye contact briefly with

the man in the black suit. He lit a cigarette and watched us drive away.

Roxy dug around in her purse. "Can't barely move without my meds."

"If you're looking for your phone, it's in there, but damn it all if the batteries aren't dead. You must have left it on too long without charging it."

"Oh, that's fine." Roxy gave a careless wave. "I just need my medicine. Don't have anybody to call anyway."

Teeth Sucker began to hum as we drove. "You must be busy, working the gas station and being a police officer," Roxy commented.

He grinned. "We're all called to serve."

I looked out through the back window, seeing the downtown disappearing behind us. Soon the police building was gone over a hill. I couldn't see any of Argentum. The panic was rising to my throat.

I could see Teeth Sucker looking at my reflection in the rearview mirror. "Don't you worry. I have to make a quick stop at the hospital, it's just around the bend from here. After that, we'll head right back to the inn."

"My ass," Roxy said, pulling out the mace from her purse.

"Fuckin' fuck!" he cried out as she sprayed his face.

The car veered wildly. Roxy kept spraying as he reached out to block her. "Fucking bitch!" When the chemicals truly sunk in, he started to scream.

"Roxy!" I cried out, watching the car weave across the road and then take a violent turn towards a telephone pole.

The impact threw me back, but not before I saw Roxy crash into the dashboard. As Teeth Sucker frantically wiped his face, I sat stunned for a moment, my head spinning. I could hear a hissing sound from the engine, and I closed my eyes to try and stop the vertigo.

"Roxy! Are you OK—?"

She moaned and then flinched away as Teeth Sucker reached out for her angrily, his sausage fingers grabbing the hood of her coat.

My wallet, stuffed with Target receipts, credit cards I'd closed but forgot to throw away, and volumes of my grandchildren's photographs, was the first thing I threw at him. Maybe it was that I was so close behind him that my aim was so true. It struck him sharply on the back of his head. The metal clasp on the wallet must have hit him in a soft spot as the impact produced another yelp of pain as he continued to wail and wipe his eyes. I started throwing everything I could grasp in my purse: a compact, a small flashlight, pencils, mints. When an eyeliner pinged off his right temple, he reached back for me blindly.

I fell back into the backseat, smacking his hand with my purse. My eyes were starting to sting from the mace as well. I could hear Roxy fumble with the door handle and she practically fell out the door, her feet momentarily in the air.

Teeth Sucker lunged in the direction of the sound. He wrestled at his waist and pulled out a gun. Gunshots rang out in the car.

"Roxy!" I screamed, once again striking him with my purse. He pivoted the gun back towards me. As I bent down, I heard the gunfire and the back windshield shatter.

The door beside me jerked opened and Roxy outstretched her hand. She yanked me out as he fired again into the backseat. The cushions absorbed the zings of the flying bullets. "You fucking bitches!" he yelled.

"Sweet God," Roxy whispered, wiping at her own eyes. "That mace works. Even the residual hurts like the devil."

We hustled down the road, hearing Teeth Sucker curse among screams of pain as he realized he was out of bullets.

"Are you hurt? You're limping—"

"Here I pretend to be old for a minute, and now I actually feel like it."

I looked back at the crashed cruiser. Teeth Sucker had fallen out now, rubbing his eyes and screaming for us.

I took her arm as I hurried our pace. "We have to get away from here."

"Mr. Black back there didn't want to dirty his hands with actually having to kill a senator's wife, so he sent numb nuts back there to do it. I guess the first security guard or whatever he is from the park couldn't stomach it. Well, we aren't so old, are we, assholes? Good thing I bought that mace at the airport. Never leave home without it. There, go down that back street."

"Who are they? They clearly aren't police. That teacher tried to warn me. I know why now."

The street off the main road was lined with more vinyl-sided houses and empty driveways. "We have to keep heading towards town."

"Our only chance now is that Fried Chicken couldn't open his eyes enough to see where we went. But it's not going to be hard to find two old women stumbling around. Damn, does my ass hurt."

"We have to get to that hospital. If William has lost his memory, then maybe he's in treatment there. Maybe Joe is at the store. He said he was cared for at the hospital. I guarantee Sarah was a patient too. I'm also sure our Suburban has been seized now. We'll have to convince someone to take us there."

"We can't get far on foot, that's for sure," Roxy said, blinking in surprise at the wetness on her temple. "Jesus. Am I bleeding?"

I looked over, feeling the same on my face. "It's starting to snow."

SEVENTEEN

It became clear almost immediately why we'd heard so many repeated warnings; why everyone from the young man at the car rental to Sarah at the inn and even the man who just tried to kill us, had cautioned us about the storm. By the time we reached downtown Argentum, the snow fell not in sheets, but in buckets, camouflaging the storefronts in walls of white.

Roxy looked over her shoulder, seeing no sign of police lights. "Hope that scumbag gets frostbite to go with the pain in his eyes. If he has a phone, he's called his boss—or whomever the suit is—to tell what happened. If it wasn't snowing like this, we couldn't even walk this out in the open. Watch your step, the last thing either of need is to break a hip right now. Though mine hurts like the dickens."

"I knew what that man at the police station meant when he said he didn't want my family to endure another tragedy. I just didn't have a plan to get away. Thank God you did."

"I knew I had mace inside my purse, and that was the extent of my plan. We're lucky all they really wanted was our phones."

We could barely see the outlines of the mostly abandoned buildings, looming in the snow like gray sentinels.

"Looks like Joe's shop is closed. We have to get to a phone. In fact, we need to do that right now, before anything else."

"We'll stop in Scotty's, use theirs. It should be right here. . . ."

The "closed due to snow," sign on the door was laminated and worn from frequent use.

"You know it's bad when the bar closes." Roxy breathed into her hands.

"That inn is old. It must have a landline phone somewhere that still works in this weather. We aren't far."

We made to the end of the boardwalk and looked across the street. Even in the pummeling snow, we could see the lights of the police cars parked in front of the hotel.

"Fried Chicken must have radioed in," Roxy said.

"I didn't see anywhere else open."

"I saw a bunch of trash cans out behind the inn. Let's see if we can sneak in. If not, we'll find another plan. But right now, we have to get inside somewhere, and it's the only place open. That's our first priority. We'll freeze out here. We were stupid not to buy some kind of parkas at the airport; these coats we're wearing are made for football weather in Tennessee."

I took Roxy's arm again. We walked across the street and down an alley, the accumulation preventing us from moving as fast as I wanted. As we emerged behind the stores, we braced ourselves to walk directly into the snow, shielding our eyes the best we could.

There was already an inch of snow on the trashcans and on a maroon Voyager van parked behind the inn. In the ferocious winds, a screened door repeatedly slapped against its wood frame. My face hurting now, I held the screen door while Roxy slowly turned the handle of the main door.

The hallway inside was dark, and the doors to the other rooms were shut. We listened for sound of voices but heard nothing.

Roxy immediately tried to open the door to one of the rooms, finding it locked. As she moved on to the next, someone turned down the hallway. I held my breath as the person stopped, and then approached cautiously.

"What have you two done?" Sarah whispered. "Why are the police looking for you?"

"Listen, we just need a phone," Roxy said.

"The phones don't work in this weather." She looked back down the hallway while fumbling with the keys in her hands.

"Of course phones work when it snows. It only started falling a few minutes ago."

"That's not what happens here. Everything shuts down: phone, internet. That's why the man who rents this room hoofed it out before the storm for his girlfriend's house. He knows there's no contact after the weather gets bad. I see his van is still out back," she said, looking over her shoulder and opening the door to her right. "He won't even know some-body's been in his room. Come in here."

We followed her into a room where laundry sat in piles. "You have to stay in here; they've already been up in your room. They're still here, outside on the porch, smoking."

"Your landline phones must work," Roxy whispered.

She shook her head. "We got rid of the landline phones at the inn. No use for them anymore. I don't know anyone who has them."

"That ancient technology shouldn't have been abandoned

by your generation," Roxy scowled. "A good old-fashioned cord would save our asses right now."

"The officers won't even say why they want to find you. What did you do?"

"We didn't do anything. I'm here to find my grandson, and my friend is here to help me. And we found him. Today. In this town. But he didn't recognize me."

"Did you understand that?" Roxy leaned in to Sarah. "Her own grandson didn't recognize her, because he didn't remember her. He didn't even know his own name."

Her eyes darted back and forth.

"We have to get to him," I said, trying to stay calm. "I don't know anything about you, Sarah, but Roxy said you don't have much of a memory either. I don't know what's happening in this town, but my grandson is just like you. Could he be at the hospital here?"

"I don't know, but this is making me too nervous. Stay here, I have to go back up front. Don't come out. My boyfriend should be over soon. He might know what to do."

She slipped out, and Roxy shook her head. "Lynn, we have to get out of here. Now."

"I won't leave him. I can't, Roxy."

"The roads are going to be impassable soon, Lynn. There aren't any phones. Even if Tom were starting to look for you, there's no cell towers to trace our phones. We will be trapped here, and they already tried to off us once."

I hugged myself, rubbing my hands up and down my arms. Roxy walked over to the desk, rummaging around. She then moved over to the dresser.

"What are you doing?"

She slid a pair of keys out from behind an ashtray. "It can't be that easy."

"What are you talking about?"

"Our ride is here. At least I hope it is. The van parked out back. It's a Voyager, and Sarah mentioned that the guy who rents this room drove a van. Don't you pay attention to this stuff? And these look like van keys. We're giving it a shot. Let's go."

"You go. But I cannot—I will not—leave here without William."

"No one knows where we are, Lynn. We get out, we find a phone, and one call to Tom will have the FBI, the CIA, and maybe even the armed forces here. We know the hospital is here. William must be there. But we can't just bust in and try to find him, Lynn. It's too risky. If they find us again—"

"Please go, Roxy. Please. You're right. You have to get help. And the roads are going to get worse. Please, go. Go now." I took Roxy's hands. "You understand, right? You understand I can't go without him."

"We have to go. It doesn't make sense to stay here."

"It does. I will make Sarah tell me more. I'll find out the location of the hospital. By the time you get back with help, I'll have convinced her to spill it."

Roxy glared and pointed. "You stay hidden. Lock yourself in here if you have to. I'll find a phone, and I'll come back for you."

"I know you will. Please be careful. We don't get a lot of snow in Nashville."

"Hell, I drive a pickup with four-wheel drive. I don't even know if these are his keys. Stealing a car is a new one, even for me."

She gave me a quick, fierce hug and went to the door, opening it gently. "Stay in here," she said, and slipped out.

I hurried over to the window, parting the heavy curtains.

To my relief, I could still see the van through the blinding snow. I didn't dare breathe as Roxy's hunched-over form scurried through the snow and held out the keys. The van blinked its lights in recognition.

She clambered inside and fired up the engine. At first, she clearly gunned it too hard. It lurched and nearly knocked over the trashcans. Then it slowly backed up and quietly moved down the alley.

"Where's your friend?"

I flinched as Sarah stepped through the door. "She's trying to find a phone."

"She went out in this? I'm telling you, there's no phones that will work."

"She took our car."

"And left you here? The officers said you would be on foot."

"She knows I won't leave my grandson."

Sarah looked back at the door. "The police were gone when I went up front. I . . . want to talk to my husband about this. Just stay here."

She again slipped out, and I turned once more to the window. Thinking of Roxy navigating the unfamiliar streets, I made the sign of the cross. I then whispered the Hail Mary, picturing a boy standing somewhere in this town, maybe looking out at the snow too, wondering about the strange lady who hugged him so tight and called him William.

How long had my grandson been in this horrible town? How many other people without memories are here, their families oblivious to the fact that they're alive? Obviously one of the Researchers had enough information about this place to start writing that poem all those decades ago.

If it was meant was a guide, how it is Steven hadn't known that, all those years ago? Fast-forward forty years, and he was set to take

me here from that hotel room, before the FBI burst in. He'd even
created that encrypted map, just in case we were separated.

Anger churned in my chest. Either Steven was telling the truth, that he'd just recently learned the truth about Argentum, or there had been decades of lies—

I suddenly looked back at the door.

Sarah said she wanted to talk to her husband about this. But she had referred to him as her boyfriend when we first came into the room.

I should have caught on to that quicker. *You don't realize it yet, but you're going to explain everything to me, young lady.*

I eased towards the door, slowly opening it to the dark hallway. I could hear static of some kind, and then a clicking. The unmistakable sound of radio communication came from down the hall.

"I don't know, Mark. I know she's driving that maroon Voyager. Over," Sarah said in a whisper.

"I can't hear you, Sarah, speak up. Over."

Reflected in the window, I could see Sarah leaning on the counter, a two-way radio in her hand.

"I can't talk much louder. She's got to take Singer Street and then Main Street. I gotta go."

When she put down the radio, I emerged, my eyes dazed in anger. "How could you?"

She gasped. I shook my head. "How could you!"

"She shouldn't have stolen that van! I didn't have a choice! They were going to find out, and then they'd know I knew! I can't go to jail, I just started to have a life!"

"Don't you want to know? Don't you want to know what happened to you? What happened to all of you?"

"It doesn't make sense, what you're saying!"

"I only want to find my grandson! Don't you wonder if someone ever came looking for you? And *this* is what you do?"

"Please. Stay here and talk to the police, they will help you—"

I turned and rushed down the hallway.

"Where are you going?" she cried out, stepping around the counter. "Miss, don't go out there!"

I reached the end of the hall and flew through the back door, the snow temporarily blinding me. Without hesitation, I plunged into the white.

EIGHTEEN

It took two steps to realize the insanity of what I had done.

The snow that had swirled and blurred before was nothing to the whiteout conditions that now pummeled the town. I could see nothing, not even the trash cans that Roxy had almost knocked down. I reached back to touch the wall of the inn as some kind of proof that the entire world wasn't lost in white. I used its wooden surface to navigate away from the door. If Sarah was still calling out my name, she was drowned out in the oppressive howl of the winds.

I reached the edge of the building. Were the security officers on their way? Were they tracking Roxy instead? Was she far enough away by now that they couldn't follow?

The temperature felt as if it had dropped ten degrees. I gauged the distance between the inn and the first building on the boardwalk as ten feet at best. But it may have well been a thousand yards away. If I lost my sense of direction, even for a moment, I could wander into the street and never find my way. But the alternative was to stay and wait for the officers to find me.

I forced myself to imagine William again, standing in front of a window, watching the snow.

My fingertips left the building, and I stepped one foot directly in front of the other, convincing myself that it was as simple as following a line. I reached out with my right hand, not unlike the way I had as a girl trying to swim from one side of the YMCA pool to the other. I hadn't been brave enough then to open my eyes, so I swam blindly, holding my breath as long as I could, aiming for the other end. More times than not, my lungs gave out and I surfaced, opening my eyes to realize I was only inches from the edge.

I'd walked fifteen feet, hadn't I? I should have reached the stores now. *My God, I'd gone off course.* I kept reaching, with both hands now. Even with my thick gloves, my fingers ached in the cold. *Just touch something—*

I felt it, then, a fleeting surface. I waved my hands wildly, striking the wood post with such force that I gasped in pain. With my other hand I clung to it like a life preserver, reaching out for the wall.

I leaned against the cold wood and took several deep breaths. I inched along the wall, at last coming to the corner. The blinding wind was just as fierce here. *How can it blow in more than one direction?*

I continued feeling along the wall, noting a jut-out of shutters. I felt a door handle at my waist and shook it frantically, finding it locked.

You are going to die here.

Keep moving. Don't stand still. Think of William.

I felt along the storefronts. Even the abandoned buildings' shutters were locked tight. I passed the empty laundromat and approached the general store. *Please let there be a light on, please let someone still be inside.*

I was met again with tightly closed shutters and a deadbolted door. I leaned my forehead against the wood. This was it. Climbers was the last of the stores on the row. I didn't dare cross the street to the other businesses, all of which were already closed.

My skin started to hurt. The temperature must have dropped again. I wanted to sit down, huddle in my coat against the elements. But I knew I needed to keep moving, keep the blood circulating. How long before hypothermia would set in—?

The roar of an engine and two blaring lights momentarily shone through the snow at the end of the boardwalk. Gears shift loudly and ice crunched.

"Wait!" I cried out, daring to hurry alongside what remained of the wall. I slipped a bit and caught myself on the edge of a shutter. "Wait!"

The headlights began to diminish as the truck went in reverse. I stepped out away from the wall and waved my arms, scuffling a few inches along the wood floor.

I misjudged, and dropped off the edge.

Waves of pain shuddered through my kneecap as I landed. The headlights were now pointed in another direction, and I could barely make out the cab of the truck. I cried out as I forced myself to stand and shuffle through the foot of snow now on the ground over to the truck window, slamming my palm hard against the glass.

"Jesus Christ!" Said a muffled voice from within.

"Wait!" I whimpered.

"Good God, who's out there?"

The door opened and a man in a red-checked hat with flaps over his ears looked out at me, astonished, with ice-blue eyes under the rim of his hat.

"Joe!"

"Miss Lynn?" said the proprietor of Climbers, sliding out

of the truck. He helped me stay upright as I hissed in pain, holding my knee.

"What in God's name are you doing out here?" He put my arm around his shoulder and helped me limp around the plow of the truck and over to the passenger door. He practically lifted me into the seat, and hurried back around.

He got in and shut the door, turning up the heat. "What are you doing?"

My eyes closed in pain. "I had to see if any of the stores were open."

"Why? What in the world were you needing that badly that you had to come out in this storm?"

"I needed to find a phone."

"And you thought you'd take a stroll? That was a pretty damn stupid thing to do. I closed up hours ago, but left some propane tanks here that I needed. If I hadn't needed to come back so desperately, you would have been up shit creek, lady. Have you lost your mind?"

I slowly looked to him. "I found my grandson. My friend has gone to get help. I won't bother telling you everything that's happened, but I have to try to get to him."

"You found your boy?"

I nodded. Joe leaned his wrist on the steering wheel. "Well, where is he, then? Why isn't he with you?"

"Because he didn't remember me."

When he didn't respond, I cautiously turned back to him. He was staring out the windshield. "He didn't remember?"

"What's happening in this town? Why can't my grandson remember me? Why do you not have a memory? Why does Sarah up at the inn not have a memory? And why would the police go to such lengths to get us out of town?"

"The police?" The lines around his eyes creased.

"I found my grandson with other children at the park, and some woman boarded him on a bus and called for police. Some men showed up and took me and my friend Roxy into custody, and then we were told we needed to leave immediately. They clearly had other plans for us, and Roxy got us away. Now the police are looking for us."

"Argentum doesn't have a police department. We have one officer, Chief Max, but he's a good ten years older than me. And there's Milford, but he's not even full time. Was it those two old boys who took you into custody?"

I hugged myself, feeling suddenly colder. "The men I met were not old. These were young men, in dark uniforms."

Joe muttered a curse under his breath. "I've seen them before. Only once. I worried this might happen, when you showed up asking about your missing grandson. I tried to discourage you. I hoped you and your friend would leave. I guess you've probably figured out you're not the first who's come here looking for someone."

"It was you, wasn't it? Who left that warning note in my room."

He sighed. "Like I said, I tried to discourage you."

"Whoever came here looking before . . . did the police take them away too?"

He turned the wipers to a faster setting as the snow began to pile up on the windshield. "It was a while ago. I don't know what happened to them. They were a couple, I guess. Young. Glasses. Tried to act natural. Said they were new to town. Wanted to know if I knew other new arrivals, so they could join a 'newcomers' group. Once they warmed up to me, they started showing me pictures of some people they were looking for. Said they were some kind of researchers or something."

I swallowed. "You called the police?"

"No. I didn't recognize any of the people in their photographs, and they left. They made the rounds, like you did. Not four hours later, I saw them hauled out of Scotty's over there, by some cops I'd never seen before and two others wearing suits. I met up with some of the old boys at the bar later, and they said some officers just came in and seized them. The regulars at Scotty's thought they were out-of-town cops with some agents from the Colorado Bureau of Investigation, which explained the black suits."

If it were possible, I felt even colder. "What happened to them?"

He shook his head. "Don't know. Honestly, didn't think much about it until you came along. I got a bad feeling . . . you seemed so nice. Not like that couple, you could tell they were only a bunch of academics. They never even said why they were looking for those people, never said they were missing. But it started to add up a bit after you left that first time. I didn't want anything to happen to you."

"Are you afraid of these . . . officers . . . too?"

"I don't even know who they are. And even if I did, am I afraid enough to turn you over to them? The answer is no."

"Because Sarah up at the inn certainly is afraid. She called one of them to let them know my friend left town. I'm sure they're back at the inn now, looking for me."

"Good God, Sarah." He whistled. "Nice girl, but as nervous as a whore in church. Forgive the language. The medical center helped her find a good job, and I think she even dates some nurse at the hospital. She brought him into the store once. How the world would she even know those poser cops?"

"They didn't seem like posers to me. And I'm worried to death about my friend, who drove off to find help. And my grandson; I know he's here. Could it be that he's a patient at that the medical center you've mentioned, just like you were?"

Joe exhaled through his nose. "I saw a few kids when I was in the hospital. Not many, though. You said your grandson was put on the bus by a woman? Was she a lady who looked like she had at least twenty years on us? Miss Cliff her name?"

"Yes! That's what William called her. And before she called the police or security or whatever they are, she told me to leave now. Like she was afraid for me."

"Verna Cliff is not the friendliest of folks in town, and she's a closet alcoholic. But she's in charge of the small day care for the hospital kids. Even though she's got to be in her late eighties—shoot, maybe even nineties—she still lives on her own. She actually stays a few houses down from me."

"Joe," I began, "I already have risked my best friend's life. I cannot fathom the idea of getting someone else getting in trouble. I promise you, I will tell no one that you took me to her house. But I would be forever grateful if you would. She tried to warn me. I have to find out why."

His response was a downshift of the gears, and the truck glided into the snow, the plow slowly descending. "If it weren't this nasty outside, we'd be there in five minutes. I'll get us there in seven."

"I can't thank you enough."

"Given my ornery tendencies, I can only imagine I must have been quite the troublemaker in whatever young life I had before this one, so I really don't mind kicking up the dirt once in a while. Even though that couple was strange, I got a bad feeling when those cops arrested them. I don't like that it happened to you too, especially now knowing that you, and maybe those other two, came here to find somebody they loved. Maybe I'm just jealous, because no one ever came to find me."

"You don't remember anything? At all?"

"Blank as a clean chalkboard. Sometimes a word or a first name will sound somewhat familiar, but that's it."

"And your whole life it's been that way?"

"My whole life. I woke up in White Crest as a teenager, not knowing anything. That first year, they gave me the name Ethan. But it never felt right. Then one of the nurse's names was Joseph, and it just felt right to me, felt authentic—more so than Ethan. So I took that name, and forty some years later, I'm Joe the snowplow guy."

"I'm not sure how old you are, but I'm guessing you're about my age. You must have friends, family, somewhere."

"I assume I do, but where? No one ever came looking, and I have no memories before White Crest. The hospital said I was found by the side of the interstate, lying in a ditch. No injuries besides a knot on the back of my head. No car accident, nothing. Who can say? I don't match any missing-persons cases in Colorado or anywhere else that I could find. Seems like to me someone wanted to get rid of me, or I was involved in something bad and ended up dumped. Who knows? Good doctors up there at the medical center, though. They taught me everything to act like a human being again. It all came back quickly, and for that I'm grateful. I'm sure your boy's getting good treatment. How it is you knew he would be here?"

"It's a long story. Let's just say an old friend thought he might be in this town. But I'll be honest with you: I had no idea there was even a hospital here. And how can a hospital even exist in this remote of an area?"

"It's too small to be a true hospital. Amnesia is their specialty. Maybe I was a mean kid who got drunk and blacked out and conked my head. Again, who knows? I owe a lot to the good people up there. And I never had to pay a dime. I guess

they assumed I didn't have health insurance, since I didn't even
have a driver's license. Some of us need to even be retaught
how to read, how to walk. I'm lucky, I guess; I picked up everything pretty quickly."

"That's where my grandson has to be. I have to find a way
to get in. I should just bypass going to see the teacher. Could
you just drive me to the medical center?"

"I'd take you right now, but you have to have a code to get
in after hours, and the staff is mostly gone this time of night,
especially in this weather. And they change the code from
time to time; there's a lot of turnover. Miss Cliff has the cur-
rent code, that's for sure. I've been gone from White Crest for a
long time, and honestly, I'm in no hurry to go back. The loneliness, the confusion, the anger, you can't imagine what it's like
to have no memory. And honestly—most of the patients don't
leave. They can't. They can barely function. Can't comprehend
light switches, microwaves, even straws. Sarah's the only one
I've ever known in the past couple of years who could even
hold a job."

"So it's not only memory problems the patients have?" I
thought of how damaged William may be. *If I could relearn, so
could he. . . .*

"Oh, it's memory problems, all right. They can't remember
their past, and many of them can't remember what happened
yesterday. It's like dementia, I think. It's awful."

"Why would my grandson be there? Be in this town?" I
clenched my hands together. "How did he get here?"

"Can I ask what happened to him?"

"I don't know if you'd even believe me if I told you. The last
time anyone saw my grandson—William is his name—was in
the forest behind our house. He simply vanished. My husband . . . is a politician. We all feared he'd been kidnapped."

"Obviously, I never get to see the news. Now I wish I did. And where do you live again?"

"Tennessee. Nashville."

He whistled low. "William disappeared from Tennessee and now he's in the Rocky Mountains? My God . . ."

We drove in silence for a while through the growing snow-drifts. *You're wondering where you came from*, I thought as I glanced at Joe's puzzled face. Maybe somebody did want to find you.

Joe slowly applied the brakes. "Here we are."

He pulled up next to a row of houses covered in the falling snow. "That's Miss Cliff's house, with the light on. My house is only three down. I'll walk you up, introduce you."

"Joe, I'm so sorry, but I have another huge favor to ask you."

"Ask away."

"I'm very worried about my friend Roxy. I told you she drove off out of town to try and find a phone to call my husband. Would you mind looping back to see if she made it out OK? I wouldn't ask, but you seem quite capable of navigating the snow."

"I start the clearing on the main drag, so I have to go that way anyway," he said with a smirk. "But I have a feeling that you don't want me to be there when you talk to Verna."

"It will be easier to turn me away if I have an escort. She can't leave me outside in this."

"Well, she might. She's pretty tough. Even though those kids could blow on her and she'd fall over, I've seen her tear into them from time to time. Well, if she does kick you out, or she won't answer the door, go down three houses, mine is 333, the one with the dead plant out front. Keys underneath that. Snow's calming a bit, but it could pick up anytime. Don't you let her toss you out if the snow kicks back up; you could have died back there. Anyhow, I'll be back. I'll take the road all the way to the interstate to make sure your friend isn't in a ditch somewhere. If you're not at my house when I get back from my rounds, I'll snoop around and see if you made it into her house."

"God bless you, Joe," I said, opening the door.

"Three houses down, Miss Lynn!" he pointed.

I gave him a grateful wave and stepped down, realizing the snow was still fierce but not as blinding as before. Thankfully, there was a light on in the front room. Mustering up my most pathetic face, I reached out and rang the doorbell. When no one answered, I knocked on the glass. The hallway beyond remained dark.

I shivered, walking down the porch and crunching through the snow to approach a bay window. The curtains were parted, and I could see legs propped up in a recliner, a hand laying limp over the armrest.

I rapped on the glass. When the hand didn't even flinch, I pounded with my fist.

The teacher from the park sat up suddenly and looked around, disoriented. I knocked again, and the woman turned to the window, her wig slightly askew. She stared at me as I waved desperately. Miss Cliff's mouth gaped a little, and muttered a series of curse words that I could easily make out.

She pulled the wooden lever on the chair and slowly climbed out, glaring as she shuffled into the front hall. I hurried around to the porch once again and waited by the door. The light in the hall came on, and the curtains on the small window in the door parted.

"Are you insane?" she asked through the glass.

"Please, I need to speak with you."

"How in God's name did you end up here?" The woman's wizened eyes narrowed, blinking rapidly.

"Please, it's very cold."

"You need to get back in your car and drive away."

"I don't have a car. I have nowhere else to go." I forced a dramatic trembling of my lips.

"Jesus Christ."

I whispered a silent prayer of thanks as I heard the dead bolt turn.

"The only reason I'm even letting you in is because there's no earthly way anyone saw you come here. Get in here quickly. Jesus, you'd think the wife of a senator would know better than to come out in the middle of this mess."

I was so astonished, I stopped pulling back my hood midway. "You know who I am?"

"I didn't at first," she said groggily, the ice in her glass clinking as she moved across the runner lying across the wood floors in the front hall. As she entered the adjoining living room, she drew together the already small openings in the curtains.

She slowly turned around. "But you're her, aren't you. You're Roseworth's wife."

"You know who I am. You have to help me get to William. Please."

"I don't have to help you do anything, lady."

She went to a decanter on a side table and refilled her drink. Her hand shook a bit as she poured the bourbon to the rim. "And he goes by the name of Al . . . Alan . . . now."

My God, she's completely drunk. "I don't understand. If you know who I am, why did you put William on that bus?"

"I didn't know who were you were then," she said, moving

with the speed of a turtle over to a footstool covered in magazines. "And I tried to warn you. But when you were making
such a scene, you cooked your own goose. Had to call security.
Dammit!" Her foot caught the edge of the thick rug and she
teetered, careful not to spill a drop from her drink. I instinctively reached out, fearing one fall would mean the end of the
woman. But she righted herself, reached down, and messily
slid the magazines on the top to the floor. "There. That's how
I found out."

"The Senator's Nightmare," the cover of *People* magazine
shouted, featuring a picture of my husband and our family
from the news conference, with William's picture in a smaller
square beneath them.

"I always thought I had seen Alan—or William, as you call
him—before. When I came home today, I started going through
my magazines, and I do love *People*, even with their stupid
Kardashian covers—"

"Where is he?" I moved towards her. "Please take me to
him, Miss Cliff."

"It's Verna, calling me Miss Cliff doesn't make you any
younger, sweetheart," she said, easing herself into a maroon-
colored La-Z-Boy, taking another long drink. "He doesn't remember you. And he won't ever remember you."

"It doesn't matter. I have to get to him. I have to get him
home."

"You don't get it. He is home. The only home he knows.
He's just now starting to sleep through the night—"

"You know he's my grandson! Why didn't you tell
anyone?"

"I think you're aware we're in the middle of a blizzard and
our phones aren't working. Otherwise, you wouldn't be here.
And it's not like they're going to let him leave."

"Who's not going to let him leave?"

"The same people who sign your husband's paychecks. Listen, have a seat. Do you want a drink—?"

"I would love a drink," I lied. As she got out of her chair for the side table where several glasses surrounded a bourbon decanter, I sat on my hands to keep them from reaching out and shaking her. I thanked her when she handed me the glass, and pretended to sip. The smell was so intense I almost gagged.

"I know you want to help William, you've already done so much for him." I spoke slowly. "And he looked healthy at the park; I'm so thankful to you."

"I love all my kids."

"It's really obvious. You're a godsend to them. But please, Verna, please. I need for you to tell me where he is, how I can get to him—"

"Now you listen to me," she brandished her bent index finger as I'd seen her do to corral the children. "I'm taking a real chance even talking to you. Don't know how you got away from security, but since you're still here, it means you're on the run. And don't think for a moment they've contacted your husband. Plus, he doesn't mean shit out here. You don't understand the mistake you've made coming to Argentum. Your husband is nothing here. *You're* nothing here."

"It doesn't matter whom I'm married to. I could be married to a truck driver for that matter. All that really matters is he's my grandson—"

"All *they* care about is that Alan—I mean William—will never leave."

"Who? The people at the hospital?"

"Oh, for God's sake, Argentum doesn't really have a hospital, Mrs. Roseworth," she snapped, finishing off her bourbon and quickly filling up the glass again.

"Of course there's a hospital—"

"It's no town either," she waved her hand. She downed another glass, and refilled quickly.

At that moment, I was thankful I was sitting down. "It's an old silver-mining town—"

"That they made into a military base. Doesn't matter what I tell you, you'll never leave here. They won't let you. Even the townies, outside of myself, don't know this whole place is basically a military prison. And anyone who ends up at the section of the base that's used as a hospital never leaves."

As frustrated as I was dealing with a person who was just moments ago clearly passed out, and had drank three additional bourbons in the last five minutes, I was grateful for the liquor. She was talking, divulging more than she would have sober. At the park, Verna was rigid, protective. Obviously, anticipating being trapped inside her home for days meant there was no limit on how much she could drink.

"How do I get to him?"

"Honestly, I don't even know if he's still there." She polished off the glass, reaching again for the decanter.

"What do you mean?" I moved to the edge of the chair.

"They know you're here in the town somewhere. They'll want him out, shipped off to one of the other bases. You might be in luck, though. The storm might have kept him here. But I saw Alan—William—before I left for the night. His room was packed up. Poor thing."

"They would move him just to keep me from finding him?"

"Jesus, you are naïve. I can't blame you, I guess. I've been around for so long, I understand how things work. Hell, all I've ever known is this town. Thought it was a pretty great place growing up. Even if my old auntie wasn't the nicest of people, she still took good care of me. All I ever knew was

Auntie. Couldn't have been easy taking on some three-year-old who nobody wanted."

"Verna, please—"

"Auntie always said my mother must have been a real degenerate, dropping me off at the fire station like she did. Good thing Auntie had a thing for the fire chief and he liked her pancakes, 'cause she's the one who found me outside the fire hall door while delivering breakfast—"

"Your auntie showed the kind of kindness to you that you, in turn, showed to the kids here, and my William in particular. Your auntie took care of you. She would be so proud of you, of what you've done. All I want is to do the same for my grandson."

"It's always been my job to protect those kids, make them feel safe after what they've been through. I don't handle the adults, but those kids are *my* kids, and I take care of them."

"I can't thank you enough for taking care of him all this time," I said, knowing I was laying it on thick. "But Verna, I don't understand. What happened to William? How did he end up here? Why doesn't he remember me?"

"You wouldn't believe me if I told you." She threw back her head to shoot the rest of the drink.

This is more than a binge. This is how she copes. "I would believe you."

"I don't think so."

"Was he abducted?" I asked carefully, seeing the woman's eyebrows rise lazily. "By something that most people . . . don't even believe in?"

"But you do?" Verna asked quietly, refilling and taking another swig.

I swallowed. "I've seen a lot."

"Oh, you haven't seen anything. You haven't seen people

show up in a field, some wearing suits, some wearing jeans, some wearing hijabs. Kids, too. Your boy. All in a field behind White Crest."

"A field?" I asked, horrified at the thought of little William standing in the cold, lost and confused.

Verna was starting to drink slower now. "He's a sweet boy, that grandson of yours. All the kids love him, they just flock around him. Took to me real quick, too. Now I understand why. He has a maw maw who loves him. Never had kids of my own, so they're all my grandkids."

"Then you know how I feel. Of course you know."

"The docs always give the line—and I bought it for a long time—that the patients come here from all over the country to get help. And once they became functional, they'd return to their families. Except, they weren't coming from all over the country, it turns out, just from a field out back. And their families never came to get them; they just get driven away from the hospital. And I never see them again."

She sighed. "I never expected to do it my whole life. I felt so sorry for them, still do. But about ten years ago, I wanted to retire. At the beach. I was too old to drive in the snow anymore. That's when they told me I couldn't leave. *'No, Miss Cliff, we can't lose you. No, Miss Cliff, the kids need you.'* And they sat me down and showed me what was *really* happening. I didn't even have a choice. They even set up this new house for me so I could get to work easier. It became very clear I wasn't leaving. Hell, I'd been there longer than anybody else. Everyone else at that damn place leaves after a year or so, even the docs. They say they can't handle it, or they're too sick to work anymore. They won't even get close to the kids. But honestly, I couldn't leave my babies. Poor things don't even realize they don't have amnesia. None of them do. Or did."

"What's happened to them then?"

"Their memories are straight up gone when they come back. Blank as a slate, standing there in the field. But then, there are the special ones," she said, raising her wrinkled index finger. "Those are the ones who present a problem."

"Special ones?"

"They don't know why for sure. But unlike the adults, a few of the kids *remember*. I've heard the docs whisper—'cause they don't think I can hear—that it's a genetic thing that their memories are stronger than whatever those bastards in the cosmos do to them. And if those kids come back, well, the Suits have all kinds of good drugs to make those memories, and everything else, go away. Remember that drug that Michael Jackson OD'd on? They love that one, cleans out those memories real good. Can't risk those kids getting out and talking and causing a mass panic."

I was so horrified all I could do was watch her sip.

"All those families . . . they deserve to know what happened. What's been done to them," I finally said.

"They wouldn't want to know." Verna licked her lips. "They're vegetables, most of the grownups. Whatever they do to wipe out their memories, most adults can't handle. Only a few even learn to talk again. The kids, for some reason, are different. They can learn what they've forgotten. There are very few exceptions with the adults, like that young Sarah up at the inn, and, of course, Joe."

Verna scowled after a sizable slurp of her drink. "Is he the one who ratted me out? Is that how you got here? Caught the eye of that old fart, and he dumped you off?"

"I swear to you, I will tell no one that I was here."

"They'll kill me, you know," she said, her eyes bulging in her attempt to stay awake.

I leaned forward. "They wouldn't kill you."

"Why do you think they won't let me retire? They won't let me *leave*, Mrs. Roseworth. And they can't erase my memories because they need me to take care of the kids. You still don't get it? If word of this gets out—what will the world think? That those assholes in DC have known about the abductions for decades? Mass chaos, lady. It's why your boy won't leave. It's why *you* won't ever leave."

"You don't have to do anything more than what you've already done. I need to know how to get to the hospital."

"No need for much security. No one remembers anything, so they have nowhere to go. There's no way you'll get in. You do have to have a code to get in. And it changes every month."

"If I could just get that code . . . And just an idea of how to get to the hospital."

"Hell, you won't survive walking. It's below zero out there."

"Joe should be back soon. . . ."

"There may not be that much time." She looked out at the windows in the dining room. "The snow is letting up a bit. They're going to move him."

"Let me have your car. I beg you. I'll never find him again. You said you considered all them your kids. There's nothing more important than William getting home."

Verna took a long slurp. "What do you think will happen? Alan—I mean William—won't know his parents. He won't know you. You are jusht a shtranger to him. . . ."

Oh God, don't fall asleep. "Then I'll spend the rest of my life reminding him that he's ours, and we never stopped looking for him."

The teacher narrowed her eyes and then closed them, leaning back into the chair. "They'll find you," she said, her eyes closing. "And you'll be like the rest of them."

"May I take your car?"

"My car is under two feet of snow . . . you're shit out of luck. And you . . . you can't go my way . . . our way . . . you'll get lost . . ."

"What do you mean?"

"You'll never find him," she said, yawning. "I can't even remember the number of his room . . . they probably moved him to the second floor. You'll never find him. . . ."

"Tell me the code. How do you get to the hospital?"

"Hell, I don't remember the code." She wiped her mouth.

"How do you get in?" I wanted to shake her.

"First thing . . . I do . . . when I walk up . . . put it on the fridge. First thing . . . every time . . . I walk up."

"Walk up?"

"First . . . thing," she muttered.

I started to ask more, then held my breath. After a few moments, the woman's mouth opened a bit, and her chest began to rise and fall deeply.

I fought the urge to slap her. She was so far gone, even if I woke her, she'd be incoherent.

Make some coffee. Make her drink it.

I went to the hall, looking around frantically. The green lights from an ancient microwave revealed the kitchen to the right. I entered and turned on a light above the stove.

The light illuminated an olive-green fridge. On its door were a few magnets, including a small dry-erase board with a dangling marker attached. Scrawled hastily on the board were the numbers 16-0-19-8-25-30.

I found a pen in a junk drawer and wrote the numbers on the back of my hand. But what good would the numbers do if I couldn't even get to the hospital? I could wait for Joe to return, but that could be another hour. And if Verna was right, and they were preparing to move William when the storm broke, I had only a small window of time to find him.

Seeing no coffeemaker, I hurried out of the kitchen. Verna had said that when she came in tonight she had written down the code, which meant she had to have gotten here through the snow. I walked down to a back door, hoping that she had been lying, that there was a covered car park, or maybe even a garage. Instead, I could just make out a Buick with snow tires parked around back, its fading blue paint barely visible under the mounds of snow.

Did they shuttle the workers back and forth? Was there some kind of hospital bus service that operated even in this weather? And if there was, what was I going to do? Put on one of Verna's wigs, throw on her coat, and call for a pick up?

I went back into the living room where she now snored softly. I hated to do it, but I found a purse on the closed lid of a piano. A row of pictures sat on top of the piano, watching as I violated a woman's most private of belongings.

Her wallet was mostly empty except for some cash and an ID that read "Verna Cliff. White Crest: child care." Nothing was written on the back.

I scavenged through the rest of the purse and found only an empty minature bottle of Bacardi at the bottom. I sighed, glancing at the photos witnessing my transgression.

It took me several moments to start breathing again.

In the center of the photos was one badly aged with time, yellowed on the edges, featuring a heavyset woman wearing an apron, with a small child on her lap. The woman appeared stern, clearly the auntie Verna had described. The girl on her lap had dark hair and a gap-toothed smile.

I had seen the girl before. Only a few days ago, sitting in the Nashville library, in an old photograph next to a newspaper article from August 5, 1934, about a girl who went missing from the woods behind my house.

That girl sat on Auntie's lap.

In the photos, Amelia Shrank turned eight, then ten, and finally became a teenager. But it was the photo of the Amelia as a young woman, probably in her midtwenties, smiling, leaning on a post, that bore a strong resemblance to Verna Cliff.

I covered my mouth with my hand while looking at Verna's slumbering body.

You don't know who you really are. That you once had a family so devastated by your disappearance that they made a grave for you in the woods where you vanished. That you, and me, and a hunter, and my grandson, and God knows how many others all vanished from the same clearing in those trees.

I doubt very much that you showed up on a firehouse stoop. I bet the military gave you to your auntie because they weren't equipped to deal with you. You weren't a baby—you were a three-year-old girl without a memory. I bet your auntie was the first in this town to start caring for a child who remembered nothing. And then so many kids and people started showing up, they had to build that hospital. . . .

I rushed back into the kitchen, scanning the refrigerator for phone numbers; anything to show how Verna got to the hospital in this weather. I searched the entire kitchen again. Nothing.

I started going through a utility drawer in desperation when I saw the boots by the pantry door. They'd clearly been tossed there and abandoned for the thick, plaid house shoes on Verna's feet. But there was no puddle, not even a drip of moisture on them.

I looked at the pantry door and saw it had a dead bolt.

I walked over, turned the bolt, and opened the door. Steps led down into the dark, barely illuminated by orange bulbs placed above a railing. The metal stairs went down far too deep to lead to just a basement.

The lights steadily increased in brightness. I could now make out the metal circular sconces holding the bulbs in place, and how, in a very clear, precise stamp, each was marked with the words, "Property of the U.S. Government."

NINETEEN

The tunnel at the bottom of the stairs extended in two directions, with metal casing on the floor, ceiling, and walls. My fears
were no longer fluid, no longer intangible; they were rooted in
this man-made tunnel buried underneath a town whose silver
mine shafts had been remade into bunker-style passageways.

Roxy was probably far along on the interstate now, closing
in on a gas station with a working phone. Whatever communication disruption occurred in the town when this kind of storm
hit, it couldn't happen all throughout the mountains. Once
Roxy reached Tom, nothing would stop him from getting here.

If Verna was right, my grandson would be gone when they
arrived.

I had to find William, convince him to come with me, and
find our way back to Verna's home. Even if she refused us, I
would have to beg her to let us through so we could hide in
Joe's house until the storm was over.

The tunnel stretched before me, with no indication which
way would lead to the hospital. I was terrible with directions
anyway, and I had no idea in which area of town the hospital
stood. All Joe had said was that it was on the outskirts.

Stepping around the stair lift that was obviously put in place to allow Verna easy passage up and down the long staircase, I moved into the tunnel, looking for any markings, any pattern of the lights that would indicate which direction to take. There appeared to be nothing—no arrows, no signs—nothing. And how did Verna get to the hospital? At the pace she moved, it would take her a day just to walk a mile. It didn't make sense.

Just like in the snowstorm. One foot in front of the other.

I chose left and started walking. *What if I encounter another security guard? What would I possibly say to explain myself? Did the houses of other hospital workers lead into this tunnel?* I could feel heat, but I was still so chilled I kept my hood up and my hands in my gloves.

I passed another stairwell identical to Verna's. At least hers had the stair lift, so it was clear which one I would need to take when I returned with William. If I returned with William—

The dead end came up so suddenly, I actually held up my hand to stop myself from walking right into the wall. Angrily, I hurried back down the opposite direction. How much time had I wasted?

Fifteen minutes later, another tunnel opened up to my right, snaking into a long darkness, again lit only by orange lights. *How many tunnels were down here? Had the military used the same shafts of the miners? Or did they do all this as the town slowly declined into near abandonment, the locals unaware of what was being dug beneath them? There had to be questions as to why the workers at the hospital never left their homes but somehow got to work every day—*

Stop it. Stop trying to make sense. Just find William.

I had no choice but trial and error. I could only guess the new tunnel headed towards town and the hospital was farther

out. But how far? Yards? Miles? It couldn't be; someone of
Verna's age couldn't walk that distance every day.

I kept walking down the tunnel and noticed in the near
distance how it began to expand quite dramatically, its walls
receding into the darkness beyond the reach of the meager
lights. The sound of my footsteps disappeared into the space
without an echo. As the far end of the tunnel came into view,
another metal staircase emerged, not off to the right or left, as
had the others, but in the center. The answer as to how Verna
arrived here each day was a golf cart parked to the side, right
by another stair-lift chair. Verna didn't walk to work. Someone
came to get her.

As I approached, I could see, at the top of the stairs, a door
leading to an upper level, somewhere above ground. I hurried
towards it, looking up at the now familiar orange lights above.

When I reached the first step, the sides of the hallway suddenly flared with fluorescent lights. I stumbled in surprise, seeing now how the orange lights at the top of the stairs were also
glowing brightly. I'd triggered a sensor of some kind.

A passing glance at the white lights coming from the walls
of the hall revealed the man staring at me.

The greenish pall of the fluorescents weren't coming from
sconces on the walls, but from rooms with glass doors. I was so
intent on reaching the stairs that I hadn't even noticed the dozens of doors stretching down the corridor, or the face of the
man looking out.

He was lying down, his head resting on some kind of bed.
I waited for him to react to me or speak. Instead, he blinked,
yet his blank expression remained the same.

I left the stairs and hesitantly stepped closer. Approaching
the door, I could see his eyes were unnaturally glassy, and
that he wasn't alone. Dozens of rows—no, maybe hundreds of

rows—of people on beds, all connected to tubing and machines, all dressed in white. All their eyes were open, faces either staring at the ceiling or turned to the side.

I stepped back to the middle of the tunnel, eyeing the doors, each with the same light. Did all of those doors lead to rooms full of comatose people?

I walked across the hall to a nearly identical sight, but this time, it was a young woman on the closest bed; beyond her were more rows of people. As she stared at the ceiling, I watched her chest rise and fall. An older man next to her appeared to be breathing as well. All had tubes going into their nostrils or mouths.

They're vegetables, Verna had slurred. They don't remember anything, Joe had said, not even how to tie their shoes.

William isn't like them. There's still time.

I propelled myself up the stairs, trying to ignore the pain in my knees. My heart was racing when I reached the top. This door had no window, no indicator of what lay beyond.

There was, however, a keypad.

I held up my hand to the orange light. My stomach sank as I saw how my hands had sweated in the gloves. The numbers were smudged a bit. I punched in 16-0-18-8-25-30.

The keypad flashed red.

I looked closer at my hand. Was that an 18 or 19? I tried it again. 16-0-19-8-25-30. No red flash, nothing. I looked closer at my hand, trying to recall the exact numeration—

The door unlocked and swung open an inch.

I pushed through it, momentarily relishing the familiar bright light of a hallway. Gone were the orange glow and the ghostly fluorescents, replaced with a stark white light illuminating well-traveled tile and undecorated walls.

I eased down the hall, looking all around for any signs of

life. Verna had said something about William being moved to the second floor. But he could be anywhere, and I had no idea how large the hospital was or even where I was in it.

If William had been taken from his usual room here, were the other children from the park still here? If I did find another child, could I, in good conscience, ask for help finding William and leave that child behind?

I came to a door with a black sign reading "Stairwell." I entered, cringing at the echo of my footsteps.

On the second floor, I peered out, seeing another empty hallway. I had no idea what time it was, but the storm must have emptied the place. The rooms here had no plates, only numbered plastic containers holding files and papers.

The windows in these doors were mostly dark, but as I walked, I saw one man sitting at a desk, his head resting on top of his arm. I stopped, wondering if I should knock. When he failed to move at all, I kept walking. Another window in another door revealed a woman standing directly in front of a wall, staring. I could feel the desolation without having to enter.

I started counting: twenty, forty, eighty rooms. I grew sadder with each step, as there were only first names on the folders; names likely assigned to them, like animals at the pound. I thought of Joe who, even without a memory, knew the name they'd first given him rang hollow.

William believes his name is Alan. Does that name sound wrong to him too?

I looked through each window, finding most rooms to be pitch black. If there was anyone inside, they were asleep. I kept moving. Room after room down the hall, no sign of anyone else awake. I prayed to Mother Mary, for soon I would have to start venturing into the darkness of each room, blindly looking for my grandson.

A faint light came from room 212. The lamp was bright enough, however, to show the red in the sheen of a boy's hair, sitting at the edge of the bed, wearing navy-blue pajamas, his knees pulled up tight.

I whispered a thanks to Mary, forcing my hands to stop shaking and reaching deep in my coat pocket, finding the one thing I couldn't bear to throw at the security officer who tried to kill us a few hours ago.

William turned when I opened the door and flinched when he saw me emerge. "Don't be afraid, William." I smiled, forcing back tears of relief. "Miss Cliff told me you'd be here."

William didn't move, looking so much like his mother that I found it difficult to speak. As I took a step closer, he slid a bit farther away on the bed.

"Honey, you don't have anything to be afraid of—"

"My name is Alan. Miss Cliff told me not to pay any attention to you. She said you were crazy."

"That's before she knew who I was. Now she knows, and she told me where you would be. That's how I found you. I'd like to show you who I am. Is that OK?"

He eyed me warily. I briefly glanced around the room, finding it completely empty. Two small bags were packed by end of his bed.

I took out the thin plastic photograph holder from my now-lost wallet and removed a single picture. "This is me and my husband, Tom. We live in a place called Nashville, Tennessee."

William looked at it briefly, and I put it away, bringing out another. "This is an old picture of my daughters. That's my youngest, Stella, there's Kate, and my oldest, Anne. Want to see my whole family?"

The boy shrugged, and I took out another picture. "Look at how many of us there are! Do you see all the boys?"

With that, William leaned in closer. "I only have grandsons. They are bigger now, including the baby. Do you want to see what the baby looks like, the one sitting in his Aunt Stella's arms?"

I swallowed and took out a final photograph. "This was taken last summer on the Fourth of July. That's Anne's family—that's her husband, Chris, and her sons Greg, Brian, and William."

William stared for a moment and then slowly reached out. I gave him the photo, letting him look closely. "That's you, my sweet boy. I know they call you Alan here. But your real name is William. William Grant Chance. You are seven and will turn eight this summer. And we've been looking for you for a long time."

"But I don't know you," he said, still looking at the picture.

"I know you don't, and that's OK," I eased onto the bed. "Maybe you will remember us one day. Your mom, your dad, your brothers, your aunts, and especially your grandpa, they all want you to come home. I'd like to take you there."

"I'm not supposed to leave my room. Plus, they told me I'm moving. They said I was leaving first thing in the morning. They said I'll like it where I'm going. They said it's warm."

"Well, where I live is really warm. We have a new minor-league baseball stadium, and even have two different water parks because it gets so hot in the summer."

"Two water parks?" William's eyes lit up, but then narrowed. "Miss Cliff said not to go anywhere."

"Maybe we can go see her right now, and while we're walking to her, I'll tell you more about your family."

His eyes softened. "You really are my grandma?"

I couldn't stop the tears from glistening in my eyes. "I am. And I have missed you every day."

"Can I keep the picture?"

"Of course. You can have all of them if you want."

"I just want this one. My shoes are by my suitcase and my coat is in the closet. Are we going outside?"

"I hope not. It's so cold!" I forced a smile, trying to appear casual. I opened the closet door and found the jacket. I knelt on the floor and opened the suitcase, finding a heavy sweater on top.

"I want to wear my jeans," he said, still staring at the photo.

I grabbed a collared shirt, jeans, a pair of socks, and a long-sleeved T-shirt.

"Do you have gloves?"

"On the hook by the door," he said, throwing off his pajama top and putting on his shirt. "Will I get to say goodbye to Miss Cliff?"

"I hope so. I know she'd like to see you before you go."

"Is Tennessee close to the mountains? I'll miss my friends. Especially Todd, he's funny. He wears red-high tops. I didn't want to move, but they said it was for my own good."

"I promise you, I will do everything I can for you to see any of your friends here again. But right now, I want to get you home."

"What if they don't want me, once they find out I don't re-member them?" he asked, slipping on his boots.

I wanted so badly to rush over and pull him into my arms. "Hon, we've all been waiting to see you for so long, it doesn't matter what you do or don't remember."

"Then why am I here? How did I get here? All everybody says here is that we don't have memories and they don't know where we came from. But somebody has to know. Why did it take you so long to find me?"

I reached out and touched his arm. "I didn't know where you were. Nobody did. And your parents would be here too, but I just figured it out first."

"Figured out what?" he asked, his sweater now over his head.

"Let's talk about all that when we get out of here. Can we go now?"

William clearly picked up on my nervousness. "I'm not supposed to leave my room, you know."

"Well, Miss Cliff told me where you would be. She knew I had to get to you. Should we go see her?" I asked, hating the lie.

"Sure," he shrugged.

"Let's go quietly." I put my hand on his back and carefully opened the door.

I led him out and we began to walk down the hall. With each door we passed, I fought the urge to grab him and run. He was coming willingly; I couldn't do anything to spook him. I didn't even dare hold his hand, although I wanted to desperately. I could see the sign for the staircase. We could be down to the first floor and out the door to the tunnel in a few minutes' time. *Roxy must have made the call by now, and Tom knows that William is here.* I did put my hand on his back, hoping the gesture would move his little legs faster. All we had to do was make it down—

"Mrs. Roseworth."

I closed my eyes. William quickly turned around, but I didn't need to. I recognized the voice.

TWENTY

The woman who I thought was my husband's press secretary, who once sat in my own kitchen giving us political advice, who then showed up in the FBI's raid of Steven's hotel room, was now wearing a black suit.

Deanna Ruck had her hair pulled back in a ponytail, just as she had when she drove me from the Murfreesboro motel back to Nashville. Walking up briskly behind her were two men dressed in white scrubs.

"Please let us go," I whispered, placing my hands on William's shoulders.

"I wish I could, Mrs. Roseworth," she said. "Hi Alan. We haven't met. But you know Josh and Rick. Josh is going to take you back to your room."

"But this lady says she's my grandma." He looked up at me. "She showed me pictures of my family. She says my name is William."

"I understand it's confusing," Deanna said with a sympathetic smile. "Tell you what: I need to talk to Mrs. Roseworth first, and then when we're done, we'll try to come to see you. OK?"

"Just let us go." I pulled William close. "I swear to you, I won't say anything."

"Mrs. Roseworth, you're only making this more difficult."

"She said my name is William," he grumbled with a sullen tone, pressing up against me.

It was that movement that made me grab William's hand and run for the door. As I seized the door handle, a strong grip clamped down on my arm. I tried to pull away, but the man held tight, closing the door with his other hand. The other tore William from my grasp.

"William!" I cried out, trying to yank my arm free, knowing the strength of the man would leave bruises.

"I'll come for you!" I struck out, trying to peel away from his grip. "Let me go!"

As I struggled, I saw William lift his hand towards me, his eyes wide with confusion, as he was carried back into his room.

"Right in there." Deanna motioned to a door across the hall. With a good one hundred pounds on me, the man led me with ease, despite my attempts to wrestle away. He opened the door and sat me down in a swivel chair resting by a row of file cabinets. Shelves lined the walls, filled with thick plastic binders.

"Give us a few minutes," she said, following us in. The man at last let go, giving me a stern look as he walked out.

"How can you be doing this?" I exploded, rubbing my wrist. "You know William's alive! You know he's my grandson! I thought you were an FBI agent! You're supposed to be protecting people like us—"

"That's exactly what I am doing, ma'am. There's only one person responsible for this situation, and it's you. I told you back in Tennessee to let this go. I told you what could happen. When we'd learned you and your friend suddenly decided to

skip town in the midst of your family's worst tragedy, I knew you'd disregarded my counsel.

"I suppose I should be grateful to that teenager in the airport terminal who tweeted out that he saw you. We've been monitoring all social media for you. He took one photo of you walking away, but failed to earn even a single retweet from his seven followers, or everyone would know you're here. That tweet, by the way, no longer exists anywhere, in case you thought someone in your family might find it. We had to fly a helicopter through that storm to get to you. Do you know how dangerous that was? Just to come and find you? I don't know how much Dr. Richards told you about Argentum, but you really made a mistake coming here."

"Made a mistake? What kind of person are you? You have seen yourself what this has done to my family. And you're telling me it was a mistake to come find him?"

"It was a mistake because what your family will now have to go through."

"And what does that mean?"

She pulled up another swivel chair and sat down, leaning forward. "Because you can't go home now, Mrs. Roseworth. I wish you could, believe me. I don't want to see your family suffer any more. I don't know ultimately what my superiors will decide, but I do know with certainty that some sort of story will have to be arranged—"

"I promise you, I will say nothing about what I've seen."

Her lips pursed in a frown. "Really? You'll just show up with your grandson and not explain where you found him? And you just won't ever explain why he doesn't have a memory? This is why we go to extraordinary lengths, such as keeping this facility secluded in this godforsaken corner of the world and

blocking it from Google maps and internet searches; to avoid exactly the kind of situation we are in now."

Deanna reached down and pulled out a laptop from the satchel she'd been carrying. She tapped on the rectangle below the keyboard and turned the screen to face me. She touched the play button and frantic green pulses raced across the screen.

"Please listen."

She turned up the volume, and at first all I could hear was rustling. Then, my own voice. "You know nothing about my life."

"Listen," came Steven's voice. "I think I know where William is."

"You think he's still alive?" I heard myself respond. Then, a pause. "Steven, please. You owe it to my father to tell me. Tell me what you know—"

Deanna hit the pause button. "You know this is coming from that hotel in Tennessee. Obviously, we had the room bugged. You need to know that this audio—along with photographs of Steven Richards being forced out of the hotel room by FBI agents, and you and I leaving afterwards—is compiled in a file that can be sent, with the click of a button, to FOX News and *The Washington Post*. Can you imagine what they'd do with this after what's already been released about you in that basement with Richards's supporters? What it would do to your family? Because this is where we're at now, Mrs. Roseworth. You either agree to go quietly into obscurity, or we release this. It will show you in a hotel room with your former lover. Agreeing to do anything he asks. Is this the last memory you want your family to have of you? For your husband to have of you?"

I heard it then, a slight tapping, coming from the corners of the room. As I glanced over, Deanna snapped her fingers. "Stay with me, Mrs. Roseworth. I need to know you understand. If you will agree to vanish—with our assistance—the recording never goes anywhere. It's also imperative that you tell me how it is you found this town. We didn't hear the two of you discuss Argentum in the hotel room. How did Steven Richards tell you about it?"

The tapping sounds grew louder now. They came from the corner of the room, directly behind where Deanna sat. Over her shoulder, I could see a tall pneumatic tube stretching from floor to ceiling. Something tiny was inside, popping.

"They have a right to know," I said softly, looking at the glass tube, then back to her. "Families all over the world spend their whole lives dying a little more every day wondering what happened to their loved ones, and you've had them all the time. And if anyone tries to find them and tracks them here or to any of the other bases, you have no qualms about murdering them, too."

"It's not that simple, Mrs. Roseworth. Surely you must realize that. We're in the containment business, not the killing business. Back to my earlier question. We need to know how you got here. The more open you are with us, the more we can be lenient in letting you see your grandson before . . ."

"Before what? The man ordered to kill us obviously failed. My husband will soon know where I am—"

"I hate to be the one to tell you this, but your friend didn't make it. And it's no one's fault but your own."

I paused. "I don't believe you."

"A tragic accident, from what I'm told. She drove off the road, crashed the van. She wouldn't have been driving in this horrible weather if you hadn't directed her to leave—"

"You're lying."

She sighed, took out her phone, punched with her finger

and then held it out for me to see. "One of our officers came upon her wrecked vehicle."

I leaned in and could see the van sunk in a snowbank. Even on the small screen, it was easy to see that the shattered back window was riddled with bullet holes.

"My God," I whispered.

"No one wants any more tragic accidents involving anyone else you love."

"You wouldn't hurt William—"

"You need to start explaining how it is you came to find Argentum," she said, having to raise her voice over the now-frantic popping sound. She turned around to the tube as the entire building shook for a moment.

In response, the long canister began to fill up, as if some sort of film was suddenly coating the glass from the inside. The building rattled again, and Deanna had to steady herself against the wall. When the shaking stopped, she began to type briskly on the computer.

"What's happening?" I asked.

"Nothing you need to concern yourself with."

The door opened and a man in camouflage stuck his head in, a long-range rifle over his shoulder.

"Ms. Ruck, you need to come. Right now."

"I'm debriefing—"

The building shuddered. The wheels under my chair began to roll.

"Right now," the soldier insisted.

Deanna held on to the wall. "You might have noticed, Captain, that I am not in your military, and I don't take orders from you. And the tremors aren't unusual. Gather them up—"

"Ma'am, there are *two* ships. And they're sending them down."

"They always come down."

"No. Not people. *They're* coming down."

Deanna stood up. She stole one more glance at the tube and grabbed the door. "You'll have to stay here, Mrs. Roseworth. I should be right back. Use this time to think about what we've talked about. You know what you need to do."

As she hurried out, a series of beeps came from outside and another tremor rippled through the building. I went to the door. The handle refused to even move.

I covered my mouth with my fingertips.

Roxy.

My oldest friend, my constant companion for so many years, dead because she wouldn't let me come here alone. My girls, my grandsons, Tom, all lost. The military would take Roxy's truck and my Volvo from the Nashville airport, crash hers off some rural road in Paducah, and have mine crushed. If they had gone so far as to frame Steven for the death of William, they could certainly go to extraordinary lengths to hide the truth about what happened to us—

No. I will not. I began to pace, keeping my hand on the wall. *I will not let it all be in vain.*

The glass tube was now emitting a low humming sound. I approached it and knew why the sound was so familiar. My throat tightened in realization.

It wasn't humming. It was vibrating.

Inside, thousands of ladybugs swarmed, frantically smashing against the glass and climbing on top of each other. The bottom of the tube was difficult to see, making it unclear where the bugs originated.

There was no doubt why the medical center kept a tube like this in the room.

The soldier said *they* were coming down.

The room shuddered violently and the lights dimmed as pads of paper and clipboards slid off the shelves and slapped onto the floor. I instinctively reached out to balance the tube, but found it firmly set into the concrete. William's room had been empty, right? I didn't remember seeing breakable things up high, heavy things, that could have fallen on him. Was he still in the room? What if they had already taken him somewhere else—?

The lights went out. I held tight to a table as darkness swallowed the room. I eased alongside the table, brushing up against a chair. I looked for the door, but the window in the door was nowhere to be seen, as the lights out in the hallway were also extinguished. I fumbled to where I thought the door was and slid up against the wall.

In the pitch blackness of the room, I saw it: the blinking light of the battery of Deanna's laptop where it had fallen to the floor. Maybe there was wifi, maybe there was a way I could send an email or something to the outside world.

I felt through the darkness. But once I opened the laptop's brilliant screen, my hopes were dashed. The internet signal was gray, with no bars.

I could still use it as a light source, try to find something to break through the door. But even if I happened upon a circular saw or a sledge hammer, I realized, I still couldn't get through the electronically locked door.

The screen glared at me. The laptop belonged to a woman who had to be one of the top officials amongst the black suits. Maybe she had the pass codes to the doors in one of the folders.

Each file appeared administrative: budget, addresses, PowerPoint presentations, research models. I continued to read the headers: overlays, contact points, spreadsheets, survivors' interviews, satellite coordinates—

I stopped scrolling down to instead use the track pad to move the arrow over to the second to the last folder in the row.

Survivors' interviews.

I clicked on it to find several internal folders. Each was marked with a code: JFAZ206, HTNY85, RJIL72, EKOK11 . . .

Get back to the main screen, keeping looking for anything that could contain pass codes.

I could barely navigate Microsoft Word on my computer, how could I possibly understand what these folders meant?

CJCA82, TRPA72, TDIL73, KVIL73, LSTN51—

Those letters and numbers . . . LSTN51 . . .

I held my breath. LSTN51. LS, my initials with my maiden name. TN for Tennessee. 51. The year I was born.

I opened up the folder. Three QuickTime movies were inside, each with their own label: subject camera, interviewer camera, and combined cameras.

The room rumbled slightly. I clicked on the first movie. After the color wheel spun for a few seconds, a screen opened up. *When the video clip proves to be nothing, I'll go back to searching the rest of the computer.*

As the video began to play, my hand raised to my chest.

A little girl sat in a chair in front of a table. Despite the grainy footage that was obviously taken from a filmstrip, it was easy to tell she was exhausted. Even though it was in black-and-white, even though the clip had several jumps from when the old film flickered, even though the camera was several feet away, I knew her.

It was me, at five years old.

"Yes," I heard myself say softly.

At the sound of the voice of an adult, I watched the much younger version of myself squirm at bit, looking around for the words. "I saw the people. The people I told you about. They change colors."

I know this. My God, I know this.

I stopped the clip and moved the arrow directly to the "interviewer" video clip. Only after the video played for a few moments did I finally begin to breathe.

I had first seen the man in the video on Doug's computer in the basement of Steven's home. I remembered Doug had clamped the laptop shut, saying he would show me the rest of the video if I promised to go public. The first known interview of an abductee, he had said.

After I'd left, he'd followed us to the street, standing outside my window. *"You'll never know. You'll never know the truth—"*

I didn't need to go to the end of the clip to see what it would reveal. But I did anyway, fast-forwarding to the end, as the man took off his glasses and rubbed his forehead.

The camera panned for a moment from the man to where my five-year-old self sat at the other end of the table.

Though the camera was on me, I heard the man whisper, his mic still picking up his words. "I'm not getting anything here. Get the Propofol ready." The film stopped rolling.

My breath caught in my throat. Every card-carrying member of AARP knew that Propofol is used before major surgeries, but can also cause memory loss. My God—

I doubled clicked on the video labeled "combined cameras." It began as the second video had—with the man in the horn-rimmed glasses and the fierce part in his hair.

"Are you comfortable?" the man asked.

The video then cut to show five-year-old me sitting at the table, looking out the window beside me. "Yes," I said, squinting in the sunlight streaming through. When the camera adjusted to the lens flare from the sun, I could see endless waves of water stretching out from a long beach.

The edited video featuring both cameras continued with the man leaning forward. "Can you tell me about what you saw?"

"I saw the people. The people I told you about. The people in the sky change colors," I heard myself reply.

"What do you remember about the ship in the sky?"

My little eyes looked back to him. It looked like I started trembling. "Mama and Daddy took me to St. Louis once, it was bigger than that. It changes colors too. Especially when they caused it to rain."

"Rain?"

I watched myself nod. "When we came back down . . . everything was clear . . . then it got stormy. All around us. Bad clouds. Big winds. They did it. They brought the storm . . . when they came down."

The man furiously scribbled and then tapped his forehead with his pencil.

"I know you've been through a lot. I need you to explain this to me. You told me before that you never actually talked to the . . . people in the sky. That you . . . understood them—like you spoke with your thoughts."

"We shared."

"You shared?"

I nodded. "Some of mine, some of theirs."

"This is very, very important, Lynn. Is this how they communicated with you? Was it like a conversation?"

"Back and forth. Back and forth. I showed them the cornfield by my house, they showed me how they fly over cornfields. But then . . . it was not nice. They . . . wanted more. Like when they wanted to see if I get sick. I showed them when I got chicken pox that one time and Mama made me take a bath in all that white stuff. And then . . . I saw how they want to make other people get sick, and eat food that's bad, and get hurt. In all kinds of ways."

"How are they going to hurt people?"

I watched as my younger self reached up behind my head and winced. "There's something . . . in me. And in the other people they bring back. They want to see . . . if everyone around us . . . gets hurt by what this does. I don't want it in my head—"

"Get hurt by what?"

"What's in here," I saw myself motion to the base of my skull. "Can I see my mama and daddy now?"

"That's all for now. Thank you, Lynn. I know it's been difficult. You're a strong, special girl—"

I stopped the video with a sharp tap.

Special ones, Verna had said. *They don't know why for sure. But unlike the adults, a few of the kids actually remember. I've heard the docs whisper—'cause they don't think I can hear—that it's a genetic thing that their memories are stronger than whatever those bastards in the cosmos do to them. And if those kids come back, well, the Suits have all kinds of good drugs to make those memories, and everything else, go away—*

No, no, no, I thought, exiting out of the folder and frantically scanning the others. *A genetic thing . . .*

The government gave me drugs—certainly the Propofol—and took everything I knew about my parents away.

WCTN11, WCTN11, WCTN11–

Oh, no.

The very last folder was WCTN11.

WC, William Chance. TN, Tennessee. 11. He was born in 2011. I clicked on it. Again, three movies. I frantically opened the third.

The video was incredibly clear, obviously recorded in high definition, and this time it was a younger man sitting in a stark white room. He adjusted his black tie and smiled with the warmth of an ice rink.

"Hello, William. Are you OK?"

My grandson sat in a chair, his short legs dangling. "I want to see my mommy and daddy."

I blinked back angry tears. *He remembered us.*

"You will, son, but I need to ask you a few questions—"

"Want to see my mommy and daddy and my nanna."

"Sure you do. But I need to talk to you first. About what you saw. And what you drew for us."

"I already told the other man. They're mad. I wanna go home."

"They're mad?"

"Really mad. I wanna go home. Don't let them take me back up there."

"You're safe now, William. You told my colleague Dr. Cody that the people in the stars who took you—"

"They aren't people. Please, can I call my mommy?"

"Why are they mad, William?"

"I already showed you."

The man opened the folder in front of him and drew out a few pieces of paper. He looked directly into the camera and indicated to the photographer to zoom in. The lens focused, and the picture came into closer view.

"William, can you confirm that you drew these?" He slid the pictures over to William.

"Uh-huh."

"Tell me what you've drawn. We know how they share memories, so you don't have to explain that. All we need to know is what you saw from them."

I heard William sigh. I leaned in closer to the screen,

seeing on the top sheet several stick figures inside a building. "Those . . . are the people they sent back. But . . . you trapped them here."

The man pointed to another group of stick figures walking on a hill. "Then who are these other people?"

"That's what all the people they brought back are supposed to be doing. Moving around. Not stuck here and in the other places you keep them."

"You mean everyone . . . with the bump like yours?"

William nodded. "Will it go away? It hurts."

"In time, it goes away. Back to the people who are supposed to be walking around, why do you have those lines around their heads?"

As the camera zoomed in closer, I saw what appeared to be waves coming from the heads of the figures. "That's what some of us are supposed to be doing."

"Some of you? But not all of you? Why?"

"Because . . . they haven't flipped the switch on everybody yet."

"What does that mean?"

William waited a moment and then took the man's pen from where it lay and added waves around all the heads. "They're almost ready for everyone to start together. But they had to be spread out. So they went to see where everybody was, and found out . . . that you stopped them."

"Stopped them from what?"

William reached over and touched the bottom of the picture, where a few stick figures lay on the ground, their eyes marked with Xs instead of dots.

"William, listen to me. I know this is hard to understand. Do the people in the stars know why we're containing the people they've returned—in hospitals?"

"Do I get to leave the hospital? I wanna go home."

"Of course."

"The monsters showed me how you trapped the people here and in all the other places like this. But the people they send back are not supposed to be trapped—they're supposed to go everywhere and cause trouble, with what the monsters put in here," William said, gently touching the back of his head and then reaching out for the rest of his drawings.

The camera moved in, showing more of William's stick figures. People emitting the waves were standing under dark clouds from which tornadoes were descending.

"Some of them make bad storms."

He turned the page. More stick figures, but this time standing with crudely drawn cows cut in half among what I thought at first was weeds, but then realized were plants with yellowed seeds in the ground.

"Some of them make our food so it's bad for us to eat."

The next picture was especially disturbing to know my grandson had drawn. One stick figure stood on a hill while people below were shooting at each other. A red crayon had been used to draw the blood.

"Some of them . . . just make other people so mad they fight and hurt each other. And then the rest . . . make people get sick. Just to see how well it all works. And when the tests are done, they'll flip the switch, and they'll all do it at the same time."

"But we've seen time and time again it doesn't happen to everyone," the man said, clearly thinking out loud in exasperation. "Why? Why only trigger some people and not all? What's the tactic?"

William waved his little hand across the picture. "Some get turned on now. Some get turned on at the end, when everyone is in place. They're supposed to be all over the world; that was their plan. The ones that get triggered now . . . the monsters wanted to see what each one of them could do on their own, how far . . . uh . . . their . . ."

"Range?"

"Range would reach." William snapped his fingers. "That's the plan. The monsters pick us up, put the bump in our heads, drop us back off, and then go back to the stars for a while. But this time, when they returned to see where everyone was, they found out you messed up their tests. They're so mad."

He then pulled out the last picture. Another stick figure, this time of a man shaking, his mouth shaped like an *O* and his eyes forced shut. Arrows rained down in a single line from the stars to the man's head, all while he held his hands over his ears in obvious pain. Once again, a red crayon indicated blood, this time seeping between the man's fingers.

"I don't want them to flip my switch. They showed me how it hurts your head, how your ears bleed. How the sound is so loud in your head, you can't hear anything else. Have you seen it happen to the people here?"

"We have, to some of them. We try to keep them away from everyone when it starts. We want to find a way to stop it, or maybe even prevent it."

"That will only make them madder if you do that."

The man rubbed his face. "You keep saying that. How do you know they're so mad?"

William finally looked up. "Because they're coming back for us."

The room rocked again.

I rushed to my feet, carrying the open computer to use as a light source. *I have to get him. I have to get him out.*

I shone the computer light along the wall to the corner, and then over the door frame. I found the handle. *I might have to get under it to see if there's some way to loosen it—*

When I yanked down on the handle, the door immediately opened. When the power went out, all the automatic locks had been shut off as well.

Good God, Lynn! Wanting to throw the computer in frustration with myself for not thinking of that earlier, I instead set it down and shoved the door open, stepping out to strange, multicolored lights beginning to flicker through sparse windows. I inhaled sharply, seeing the hallway jammed with people all wearing the same gray pajamas, wandering or standing still.

I rushed through them, nearly colliding with a man who was pacing, a look of utter confusion on his face. I thought of the dozens of rooms I'd passed before finding William; people without memories, already unable to remember how to do anything, now completely confused as to what was happening.

I edged along the wall. 216, 215, 214, 213, 212—

I seized the handle and pushed open the door. "William?"

"Yes?" a small voice came from the blackness.

"Honey, it's your nanna. I'm here in the door. Can you come to me?"

I expected him to hesitate, but in a moment be was right in front of me.

"My sweet boy." I knelt down to hug him.

"Why did they take me away from you? Josh said that we were going to play UNO until it was time for bed, but then everything started shaking and he ran out and the doors locked. I hate it when the doors lock at night. Why are all the lights out? Why is everything shaking?"

"I don't know, honey, but I really want to go. Let's go find Miss Cliff."

"What if they find us again? Will they take me away from you? Hey, those other boys in that picture you gave me, do they like Transformers?"

"They love Transformers. And they have dozens of them, and you can play with all of them as much as you want. But we have to go."

He let me take his hand and step out into the hall.

"Why is everyone out of their rooms?" he asked. "I wonder if my friends are out too. They're in a different building. My room used to be there until they moved me over here tonight."

I can't go for them too, I thought in despair. *All those children whose parents don't know they're still alive.*

The lights dimly came back on, and the doors down the hallway started to beep again. *Down to the first floor, then the tunnel.* I reached the staircase door and turned the handle.

A panel underneath the "Staircase" sign flashed red. I yanked the handle again, and the red flash repeated. *They lock them in, all of them on this floor. The staff can come in, but no one goes out without the code.*

"What's wrong?" William asked.

I looked at my hand, my writing now completely smudged.

"Honey, is there another way out of this hallway? Another staircase?"

William shrugged. "I think so. I remember seeing it once. Don't know where, though."

I moved us down the hallway. Most of the patients didn't appear to even notice us. I checked the sign next to every door, hoping one might to lead to a staircase, anything to lead us out.

Five doors down from us, there was a long beep, and three men in white scrubs emerged from a room. I swept William into the crowd of patients.

"Jesus, they're all out!" said the first man. "Round them up and hurry, before the power goes out again. Tony, go right to room 220, make sure she's still in there—"

The building shook and the lights dimmed, but the power stayed on. I guided William slowly towards the wall, thankful for the slow-moving, clogged group around us. I watched as one of the workers stuck his clipboard in the door to keep it from closing and then hurried down to the other end of the hall, followed by the two others, who began to usher the patients into rooms.

I lifted William into my arms. *Please don't turn around, please don't see us.*

I reached the door, caught it with my foot and held the clipboard. I quietly slipped through the door and put the clipboard back in place. Through the slight gap, I heard one of the men call out from down the hall, "She's not in the room!"

I ignored my throbbing knee and hurried down the hallway. This wing was just as stark, but with no windows and no patients wandering about. I frantically scanned each of the nameplates.

The building rocked, and William cried out as the lights went off. *We'll never know which door leads to a staircase now.*

He began to cry, and I held him close, my arm beginning to ache with his weight. "Don't you worry, I'm with you," I whispered in his ear. "Won't you walk with me? Hold my hand?"

Keep moving. Put as much distance between you and those men as you can.

The hall was almost pitch black. I took William's right hand and used my other hand to feel along the wall. I reached one door, opened it and could tell immediately from the smell of cleaning supplies it was a closet. I moved on, opening the next, and again could sense it wasn't open enough for a stairwell. I slid my hand along the wall and came to a sharp turn. *Oh God, another hallway, we'll never find our way—*

I almost fell on the first step, and yanked William back.

There's no door. There must be no patients on this wing.

I lifted him again. "Nanna's going to carry you, baby, down the stairs."

"I'm not a baby," he grumbled.

"No, you're Nanna's big boy, but I don't want you to fall," I said, feeling out with each footstep.

After several stairs, the floor stopped dropping, and I followed the railing to another landing and another flight. I knew if we moved too fast, we would tumble into the dark.

When the railing ended, I reached out with my foot and felt no more decline. I set William down and reached out for the wall, following it to an angle and then a slight crevice. Finally, I reached a cold door handle.

"Don't go out there," whispered a voice from the dark.

I whirled around, a protective hand holding William back.

"Don't do it," said the voice again, originating from under the stairs. The light from the screen of a phone flashed briefly across the face of Deanna Ruck.

"What are you doing?" I whispered back.

"They're out there. They're in the hospital." The panic in her voice was so thick that I squeezed William's shoulder.

"What do you mean?"

I heard it then, the click of a safety going off on a handgun. In the light of the phone, I saw her pointing her gun directly at us.

"Stay away from us," I said.

I hear her cock the pistol. "Don't go out there!" she begged.

I opened the door and rushed William through.

"Why is she hiding under the stairs?" he asked.

I began to hush him when I nearly tripped, reaching out to steady myself on the wall. In dim, pulsing lights coming from down the hall, I could make out a shape on the floor. A long semiautomatic weapon lay just beyond the motionless body of the soldier who had come into the room to summon Deanna.

To the left of the body was another soldier, bent in an unnatural way, his face turned towards us, eyes open but not blinking. Crouched over that second soldier, something turned towards us.

At first, I thought it held the tip of another rifle, for something long extended from its arm. Then it twitched—too long and too curved to be a barrel. Several other membranes then moved alongside it.

William started to scream.

It rose to its full size, about a foot shorter than me. If it had a color, I couldn't recognize it, for it seemed to constantly change. For one moment, it was the camouflage of the soldier's uniforms; for the briefest of seconds, it bore the face of the dead man sprawled before it.

"*The people in the sky change color,*" my five-year-old self had said in the video.

Then, that face was gone, morphing into almond eyes under a large, smooth forehead. It lacked a nose, had only a tiny lipless mouth above a pointed chin.

It was a face I had seen drawn by people all over the world.

Its head tilted sharply, its eyes without pupils, and for a moment, William's terrified face reflected in its inky eyes. Then it turned to me, made a clicking sound, and it gave me the same stare.

I began to feel it. A numbing in the back of my head. It was an almost calming feeling, all of the anxiety I had felt for days starting to drain away. William wasn't screaming anymore, either. My shoulders relaxed, and my fingers let go of his hand—

I immediately reached back down and snatched his fingers, shaking my head, trying to clear my suddenly cloudy thoughts.

I felt the numbness again, this time stronger than before. The creature had moved closer to us now, making the clicking sound more intensely.

A kind of comfort I hadn't felt since childhood swept over me, and the hallway around me vanished in a wash of white light.

From the light came Daddy.

He held my left hand so firmly that I could feel the calluses on his skin. In my other hand, I carried a purple balloon that danced above us. I could taste the cotton candy, smell the diesel fuel from the rides, hear the laughter from the crowd

"I knew you'd love the fair," Daddy said.

I tugged at him to leave the midway, pointing towards the livestock tent. He happily obliged, laughing as I wrinkled my nose at the scent of hay and manure. I shooed away the goat that chewed on the hem of my dress, and grinned at the baby pigs squealing and running in circles around their slumbering mother. We wandered over to the cows, and I reached over the divider to pet the coarse, white hair—

In a flash of light, a cow was on its side, split open. Not the cow from the tent, but a different one, lying on a vast sea of grass. In its open mouth, I could see its tongue had been removed. Other incisions riddled its body.

I wanted to scream, but realized I wasn't there.

I was the inside the alien's memory.

It stood over the mutilated animal, observing an angular box with strange writing hovering over the animal. With a motion of the creature's hand, a searing red light from the box continued to slice into the cow's abdomen, precisely removing the skin to expose the small intestine.

When the incision was finished, a rapid series of flashing lights penetrated the wound. I desperately wanted to look away but my gaze was fixed, horribly tied to the alien's examination of the animal's organs—

A searing shot of white light, and Daddy helped me into the car.

"Don't let go of my balloon," I said.

Daddy had eased it into the backseat, making sure it and the string were safely inside before he shut the door.

I leaned back against the seat, looking at the carnival lights through the window. I was stuffed with funnel cake and French fries, and was beginning to feel drowsy. As my eyelids drooped, my eyes adjusted, and I could see my own face reflected in the window. On my rounded cheek, was a dab of ketchup from that delicious hotdog—

From the blast of light, came a face so similar to mine that there was no doubt he was my grandson.

The creature stood above William as he lay on the triangular table, a webbing of sorts covering his body. Lights pulsated behind the boy's head.

The creature leaned him over and clicked. Once more, I shared its memory.

Each has a role, it thought as it studied William's face. *Summon the storm, bring the disease, damage the food, start the war. But not you. You are different. You are the center. You are the nerve system. You are our conduit. You will unite them all. You are the final stage—*

A softer white light, but still just as jarring, showed Daddy opening the door for me. "Did you fall asleep, sweet girl?"

"Uh huh," I muttered from the backseat.

"Come on, let's get your pajamas on," he said, lifting me.

I snuggled into the collar of his shirt, smelling pipe smoke, fried fair food, and aftershave. I held him tight, and he squeezed me in return. With Mama gone, he was my whole world.

It had been such a fun night. I didn't get a stuffed animal, but I did get—

"My balloon!" I cried out.

He turned and I lifted my head, seeing the balloon, starting to already lose some of its helium, drift into the trees.

"Daddy, we have to get it," I whined.

He paused for a moment. "No, Lynn. It's just a balloon."

"It's not!" I reached for it. "Daddy, you won me that balloon."

"No, Lynnie," Daddy pulled back so our faces were just an inch apart. "We never, ever go into the woods."

Never go in the woods.

I jerked my head back, breaking the creature's hold. The hallway in the hospital came into clear view, along with a clarity that nearly brought me to my knees.

Summon the storm, bring the disease, damage the food, start the war.

The creature stood just a foot away. On seeing my dazed expression, it began to click again.

I knew what it wanted. From me, from all the returned.

It began to click faster, its head tilting. It stepped forward to where there was only a few inches between us.

All it needed was a few memories more, to determine what they'd put in me. What they sent me back to do.

What weapon I carried within me.

"No!" I cried out. "Stay away!"

I stumbled back, trying to steady myself. I awkwardly

swept up William and blundered down the other side of the hallway, ignoring the screaming pain in my knee. The further I moved away, the sharper my thoughts became.

We're their weapons. Whatever they put in us, whatever we carry in us, they activate and watch the chaos unfold.

William's drawings flashed through my head like videos on the evening news. The unexplained rise in hurricanes, tornadoes, cancer, and even deadly allergies to food—science struggled to understand why.

It was all by design. Our world is where they test these weapons.

And whatever they planned to do in the end, it said William was the final stage.

They cannot have him. Whatever happens, I have to get him out.

The frantic, strobelike lights made me feel as if I could go crashing into a wall at any moment, but I kept running. The lights were growing brighter now, coming through wide glass windows of the room beyond.

The hallway led into a lobby. Several men in heavy camouflage coats, their rifles pulled up to their shoulders, ran past the windows outside. The light fell on the drifting snow, making it look like it was raining confetti.

William was still entranced. I carried him to the glass entrance doors and waited a moment for them to open.

The power's out, they won't open.

I set William down and tried to pry the doors open at the seam. "Come on," I pleaded.

Through the glass I saw a man, standing a yard or so away. He wore a heavy coat and a sock hat and stared up at where the light originated, transfixed by whatever he saw.

"Joe!" I cried out, banging on the glass. "Joe!"

I even saw his massive truck parked nearby, its plow

covered with a layer of snow. "Joe!" I said, striking the glass repeatedly.

He continued to stare, his eyes wide, the lights spilling over his face. *He isn't even blinking.*

The lights in the lobby came roaring back on. I hurried to stand before the doors.

The glass didn't part. I looked around, seeing another key-pad flashing beside the door. *Of course there would be a code here, they wouldn't just let anyone in. Or out.*

I heard the sound of William's feet scuffling.

I whirled around, seeing him beginning to walk back to where we came from. At the far end of the hall, I could see several shapes emerging.

I ran and seized William, rushing back to the door. I smashed my fist on the glass, screaming for Joe. I scanned the lobby for anything I could use to try and break the glass, but the only thing I could see was a computer monitor on the front desk, and it wouldn't have made a dent.

I could feel the numbness growing on the back of my head. I kept pounding. The memory of Daddy's warning about the woods broke me free of the creature's control before, but I didn't know if I could snap out of it again.

I looked out to see the interior light come on in the cab of Joe's truck. The door opened slightly, and someone peered out.

Despite my staggering panic, I gasped. Roxy's face was so bruised, so swollen from the ugly gash down her forehead, that I almost didn't recognize her at first. I cried out her name, waving my arms wildly. I saw her limp out of the truck towards Joe. She looked up in the sky, her hand covering her mouth in astonishment. She looked back at the truck, and then briefly towards the medical center.

I screamed her name, striking the glass. She did a double

take, and I could see her yell out my name. She moved towards Joe, pointing in my direction. Roxy shook him, but he continued to stare upwards.

I watched her give a frightened look in the direction in which Joe stared, and then she painfully moved towards us.

"Come on!" she motioned to me.

"The door won't open! We can't get out!"

Roxy went back to Joe, this time hitting him in the arm. When he didn't respond, she gave me a frantic look, made an obscene gesture at Joe and limped back towards the truck. She was practically dragging her right foot. I watched her open the driver's side door and haul herself in.

The lights went out again, and as soon as I turned back to the lobby, the numbness was back. All I wanted to do was relax. The feeling was so refreshing, such a relief, the euphoria almost too much to fight.

There were five, six, no . . . *ten.* They were like tall children, some walking, others . . . arranging themselves, twitching in rickety sections, angling and reaching out like a scurrying insect.

None of this was alarming. It was such a delightful feeling. I wasn't even worried that William was a few feet ahead of me, walking—

I heard the roar of engine. I groggily turned back to look outside, seeing Joe's truck move in reverse and make a sharp turn towards the lobby. The light in the cab came on briefly, and Roxy was motioning wildly at me from behind the wheel.

"Get back!" I could see her yell.

The headlights of the truck shone out over the plow as it barreled towards the doors.

I rushed forward and grabbed William, stumbling away, closing my eyes as the glass exploded behind us.

As the plow smashed through the doors, I heard them scream. The sound, metallic and feline, made me want to cry out myself. The numbing feeling was immediately gone.

The truck tore back in reverse. I seized William and carried him over the shattered glass, wincing as an icy blast hit us both.

"What the hell?" I heard Joe call out, now turned in our direction. "What are you doing?"

"What are *you* doing, you moron!" Roxy hollered while she rolled down the window. "Took me driving through a building to get you to pay attention! Lynn, get in the backseat! Joe, get the hell in here! I had to use my bad foot to hit the gas, and it's hurting like a son of a bitch!"

I opened the door and lifted William inside, looking back towards the lobby. "Go! Get away from here as fast as you can!"

"What the hell is going on out there?" Joe said, climbing in to take the wheel, rubbing the back of his head.

"Holy Mary Mother of God! William, is that really you?" Roxy reached out to brush his knee, and then winced in pain at the effort. "Lynn, you found him, you found him. . . ."

"Roxy," I said, my heart in my throat. "What happened to you?"

She leaned back. "Joe, get us the hell out of here."

Joe sat, still dazed. "I . . . froze. I just can't believe it. My whole head felt like I was doped up. What are those things? I mean, it can't be—"

"Shut up and drive."

The comment came from what I first thought was a pile of snowsuits on the other side of the bench. Instead, the groggy and wizened face of Verna Cliff revealed itself from within the hood of a long maroon coat. After scowling at Joe, she reached over and touched William's shoulder. "Sweet boy. Your grandma found you."

"How are you here . . . ?" I stammered.

"Cover his eyes, Grandma." Verna leaned forward. "Or he'll be as useless as Joe was out there. Hard not to be; even I couldn't look away."

I realized that William hadn't stirred. He was sitting on the edge of the seat, staring out the windshield.

I followed his gaze and immediately felt the numbing again. Beams of light spilled down from the snowing sky. Dozens of columns, white and gold, amid a flurry of colorful pulsating lights high in the gray night sky. As I looked beyond, I could see even more of the light beams behind the hospital.

Walking into the lights were people.

Even in the heavy snow, I could tell there were hundreds. They stood within each pillar of light, each wearing a hospital gown, looking up.

I knew with certainty that the basement to the hospital was now empty, and all those comatose people had risen for the first time. The power was out, so the door to the stairs was open. They had streamed out, a mindless mass, responding to the call.

I understood why. The closer we could all get to those lights, the better we would feel.

I reached over for the door handle when a large group of men in camouflage flooded past us, running to the hospital. I saw one point and sharply direct a few of his subordinates towards us.

Three soldiers broke off and ran to the driver's side of the truck, pointing their rifles at us. As soon I focused on them, the calm feeling was gone.

"Oh shit," Joe said.

"Put your hands where I can see them!" one of the men shouted.

One of the soldiers leaned into the glass and quickly spoke into the radio on his shoulder. "The boy and the old lady are in there. Do you copy? We've have them. They're here."

Drive, Joe! I wanted to scream.

"All of you, get out of the truck. Keep your hands up," the first soldier ordered.

"Tell him his buddy made me too sore to move," Roxy grumbled, her hands barely raised.

The soldier tapped the edge of his rifle on the glass. "Ma'am, we don't have time for this! Do you hear me? Get out—"

Four beams of light shot down before the now-shattered entrance to White Crest. One beam was so close to the truck that Joe cried out. The soldiers turned, blinded by the searing light.

Seconds later, more shapes began to emerge from the hospital. All in the same stark hospital garb, all their faces calm and serene, walking towards the lights.

The feeling was so strong to join them that I opened the truck door, and heard Joe's door ding, signaling he was feeling the same. William was already sliding across my lap to jump out.

"What the hell is wrong with you people?" Roxy cried out. "Drive, Joe! Dammit! And close the damn doors!"

"Shit," Joe said, wiping his eyes.

"Don't look at it!" I covered my own eyes. "Just drive Joe!"

Joe slammed on the gas. The pickup truck bolted forward, heading directly for the emerging masses.

"Turn!" Roxy yelled. The people in the light made no attempt to get out of the truck's way. Joe spun the wheel and barely cleared a man and a small woman. Joe made another wild turn and drove directly towards two armored cars.

Again Joe turned, this time too late. Despite its snow tires, the truck slid into the front end of one of the military vehicles. We were all momentarily thrown forward, but Joe gave us no time to recover. He immediately took off again, driving down the row of vehicles and hanging right on the wrong way of a circle drive. He headed down a long road leading away from the medical center.

"Everybody OK?" Joe asked, out of breath.

"I'm gonna puke if you keep driving like this!" Verna said.

"Serves you right," Roxy muttered.

"Whatever happens," I said to Joe, "do not—I repeat—do not look into the lights."

"What's happening to us?" he asked, looking at me with genuine terror in his eyes, reaching out to touch the back of his head.

Knowing I couldn't explain at this moment, I scooted to the edge of my seat. "Roxy, what happened to you? They showed me a picture of the van, they told me you'd been killed—"

A rifle shot suddenly sounded, and the back window of the quad cab cracked. I covered William's head.

"Dammit," Joe said, looking at his rearview mirror.

I turned to see three Humvees now following in the distance, their headlights beaming through the snow.

"Come on, Moses." Joe pushed hard on the gas as houses started to appear. "Why are they shooting at us?"

"You think the government wants to you cruise on out of town to tell the world about this shit show?" Verna said.

"Aw, hell." Joe took a sharp left down a side street. I was thankful for the chains I'd noticed on his tires. Otherwise, even on the recently cleared roads, we could have hit an icy spot and gone crashing into a building. Then another right, and another left, knocking down several snow-covered trash cans in an alley.

We heard another gunshot. "Can we get out of town?" I asked, feeling waves of carsickness.

Joe then swung another left and tore down the main drag, where he had earlier made the first pass in trying to clear the streets. Large mounds of snow lined the curb in front of the stores, making the street a single lane.

"They'll chase you to the ends of the earth. They won't let any of you leave," Verna said.

I saw Joe's jaw clench as he took a rough left turn. "Please don't have locked the shop. Please don't have locked it."

"We're going to your store?" Verna asked.

"Not my shop," Joe grunted as he turned in an alley. "Ron's place. When he's slow on business, he lets me park the truck there if it's gonna snow and I have to work late. I hope he's not working on anything."

The truck came to a sudden stop and Joe jumped out, leaving the truck running. "Roxanne, you'll have to take off if they come. Got it?"

"Yep." Roxy winced, touching her leg.

I held my breath, waiting to hear the engines of the Humvees as they tore down the alley. Instead, there was the small squeak of worn hinges as Joe opened two huge, metal double doors. Once he opened them as far as he could, he slid back into the truck.

He quietly pulled into the mechanic's shop and turned the engine off, running back to close the doors behind us.

We sat in silence, looking back to see Joe peering out a rectangular window to the alley. We waited for military vehicles, expecting angry pounding on the door.

After several minutes of nothing, Joe crept over and leaned in the cab. "Stay in the truck," he whispered. "Ron's got the heat way down low. Don't dare turn the lights on. You'll stay warmer in there. I'll keep watch out the window." He shut the door.

I turned back to Roxy. "Tell me what happened."

"It's not as important as what happened to you. William, I can't believe it. You're here. You're really here," Roxy said, touching his head.

"It matters to me," I whispered. "I thought you'd been killed. Did you crash?"

Roxy shook her head. "These bruises are courtesy of one of this town's finest after I got the van stuck. He was on me as soon as I slid off the road, like he knew where I would be. He didn't like my response when he asked for my ID and proof of insurance. I knew I was a goner at that point. Things got ugly fast, and it became clear very quickly I was not supposed to walk away from that encounter. But he didn't know how mean I can be. I even got his gun, can you believe it? But I've got terrible aim, and I shot up more of the van than him."

I almost laughed in relief, then, thinking of the picture Deanna had shown me on her phone. It had been Roxy shooting, not the other way around.

"He got the gun back fast, but it was out of bullets. He was a sick son of a bitch too—started taking pictures of me laying in the snow, and the van, I guess someone wanted proof. I was in a real bad way when Joe rolled up and saw the guy using me as a punching bag. He underestimated Joe too. For an old guy, Joe used that crowbar in the bed of his truck and showed him who was boss—"

"Are you OK?" I reached over to Roxy's swollen cheek.

"I hurt everywhere. My foot and face are the worst. But I insisted Joe get me back to you, and when we got to Miss Congeniality's house, she was so bombed she could barely make it to the door. Joe thought some sudden exposure to this wonder-

ful Colorado weather might perk her up, so we went for a ride—"

"Kidnapped, more like it," Verna grumbled.

"Didn't have a choice," Roxy said with a glare. "Joe said we needed that damn code of yours from the kitchen to get in. If Armageddon hadn't started when we showed up, I would have personally forced your butt through that hospital till we found Lynn and William."

"Didn't you want to come get me?" William asked quietly, looking at his teacher.

I watched whatever was left of her binge seep from the old woman's face. She reached out and gently squeezed his arm. "Miss Cliff was just tired, honey. And I'll admit it," she sighed, "I was a little afraid of the sky tonight."

"Afraid?" I whispered. "You knew . . . this . . . those ships, those . . . things, were coming?"

"Things?" Verna asked.

William curled up closer to me, burying his face in my side.

"Oh God, you actually saw them? I don't know if anyone here ever has. When I saw what kind of storm was brewing, I knew the ships would come. They always do when the weather gets this bad. And when all the phones and computers stopped working, I knew it for sure. But it didn't happen . . . like it usually does. They aren't dropping off people. They're taking them back. Everyone who's been marked. All those people, all my kids . . ."

She looked out the window, her eyes glinting with tears.

"You know . . . about the markings?" I asked in a hush, knowing I should cover William's ears.

Verna ran her fingers over the back of William's hair. "Honey, do you still have that bump on the back of your head

from when you fell off the bed that night? The one that hurts sometimes?"

"Yep," William yawned. "Are we gonna be here for a while?"

"Close your eyes honey," Verna said, looking at me. "That bump, it's always hurting him. The other kids complain about it too, but it goes away in time. It's under his hairline, you'd never see it. You have to *know* it's there."

"I don't know what you're talking about," Roxy whispered from the front seat, "Why does the military stand there and let those . . . ships . . . take those people?"

Verna smiled with traces of anger. "Because the government can't stop them. Believe me, they've tried. It hasn't been pretty. The military has tried to communicate with them, but they're not interested. It's like pigs trying to negotiate with a butcher. They've always just dropped off the ones they've abducted. I don't know why they're taking them back."

I do, I thought. You don't want to know.

I understood then that Verna's drinking wasn't to momentarily escape the sadness of what she'd seen. It was how she survived all those long years, watching the doctors and staff leave after working at the hospital for just a year or so—

I quickly looked to her, remembering her own words: *They say they can't handle it or they're too sick to work anymore. Won't even get close to the kids.*

Those doctors found out, too late, what happens if they're around the returned who have been activated. How not long after the patients scream in pain, their ears ringing and bleeding, the doctors themselves start dying.

Only Verna remains unaffected, and she doesn't even realize why. Even though she said she was mesmerized by the lights from the ships, she doesn't even realize she's one of us too—

"Lynn Roseworth," came a loud voice from a megaphone.

William sat up whining, and I looked around in panic. The voice came from outside the shop.

Joe ran from the garage window to the front of the building as the voice continued. "Lynn Roseworth, please come out. We know you are inside. Do not make us open fire. We do not want to harm you or your grandson. Come out, now."

Joe hurried back from where he peered out the small window facing the street. He slid into the front seat. "They're sitting there at the intersection, looking all around. They must not know where we are other than downtown somewhere."

"Don't doubt them. They will start shooting," Verna said.

"This is a mechanic shop, can we hide somewhere? Down in a pit or something?" Roxy asked.

"Where's the bathroom in this place?" Verna asked.

"Are you kidding me?" Joe hissed.

"Listen, I've drank enough tonight to put all of you under the table. When you're this old, and you gotta go, you gotta go, or you go on the spot," Verna said, sliding out. "I'll find it myself."

"Joe, what about Roxy's idea of the pit?" I asked.

"We're on top of it, and it's covered. I'd have to move the truck and pull off the metal cover—"

"Give me your coats," Verna commanded from outside the truck. We looked to see her standing by the light switch, her finger prepared to flick it up.

"Jesus, what is wrong with you?" Joe whispered.

"I will turn on these lights and they'll know in a second where you are. Give me Lynn and William's coats. Now."

"God damn you, woman," he said. "You're gonna go hunch down in the bathroom under all those coats and wait this out—"

"I'm counting down. Starting now: five, four—"

"Shit!" Joe yanked off William's coat and took mine as I shrugged it off.

"Miss Cliff," William said groggily. "Are you leaving us?"

"Sorry kid. I'm done with all this. I know what they're capable of doing. And your coat, too, gimpy. And that stupid sock hat of yours too, Joe. It will be cold in that bathroom."

"I hope when they start shooting, they aim for the bathroom." Roxy winced as she took off her coat.

Joe threw the coats out. As Verna slowly gathered them and walked towards the bathroom, the voice came again from the street. "Lynn Roseworth, you have one minute to come out. Please don't make us harm your family."

"Jesus, what are we going to do? We have to go," Roxy said. "Just gun it out of here, Joe. We'll have to take our chances."

"They'll be on our asses in two seconds, they're right outside. They missed before, but now they're at close range."

"There has to be another place we can hide," I said. Hearing the panic in my voice, William started to cry.

"Joe," Verna's voice came from the door. "Give me twenty seconds and then follow the alley down to where Janice Stoney had that crappy secondhand store. You can follow Sugarhill Street out."

"What are you talking about . . . ?" Joe said, watching Verna shuffle to the front of the building towards a door. Instead of her long coat, she now wore mine, and had the hood up. We could see she'd stuffed Roxy's coat into William's with the hood sticking out, and had placed Joe's sock hat in the hood.

To complete the image, she'd tied her own coat around the waist of the makeshift boy, to cover his legs from the cold.

"What is she doing?" Joe demanded.

"Verna!" I whispered, covering my mouth.

She couldn't have heard, but she did turn around and look

at me. "Tell him," she mouthed the words. "Tell him what I did. And *get him out.*"

Verna unlocked a door and stepped out of the building onto the main street, closing the door behind her, holding the crudely assembled dummy in her arms. "I'm here! Don't shoot!" she cried out.

"Put the child down, Mrs. Roseworth!" the voice boomed.

"No!" Verna yelled out. "I won't let you have him! I want a phone!"

"We have to go," Joe said, jumping out of the truck and gingerly opening the doors to the alley.

"Mrs. Roseworth, put the child down. Walk over to us with both your hands in the air."

"I'm not coming a step closer until you get my husband on the phone! He's a US senator!"

Joe slid back into the truck. "What's going on?" William asked. "We can't leave Miss Cliff—"

"Now, Mrs. Roseworth!" the soldier on the megaphone ordered.

"No! I want my husband on the phone—"

There was no order to open fire, only the sound of automatic weapons unloading. Joe threw it in reverse. I covered William's face as we slid out of the garage and into the alley.

The shooting continued for several seconds more, masking our noise enough for us to make a sharp turn and approach another street.

"Jesus," Roxy's voice was tight. "Oh my God. . . ."

"God love you, Verna," Joe murmured quietly.

I made the sign of the cross across my aching chest.

"What happened?" William asked.

I held him close. "Miss Cliff wanted to save you."

"Shouldn't we go back and get her?"

I kissed his forehead and told him to close his eyes and try to rest.

Joe drove at a slow pace, unable to use his headlights. For the first time since arriving in Argentum, I was grateful for the fact that this was a small, isolated town. There were no streetlights on the side streets, which allowed us to creep along without being seen.

"Do you even know where you're going?" Roxy whispered.

"You could blindfold me and I could still make it around town. At least, I hope so."

"Once they . . . look closer at the coats, they'll know. They'll start looking for us," Roxy said.

"If we can get up and over the rise . . . ," he said.

"Well, I sure couldn't," Roxy said. "It's complete ice and snow. You better have a plan B."

"It's the only way out of town." He leaned in to the windshield.

The lights of Main Street were still in view off to our right. Joe drove as far on the side street as he could before it dead-ended. Then he had no choice but turn towards the town's main thoroughfare.

When we reached Main Street, he edged out just enough to look. We all leaned forward, seeing the Humvees along the boardwalk start separating. One disappeared down the alley where we'd gone to reach the mechanic shop, and the others turned towards the medical center before splintering off onto side streets.

"Hold on," Joe said, turning left. Almost immediately, we began to climb the incline that had stranded Roxy only hours before. I whispered a silent prayer for the sharpness of Joe's snow tires. We passed the crashed van and the police cruiser, its lights still flashing.

"Looks like my dancing partner survived after all," Roxy said bitterly. "He was lying by the car when we ran off. Someone must have come to get his sorry ass."

As we crested the hill, I looked back, certain we were being pursued.

My eyes lingered on the empty street for a moment before they were drawn to the heavens. Even the snow was unable to block out the two massive shapes hovering miles above the far edge of town. Their color was difficult to determine, but the thousands, maybe millions of lights, outlining their diameters and edges were clear. Comprehending their size brought on a wave of fear, like a child seeing a whale for the first time. I could only gauge they were the size of cruise liners, maybe even the battleships I'd seen on TV. I felt nauseous at the thought of William in one of them and looked away, but felt compelled to return my gaze, to make myself believe I'd really seen them.

Of course I had. I'd been in one too.

As we went over the hill, the last thing I saw was another beam of light shoot to the earth below.

Joe then stopped the truck, switched gears, and began to back up while turning the wheel.

"What are you doing?" Roxy demanded.

Joe ignored her, and pulled down the stick shift. The plow on the front of the truck slowly lowered.

Roxy's hands flailed. "Joe, just keep driving—"

"Woman, I'm telling you what," he said, waiting for the plow to crunch against the earth. He then drove off the road, the snow immediately piling up before him.

"They can't chase us if they can't get through," he muttered.

Joe continued to drive a half circle and promptly dumped

a huge amount of snow and ice on the road. He backed up and took another scoop, piling it behind the first.

"Now, we go," he said, slowly advancing onto the road.

I glanced back to see lights coming up over the hill from the town. A Humvee was over the rise a moment later.

"Joe!" I cried out.

He swore and gunned the gas, and we started to slide. I looked back out the window and saw that the driver of the Humvee apparently had the same notion when he saw us. I watched the army vehicle race down the road and weave as he tried to avoid the mound of snow and ice. But instead, the Humvee crashed into it head on, the snow falling onto its hood and covering the window.

"Drive, dammit!" Roxy yelled. Despite the heavily falling snow, I could see the headlights of the Humvee rock back and forth as the driver tried to steer it free.

"Eat that, asshole," Joe said, driving down the road as fast as he could while still controlling the truck on the ice. I saw one soldier get out of the Humvee with a long rifle and try to aim in our direction, but then we were off the road and onto the state route.

We crunched along, and Roxy patted Joe's arm. "You did good."

"Keep looking back," he said. "They'll be radioing in for anyone else to follow. It will be even more treacherous on these mountain roads. And it's night. I'll go as fast as I can, but the last thing we need is to end up in a ditch."

"Been there," Roxy said, holding up a finger, her eyes closed.

We drove in silence, the wipers pushing aside the snow that continued to fall, the pine trees rushing by in the dark.

"Joe, I'm so sorry," I said quietly. "I'm sorry you're caught up in this."

"Miss Lynn, looks like I've been part of this for a long, long time, even if I didn't realize it. I . . . can't believe it. . . ."

"How are we on gas?"

"I keep reserves in the wintertime, so I filled up before I started clearing the streets this afternoon. I have a reserve tank too. We'll be fine to get to Denver."

"What's to keep them from following us from above? Helicopters? Planes?"

"Would be hard to follow from the air in this blizzard. It is the government, however. They're probably tracking us by satellite at this very moment, following my cell signal."

"Do you have one? In the truck?"

"In the glove compartment."

Roxy opened the latch and pulled out the phone, handing it back to me. I powered it up and found it had no service. I shook my head and looked over to Roxy, who was clenching her eyes in pain.

"We'll get you to a hospital as soon as we get into the city."

"No," she said. "We're going straight to the airport, getting you and little man on a plane."

"They'll expect that. They'll have people waiting for us there. I have to be able to make a call. Just one call."

I knew Joe was doing the best he could in the conditions, but it felt like we were moving at a crawl. I kept looking back, expecting to see glaring headlights, or hear the thumping whirl of helicopters above.

We drove on, the snow pelting the windshield, the wind rushing against the glass. Roxy sat with her eyes closed, and

Joe kept whispering to himself, shaking his head. I held tight to William, and constantly looked in the rearview mirror.

It seemed like an hour later, but we finally reached the highway. "Honey," I whispered to William.

The boy had curled up deep under my arm, dead asleep. Delicately, I touched the camera app on the phone and took a quick photo, hoping the flash wouldn't wake him. As I looked at the sweet image of the sleeping boy's face, my heart leapt at the three strong bars of service.

I quickly dialed, and held my breath as it rang.

"Hello?" Tom answered immediately.

"Tom," I turned to face the window, speaking softly.

"Lynn? Jesus, are you OK? Where are you?"

"Listen to me. I can't speak loudly. I have William. Do you understand? I have William."

"What?"

"I am in Colorado approaching Denver. I am going to send you a picture you must immediately share with Anne and Chris. Roxy is banged up bad and we're heading for a hospital. Tom, William is alive."

"Lynn, honey, I don't know what you're talking about. Just tell me where you are—"

"I love you, Tom, but I'm hanging up. Look for a text from this number. I have many calls to make, then I'll call you back."

"Wait, who are you calling—?"

"I love you," I said, and hung up.

The phone immediately rang with Tom's number appearing. I ended the incoming call, touched the picture of the photo, and texted it to his number. He called again, and the phone made a swishing sound as the text went through.

A few seconds after the text went out, the phone stopped ringing.

I pulled up Safari and quickly typed, pulling up a number of different websites.

"You finally learned to use another app," Roxy observed, with a pained voice.

I touched one of the numbers that appeared, and I held up the phone to my ear. The phone rang three times before someone answered, "KUSA-TV, can I help you?"

"Is this the NBC station? Do I have the newsroom? My name is Lynn Roseworth, I am the wife of Senator Tom Roseworth of Tennessee. My grandson William has been missing for several months. Are you familiar with the story? Good. I am calling to tell you that I have located my grandson here in Colorado, and we are driving to the Denver Emergency Center, where I will be bringing him in to be evaluated. That's right, my grandson. The one who is missing. I am calling every television station in town, as I intend to make a brief statement after we arrive. I will also be sending you a photo of my grandson for verification purposes. I will call again as we approach the hospital. You can call my husband's press secretary within the hour to confirm that I have spoken with him. I hope you'll be there. I can be reached at this phone number as we drive into Denver, but if I don't answer, it's because I'm calling your competitors. I hope to see your crew there. What is a good phone number to text you this picture?"

When I hung up and began to search online again, Roxy painfully leaned forward. "What in God's name are you doing?"

"It's our only protection. If every TV station and newspaper sees that William is alive with me, they can't try to take him from us. It's the only way."

"What exactly are you going to tell them when we arrive?" Joe asked quietly.

I put the phone up to my cheek. "Are you the ABC station? Good. My name is Lynn Roseworth."

Two hours later, when we at last reached Interstate 25, the cell phone was hot from constant use. If it hadn't been for the phone charger Joe thankfully kept in the glove compartment, the phone would have died long ago.

Tom had called several times, as had Kate, Anne, and Stella. I hadn't answered, only texted them the picture. I felt so tired after talking to all the journalists, knowing they were all wondering what the crazy alien lady would say at the hospital. It was only a taste of what was to come.

Roxy knew it too. "You need to call Anne."

"I will, in a minute. I need to get my head together."

Roxy reached back across William and took my hand.

I squeezed. Tom was no doubt on a plane, probably having called in a favor to a wealthy donor to get on a private jet. He would bring Anne and Chris. Stella would probably muscle herself on board. Kate too. There would be so many questions, but I would insist that word of William's discovery be sent to Nashville's metro police immediately. Steven had to be released. And Barbara as well—

I quickly turned to Joe, who was whistling softly. For the first time, I noticed the silver swirl of his hair that lay over the back of his collar, and how he was twirling it, round and round.

The angle of his jaw. The sharpness of his nose. The light shade of his blue eyes. None of it registered then, but it did now.

It can't be.

When Barbara was a teenager and had come to ask for our help all those years ago, she had twirled her hair. She did it again in that basement in Champaign as well. Barbara Rush, silver hair, soft chin, sharp nose, brilliant blue eyes. Barbara, who never stopped looking for her brother Don.

Twins, from St. Joseph, Michigan.

"Joe," I asked. "You don't remember anything of your past?

"Nope."

"So you don't even know . . . if you had . . . maybe a sister?"

"Not a thing. My God, all that time . . . was I . . . taken?"

"So you don't remember anyone named Barbara?"

"Barbara? You know, funny you should ask," Joe said, a sad smile coming to his face. "Remember when I told you that some names sound kind of familiar? Like how I chose Joseph? Well, of all the names of women I've heard, Barbara has always been my favorite."

EPILOGUE

I rested the tip of the pen on the blank square of the question, tapping it repeatedly. The capitol of Maine. Seven letters.

I swear it's Bangor. But the "b" doesn't fit, and it's not long enough. I know this. I know this.

I looked out across the garden, laying the crossword puzzle on the arm of the Adirondack. The chair was by the lavender bush for a reason: Daddy always said the scent had calming effects. I breathed in and closed my eyes, trying to slow my racing heartbeat, looking down at my watch for the thousandth time in the last fifteen minutes.

I tried to focus on the billowing hydrangea bush in its myriad blues and pinks, taking long breaths to slow my heartbeat. The garden has come back after so much neglect—isn't it remarkable?

We agreed to meet at three o'clock.

Yes, I'd lost some finicky gardenias, and my pots all had to be replanted, but they had been filled with annuals anyway.

I won't have much time with him, but there's so much that has to be said.

The hydrangeas are suffering, and they'd be wilting right now in the early evening heat, even if I hadn't abandoned them late last summer.

I have so much to ask him.

Augusta. Augusta, Maine. I wrote down the word. Now move on to the next, stop thinking about what could be within us—

All those terrible diseases. Horrible storms. People getting sick after eating meat—

"Miss Lynn?"

I looked over, across the fence. It needed its yearly painting, but I planned on having that done in the fall, when the temperatures were bearable. The man just beyond the fence stopped and wiped his brow with a handkerchief, setting down the wheelbarrow full of mulch he pushed. "Do you want me to take the mulch up to the garden by the shop, or dump it here?"

"I'll use it for the rose bed by the Peddler's front door. You can dump it there."

"Uh, no, you cannot."

Roxy huffed from the other side of the garden. I could hear the keys jingling in the front of her overalls, indicating she'd just closed up the shop. She walked with a cane, and would for the rest of her days, Dr. Burcham said. He had suggested plastic surgery for the deep gash on her forehead that required a series of ugly stitches and had left a wicked scar, but she said at her age, she wasn't concerned about smooth skin. "Jesus, Lynn, are we running a trailer park here? No, you can't dump that mulch there, Don. Wheel it around back and we'll get to it tomorrow."

"Yes, Miss Roxy." Don winked at me.

"Don, you really don't have to do that," I said, fanning myself with the newspaper.

It's the heat. That's why I'm sweating. My nerves can't be this bad already.

"Trying to earn my keep," he said with a grin. "Any foxes in the garden today?"

"Oh, I think I saw one a while ago," I said, looking around.

"Not too hot for foxes, I hear. I've found the more I expose myself to this Tennessee heat, the more I become used to it."

Just like you got used to everyone calling you Don. Just like you got used to your sister hovering around you constantly. It didn't take you long to see how your mannerisms are exactly the same, and how you both have the exact same color of silver in your hair. You knew it as soon as you met. And now . . . how your eyes light up when she comes to visit you, driving down from Illinois every other weekend.

Has Don told you, Barbara? About our pact, our promise to each other? That, if suddenly, we have blinding pain in our heads, our ears begin to bleed, and we hear a terrible ringing, we know what's happening. We know they've activated us, and God knows what we could do to you and to everyone around us.

Don said that from time to time he saw it happen to patients, when he was being treated in the hospital. He said the doctors whisked them away, and he never saw them again. He says it never happened to him, and I know it has never happened to me.

But if it does, Don and I agree to leave and disappear. Despite the pain I know all too well of having a loved one suddenly disappear, I would vanish in a heartbeat, jump in the closest car and keep driving away, if it meant protecting my family.

And William. What did those monsters mean that he was the conduit? That he wouldn't harm people when he was activated, but instead, he was the final stage—

"Looks pretty busy in the kitchen right now." Don motioned with his chin to the house. "I think I'll break into the back of the shop and get some water. Clean up a bit."

"Clean up a lot, please," Roxy muttered.

"I'm just happy to have a job with you, Miss Roxy!" he called out.

"The man thinks because he rents my back room that I like him," she said, carefully navigating the paving stones through the grass. "Husband enjoys his company, though. Two peas in a pod, those two, pickin' at guitars, thinking they're Johnny and Waylon. Ed may have advanced cancer, but he's healthy enough to stay up and smoke cigarettes with Don. Good thing you've found room for him on the payroll, or else all they'd do is play guitar and drink beer. I guess Don's not planning on going back to Colorado."

I knew Roxy saw me purse my lips and what that meant. She came to sit down next to me. "Crossword puzzle. The vacuum must be broken. What's got you all riled up—?"

"Nanna!"

The screen door screeched open, and Brian stuck his head out. "Where's the Nutella?"

"Pantry, second shelf. Next to the microwave popcorn."

"I didn't see it!"

"Jesus, boy, are you hoping the neighbors will be able to help you find it?" Roxy asked.

"Sorry Roxy! Brian waved.

You yell all you want. I could listen to you yell every minute of every day for the rest of my life. From the moment you saw William and said his name, I swear I cried for two days straight.

"Will! Mom says to come inside soon!" Brian yelled, and then slammed the screen door.

"Don't want to."

We both turned to the boy crouching down next to a turtle statue, barely visible under a rose bush.

"There's that redheaded fox we've been looking for!" Roxy smiled.

"I know Don saw me," William said, his hand in his pocket. "And you're wrong, Nanna, about the turtle."

I loved his jutted-out bottom lip so much. "No, I'm not, William. You will. I promise."

"I won't," he said glumly, walking over to the chair. I reached out and rubbed his head, careful not to irritate the bump of his head. Already, I'd noticed it was starting to diminish, but he still winced when anyone even came near it. I didn't dare mention to anyone what that bump could indicate.

"I won't ever remember."

"It was your favorite statue, and it will be a memory one day."

"I don't remember anything," he pouted. "I don't remember that stupid turtle. I don't remember you, I don't remember Mommy or Daddy or Roxy or Grandpa or anyone."

I leaned in towards him. "Here's what I promise you: One day, when you're all grown up, you will remember that turtle and how I told you that when you were a really little boy, you loved it. I tell you that every day, so it will become a *new* memory for you one day."

You will relearn, as I did.

"But I want to remember it *now*."

"I know," I said, looking down at my watch. Three o'clock.

"William, why don't you show Roxy where we found that frog yesterday by the fountain? That foxglove is really spreading behind the Peddler, and I may want to make a bed there. I might have Don put the mulch back there."

I quickly walked towards the shop, as Roxy's raised

eyebrow was like a stick poking me in the back. She knew I hated foxglove.

"Nanna, how long will you be gone?"

"Not long," I said, giving him a wave without looking back.

I left the garden, pausing only to pick a few daylilies. The red bell jeered at me from the pitch of the roof of the Peddler. *Look what happened to your life once you disregarded your father's warning.*

I glared back. I would have it removed this week. I certainly didn't need it anymore.

Even though it was in deep summer and the trees were heavy with leaves, I could see the iron fence that now lined my property. It had been a massive expense; jaw dropping to get the final bill. But to install an entire eleven-foot tall fence, with extending upper rows of wicked barbed wire, around the entire perimeter of the woods, was an expensive project. And pricier still when I demanded the keyless entry.

I looked back to see Roxy and William deep in discussion near the fountain in the garden. I stepped past the first tree and reached into my pocket for the tiny remote. I'd practiced the code many times, for I was the only one who possessed it. Though my memory was legendary in my family, I still forced myself to recount the code every morning, to make sure it was set in my mind. I didn't dare write it down. No one would ever be able to enter the woods again.

I had already activated the gate earlier that afternoon. As long as I was within a mile of it, the remote prompted it to unlock. So I had casually stepped outside, punched in the code, and went back inside.

Exactly an hour later, I was now standing directly in front of the gate. You couldn't tell where the fence would open; there was no visible gate, at my request. The ironworkers who made it had looked at me with confusion at my request, but ultimately worked with a locksmith to design the hidden mechanics.

The remote looked like a small calculator in my hand. Once I touched the right combination, I heard a buzz, a click, and one section of fence opened.

I quickly seized it, for it was also manufactured to close within five seconds. I stepped inside and shut it behind me, making sure it locked.

The woods were bustling with a crush of squirrels, buzzing in the branches above. I was careful where I stepped. I was grateful for the way the woods were stubbornly territorial, trying to cover as much of the earth as possible with tangling underbrush and fallen limbs, preventing encroachment of the outside world. The fence was my contribution to the effort.

It should have been difficult to locate the clearing, with the crime-scene tape long removed and the evidence of hundreds of searchers now covered in decaying leaves under a new growth of weeds. But he still found it, as I knew he would. He'd come just as I'd opened the gate remotely and slipped in.

"Hello, Lynn."

Steven stood in the center of the grassy area. Perhaps it had been the unflattering light of the hotel lamps the last time I saw him, in that frantic meeting before the government agents stormed in, but his skin seemed healthier now, his tan showcased nicely against his closely cropped white beard.

"Thank you for agreeing to meet with me," he said.

I nodded. As he slipped his hands into the pockets of his jeans, I walked to the far end of the clearing. A few butterflies flew drunkenly before me. In the shadows of the tree line, I knelt down in front of the gray headstone I'd had delivered before the fence was finished. I laid the lilies before the stone.

Amelia Shrank, 1931–2018. Beloved Daughter, Friend to Children.

I traced my finger across her name, and then turned to Steven. "I'm here because I am indebted. Especially to you. To say a proper thank you for leading me to William. And also . . . to say I'm truly sorry for what all of this has cost you."

"It wasn't your fault. The government forced my hand when they planted the trumped-up investigation and then labeled me a child murderer. Even after the charges were dropped, I knew the damage was done. I should have left academia a long time ago and devoted all my time to investigating the disappearances. Not that I've had much of a choice, but I've chosen to go underground."

"With this group you mentioned in the hotel? The Corcillium?"

"They've shown me so much, Lynn. The Researchers are just the front lines. The Corcillium guides it all. The Researchers are necessary to gather the intelligence, but the Corcillium is truly the heart of the effort. Through them, I finally learned the truth about Argentum."

"So all that time, when you said Argentum was just a debunked theory . . . you truly didn't know?"

He nodded. "Not even what it meant. The Corcillium wanted it that way. To protect all the Researchers."

"I don't understand."

"You will. It all started when one of the members of the Corcillium came in contact with, of all things, a janitor," Steven said, and then chuckled sadly. "A janitor in love, who fell for a woman with no memory. Helped her escape some sort of hospital in a remote town in Colorado."

Despite the summer heat, I rubbed my arms.

Steven continued. "Of course, that colleague took extensive notes of his discussion with this janitor and his girlfriend. But not a day later, the two were killed. Tragic accident. Their car exploded. Brand-new car, too. Then that member of the Corcillium went to Argentum himself, to confirm what he'd been told . . . and was killed in a skiing accident. Strange, don't you think? And when the Corcillium sent others to try and verify, they all disappeared. It became simply too dangerous. They knew what the janitor said—about people with no memories appearing in shafts of lights from the heavens—but could never prove it. And anyone who tried to find out never returned."

I remembered what Don said about the academic couple who came to Argentum and were seized by the police and never seen again. And, of course, what almost happened to Roxy and myself.

"The janitor and his girlfriend had no proof, and when they died, their stories died with them. All the Corcillium had were the notes from the interviews with the janitor. To honor their sacrifice, they developed the idea of the poem to send to all the families of the missing. The idea was to give the families part of the key, and if the day came when we could prove the abducted were returned to Argentum, then the answer was there. In the last line of the poem. But I, and all the other Researchers, never knew."

"The Corcillium did that to protect you."

His mouth formed a straight line. "They assumed in our web of research, someone might come across a mention of Argentum. They couldn't risk any of us losing our lives pursuing it. So they purposely disseminated what came to be called the Argentum theory. It was one of the first pieces of information a Researcher learned: never to believe anything that mentioned 'Argentum.' It was part of our vernacular. We debated it endlessly. I still remember getting my first piece of encrypted information, containing what avenues not to explore. The Argentum theory was at the top of the list. We all learned to dismiss it."

I exhaled. "When I was in Argentum, I was told of a couple—academics—who came to Argentum. They were seized by who the locals thought were police."

"Dr. Adam Abraham and Dr. Nancy Little. Two members of the Corcillium. They were never seen again. It was only when the Corcillium rescued me, and I acknowledged that it was my own grandson who was abducted, that they told me. And warned me I would likely never return. But I was willing to risk it. I knew you would risk it as well. Of course, in the end, you were the only one to ever come back."

"Steven—" I took a deep breath. "I need to know . . . if this Corcillium has determined . . . what we carry inside us."

Steven rubbed the back of his neck in response.

"Then you know about it," I said. "I am hoping you have uncovered more. I'm deeply worried about my family and their safety."

He shook his head. "I wish I could tell you more, Lynn. But there's a lot that I have yet to learn. Even though the Corcillium has investigated this, I know there's no physical evidence. There's never been any device or implant ever discovered in someone who claims to have been abducted. Now, we've never had someone like you or William—"

"There will be no inspection of my grandson."

"But, there is . . . you."

I smiled sadly. "Observing me all those years ago wasn't enough, was it? Do you want to dissect me now?"

"Of course not. But . . . we have to try to determine what may be within you. You're the only one, Lynn. The Corcillium understands allowing them to run tests on you would be . . . taxing. That's why they're offering up your father's letters. About your mother."

I blinked. "There are more letters?"

"I was shown the first just before I came. There are several, I'm told. They explain how your parents found you. And honestly, it led to a great discovery. It's incredible where they found you—"

"That I wasn't returned to Argentum but to one of the other bases the government set up to contain us?"

His eyes widened as I continued. "Obviously you've seen the brief footage of me at the end of that interrogation film. I'm looking out a window, and beyond that window are a beach and an ocean. At my last recollection, there is no ocean in Colorado."

"You're as sharp as ever, Lynn. You see a brief flash of something in an old film, and you connect the dots."

"I've also seen the entire film, including my responses to the government agent's questions. I know what I described aboard that ship. I know what William saw too, because there's a recorded interview of him as well. And . . . I saw *them*."

I could see that Steven had stopped breathing. "You saw one of them? What did it say?"

"I want those letters, Steven. I want to know what happened to my mother."

"And you should have them. You must have them. We asked Barbara to give you my message asking to meet here for two reasons. One—we need access to this site to study. There are so few places in the world that we know of where multiple abductions have occurred. It's vital we try to understand why. And two, because . . . because they want you to come join us."

I brushed an unruly curl from my face. "I risked everything to keep my family together, Steven. There's nothing that could convince me to leave them now. Or ever."

"I'm not asking you to leave them forever. But Lynn . . . what you've seen . . . the fact that you had some sort of communication . . . it's essential we learn from you. And you from us. What the Corcillium has uncovered. What they know about the abductions—"

"I'm not leaving my family. Ever again."

"If those letters were mine to give, you'd have them right now. But I don't. Only the Corcillium has them."

I breathed out slowly through my nose. "I get it. They entice me with the letters, show you just enough to whet my appetite, as a way to draw me in. Well, you will remind them that this is my land, and neither you nor any of your peers will ever step foot here again without my permission. So here are my terms: If you want to come to this site to study, you will only be given access when and if I deem it possible. I don't know what you hope to find, but whatever you do, you will then report to me and answer my questions. *All* of my questions. You will share every single shred of information, regardless of how minute, about what may be implanted within us. And as a token of your appreciation, you will deliver all the letters from my father. It's that simple. If you agree, you can pass your requests to come here through Barbara and I will reply with the appropriate times. There's no negotiating on this."

Steven managed a smile. "You still hold all the cards, Lynn. It's why the government and the entire world is waiting on you to explain how you found William. What is it you said when you gave that statement to the reporters in Denver? 'There is a vast government conspiracy, and I'm working to uncover the truth.' No wonder the government still has Argentum shut down and closed off for 'homeland security' reasons. And all those people with missing loved ones are still rallying outside, protesting, demanding to know if the person they've been searching for is in there."

My face softened. "I wish I could tell you that I saw your

sister, even though I wouldn't have begun to know what she looked like. The people who have called me, written me, asking if I saw their missing friend or relative—I can't bear to tell them the truth."

Steven hesitated. "The truth?"

"That if their loved one was once abducted and then returned, only to be contained in the government bases, they're gone now. All those people were taken back into the ships that arrived above Argentum. What they intend to do with the people, I don't know. But there is another stage, something else is coming. If your Corcillium has any information about what's happened or may happen, I must be told."

"I have to warn you, Lynn, that the Corcillium closely guards what it discovers. Of course, they want to share everything with the world, once they have all the proof they need. But they have concerns . . . about Tom. They can't risk this information being leaked. All Tom has ever said publically is that he believes you, just before he withdrew from consideration for vice president. Would you intend to share everything with him? They don't feel they can trust someone who still very much serves the government."

"I trust my husband completely–" I paused and cocked my head slightly. "Your Corcillium doesn't want some simple grandmother exposing the truth. *They* want to do it. *They* want the credit. You can tell them that I started discovering their secrets forty years ago. Sitting at that desk at midnight, unraveling how to read documents with so many words blacked out. You can remind them how quickly I figured out the rest."

My hands joined at my waist. "Those are my terms, Steven. Tell your Corcillium that I am eager to learn of their findings. Ten minutes from now, I will remotely open the gate, and it will be your only moment to slip out."

I nodded to him once and headed back to the gate.

"I know you've seen it, Lynn," Steven called out after me. "The book that's coming out. *The Senator's Wife*, they're calling it. It doesn't seem fair to you. You shouldn't be known as just a politician's wife."

There was half a mile of woods between the clearing and my house. The leaves obscured the view so entirely that I could see nothing. But I knew that beyond the trees, Brian, Greg, and Anne were inside, sitting around the kitchen table, waiting for me to start making a promised chocolate cake. That soon, Chris and Stella would arrive hungry for Friday night dinner. That Tom and Kate would be on the five o'clock flight from DC. That a little redheaded boy was leaning on the fence, waiting anxiously for his grandmother to return.

"It doesn't matter what they call me," I said, feeling the scattering of sunlight falling on my face as I walked towards my home. "I know who I am."

ACKNOWLEDGMENTS

You hold in your hands a dream thirty-four years in the making, and these are the people who made it happen: My agent at Donald Maass, Paul Stevens, whose editorial insight and constant support makes him a hero to me and to other aspiring writers. I am indebted to the incredible team at St. Martin's Press: Pete Wolverton, who fought for this book, found the answers when I couldn't, and ripped the Band-Aid off when necessary; Jennifer Donovan, whose attention to detail saved the day; Jen Enderlin, who was right all along about the title; Sophia Dembling, a copyediting savior; Ervin Serrano, who plucked an idea from my head and designed a cover I've waited my whole life for; Janna Dokos, Meryl Gross, Paul Hochman, Joe Brosnan, Kris Kam, and Omar Chapa, thank you for leaving your imprints on this book.

This is a book about the love of family: My mother-in-law, Linda Howerton, who inadvertently gave me the idea for this book, but truly inspired it based on her unwavering support for her family; my mother, Pam Finley, who would cross the stars for her sons and granddaughters; my brother Jason, for helping me talk through the specifics of alien technology; my late father,

Dr. John Finley, and my father-in-law, Robert Howerton, whose actions allowed me to write about heroic grandfathers. A reader once asked me how I knew so much about the love of grand-mothers, and the answer is the women who were mine: the late Freda Finley Stephens and Christine "Teeny" Blondi.

To my wife, Rebecca, who endured seventeen years of late night and early morning typing and was the first to put my name on the spine of a book. Because of you, because of Eve and Charlotte, I am able to write about unconditional love.

To my earliest supporters and readers: Karyn Esbrook, Bill Applegate, Janet Smith, Jayme Robinson, Anna Beth McKeown, Amy Goodhart Koepsell, and Michelle and Mary Ann Gaffney. Thanks for believing. To my literature and English teachers, from elementary school to college, for opening the door.

While this is a work of fiction, I relied heavily on the research of people who are seeking the truth about the mysteries around us: The Mutual UFO Network, The National Investigations Committee on Aerial Phenomena, and the Aerial Phenomena Research Organization. And to Whitley Strieber and Carl Sagan, for paving the way.

My heroes have always been writers, and I could fill a book with my gratitude to them. J. T. Ellison resides at the very top. If there is a patron saint of aspiring thriller writers, you are he.

To the person who is both friend and family, Todd Doughty, who never, ever, gave up, even when I threatened to. I am forever grateful.